The Origin Project

Randy Patton

COVER ART CREDITS

Front cover: The background image titled *Cosmic Heavyweights in Free-for-All* is provided courtesy of nasaimages.org. No endorsement by NASA is expressed or implied.

Rear cover: Photo by Mary Patton

TASER is a registered trademark of TASER International, Inc., registered in the US and several other countries. All rights reserved.

All brand and model names contained herein are the registered trademarks or trade names of their respective owners.

Library of Congress Control Number 2011960793

Printed in Charleston, SC, United States of America

ISBN: 1-4609-4834-3
ISBN-13: 9781460948347

*"Evil comes in many denominations,
the highest of which poses as the Good."*

Jeremy Scott King
44th President of the United States

Prologue

Six United States Secret Service special agents from the Presidential Protective Division had been assigned to guard immediate past president Jeremy Scott King. On this spring day in 2017, they occupy three black Chevrolet Suburbans, one preceding and two following King's vehicle, now headed eastbound on the Pennsylvania Turnpike. The former president drove a slightly more exotic Chevrolet, his prized Corvette ZR-1.

It had been eight weeks since King left the presidency after serving two full terms in office. Unmarried and having no family, he'd returned home to his residence in western Pennsylvania in a tony suburb of Pittsburgh. By virtually all accounts, his presidency had been one of the most successful in modern history. His immediate predecessor, Harold W. Tate, from the conservative party, had managed to involve the nation in two bloody and costly wars in the Middle East, and brought disaster to the country's economy through tax cuts and deficit spending at a time when the country was actively engaged in the two major military campaigns. Much of King's first term involved winding down the wars, bringing home the troops, and improving the economy. His second term restored and reinvigorated NASA's civilian space program, including the establishment of a small but self-sufficient lunar colony. During this same time, he also established another scientific research project under a dark cloak of secrecy.

"How long is he going to do this?" special agent Cliff Donovan asked his supervisor and partner, Rosalie Dunn.

The senior agent replied from the passenger seat, "Remember Cliff, he has been deprived of driving any of his vehicles for the entire eight years of his presidency. He loves these things. It's one of the few pastimes he really enjoys. He doesn't have a family of his own, and his official family from the White House is now mostly dispersed back into civilian life."

"I know, but he hasn't stayed home a single day since he left office. I can understand visiting friends and former staffers, but these extended road trips are becoming a bit boring, don't you think?"

"I think boring is a great thing in our line of work. And I'll bet you wouldn't be bored if you were driving his vehicle."

A minute later, the ZR-1 accelerated to a velocity significantly above the turnpike's seventy mile per hour speed limit. "There he goes again, Rosie. What happens if the state police appear and want to pull him over?"

"We pull over with them and respectfully show our badges. Don't worry, a former president, and oh, by the way, a former governor of this state, isn't likely to be issued a speeding citation, especially when he's under our protection."

"I suppose you're right," Cliff grinned. "You always are, boss."

Rosalie smiled at her partner's acknowledgement of her supervisory authority. A fifteen-year veteran of the Service, she took her job very seriously. And, if the truth were known, she held considerable affection for this former president. He had always treated his Secret Service detail with kindness and respect, something that couldn't be said for some of his predecessors.

The ZR-1 again picked up speed. Donovan said, "Boss, he's doing ninety. Can't we slow him down?"

"Let me get this right. You want to pull him over yourself because he's going too fast? I don't know about you, Cliff, but I don't want to be stationed in Alaska looking for counterfeit dollar bills for the rest of my career."

"Okay, okay, it was just a thought."

Rosalie looked at the sky and reassessed the risk. "He is going pretty fast though. That vehicle has amazing maneuvering capability, but those clouds look like it's about to rain, and then our driving conditions are going to deteriorate quickly. At the first drop of rain, I'm alerting the lead vehicle to light up and slow down gradually. Hopefully our president will follow suit."

Not five minutes later, Rosalie's weather prediction proved to be accurate as the skies opened above them. "Okay, that does it." Speaking into the microphone, "Marcus, this is Dunn, turn on your flashers and gradually slow to the speed limit. I want Victory slowing his vehicle to a safer speed."

"Roger that," the lead vehicle replied.

Approaching the on-ramp at the Valley Forge interchange, Donovan said, "Look at that tractor-trailer speeding up the ramp. Doesn't the idiot know how slippery these roads become right after they get wet?"

The truck continued its rush onto the first lane of the roadway as the rain fell even harder. It affected their visibility as well as the traction of the road surface. Rosalie was experiencing that slightly panicky feeling in the pit of her stomach that told her the situation could turn dangerous very quickly. All four vehicles in the presidential convoy were occupying the left-most lane of the highway, and the truck was entering from the right. "Turn on the light bar, Cliff. Maybe if the driver sees our red lights he'll think 'law enforcement' and slow down."

But it didn't work. The following sixty seconds would later prove to be a blur when the agents were being debriefed. The speeding truck moved quickly over to the center lane and lost traction just in time for the trailer to skid and plow into the right side of the Corvette. Losing control completely, the truck continued to skid to its left, taking King's vehicle along with it through the guardrail and into the slight valley of the median greenway.

"Oh my God, oh my God!" screamed Secret Service special agent in charge Rosalie Dunn as she watched the Corvette turn over 360 degrees and then burst into flames. "Pull over there, now!" She grabbed the microphone, "Red alert. Red alert. All vehicles pull into the median. Victory has been in an accident!"

They were on scene within seconds, but clearly it was too late. The agents ran down into the median decline between the eastbound and westbound lanes, only to see the ZR-1 completely demolished and in flames. The other five agents quickly grabbed fire extinguishers from their Suburbans while Rosalie Dunn placed what would prove to be a fateful and historic 911 call. Pennsylvania State Police troopers along with fire trucks and paramedics from the Valley Forge Fire Department appeared within minutes, but when the flames were extinguished, all that was left of their beloved former president was his charred remains. Ironically, the truck driver sustained just minor injuries and ultimately was cited only for driving too fast for conditions.

Within ten minutes, every broadcast and cable network would carry the breaking news flash that former president Jeremy Scott King, Secret Service codename Victory, was no longer a member of the elite club of living past presidents. The nation would mourn the loss of its beloved former head of state during the days and weeks to come.

Chapter 1: Departure

The instructions he had received were extremely specific and detailed. And he had been warned: any deviation or failure to comply with any provision of the document would result in immediate and permanent rejection as a candidate for the Project. And since admission to the Project, which began as a top secret government research facility under President King's administration, and which had since been handed over to a wealthy private foundation, was extremely limited and highly selective, he intended to follow every provision very meticulously.

Thus his arrival at a private airstrip in Maryland, just outside Washington, DC, at exactly the time and date specified. Public conveyance had also been specified, so his taxi pulled up just outside the only building at the field. But just to be certain, he looked for the sign that read "Clark Aviation, Fixed Base Operator." He removed his kit bag from the car and paid the driver, who then departed immediately.

Standing outside the building on a quiet and sunny day, interrupted only by an occasional breeze, he came to fully appreciate that he was standing on the precipice of changing his life forever. This was due to the fact that joining the Project required the execution of a contract that obligated him to remain in some secretly located research facility for the remainder of his life, and at age 34, he believed that could mean a very long time indeed. He realized that this would be the last opportunity for him to change his mind. But being a thoughtful and introspective person by nature, he had already thought it through and had made his decision.

Standing six feet tall, with a trim build and a handsome face by any definition, the slow breeze ruffled his dark brown hair and brought him back to the present. He looked around, but there was nothing to be seen except for the building in front of him and a long, empty runway that stretched off into the distance. He was about to enter the building when he heard the sound of a vehicle approaching from the same dusty country road his driver had just used. Curious, he stopped and waited. A taxi from a different cab company pulled up, and the driver got out and opened the rear door for the passenger. An extremely attractive woman, perhaps a few years younger than himself, stepped out of the car. She was dressed in a tight denim blouse and blue jeans, fashionably accented with a wide leather belt and ankle length boots. Her medium-length blond hair was styled in such a way that seemed to frame her face perfectly. Virtually replicating his own actions from a few minutes earlier, she grabbed her bag and paid the driver, who then departed, leaving them standing together but alone in front of Clark Aviation, Fixed Base Operator.

He looked at her and said, "Hi, I'm Steve Sinclair. I can't help but wonder if you're here for the same reason that I am?"

She briefly looked him over and apparently decided that he didn't pose a threat. "I'm Julie Reynolds, and

I really don't think that I can say anything about why I'm here."

"Okay then," Steve replied, "shall we go inside?" He opened the door and held it for her, and she stepped through the doorway without comment. Steve caught a trace of her musky perfume and felt himself becoming intrigued by the so-far mysterious Julie Reynolds. He followed her inside and came to a counter with a sign reading, "Please ring bell for service." He looked at Julie, shrugged his shoulders, and pressed the actuator button for the bell. They heard it ring from somewhere deep inside the structure, and then they waited somewhat awkwardly.

There were a few commercial aviation magazines lying on the counter, and, sensing that Julie wasn't in a talkative mood, he picked one of them up and began flipping through the pages. Aside from articles of interest to private and commercial pilots, the magazine consisted mostly of full-color advertisements for various brands and models of aircraft, instrumentation, leasing services, and so on. He was about half way through browsing the pages when a middle-aged woman dressed in blue nurse's scrubs came to the counter, looking totally out of place in this facility.

"Good afternoon, Miss Reynolds and Mr. Sinclair. Please give me the required documents now, including your photo IDs, medical clearances, sterilization certificates, and notarized contracts."

Steve and Julie both reached into their respective bags and produced file folders which they handed over to the woman behind the counter, who rather pointedly hadn't introduced herself to them.

She said, "I'll see each of you privately. Who would like to go first?"

Steve deferred to Julie, who indicated that she was ready. This left Steve totally by himself with his magazine. With nothing else to do but to wait, ponder his decision, and flip through the magazine, he continued to admire the high-quality photographs of sleek private jets, high-tech avionics, and other things he really knew nothing about whatsoever.

Approximately twenty minutes later, Julie returned, walking just ahead of the woman they assumed to be a nurse, and she rolled her eyes at Steve as if to prepare him for what was to come.

"Mr. Sinclair, please come with me now."

He followed scrub nurse into the rear of the building where they entered an examination room like one that might be found in any doctor's office or clinic. She told him to remove all of his clothes for the purpose of a full-body cavity search. He replied, "You've got to be kidding me!"

The nurse was not amused in the least. "You can submit to the search or be on your way back home right now. I'll step out for a minute while you undress." She closed the door behind her without even giving Steve a chance to reply.

Oh well, he thought, and did as he was told. Mercifully, when she returned, she performed the search quickly, gently, and professionally.

"I'm sorry if this came as a surprise to you, but it is required of all new inductees."

Steve mentally recoiled slightly over her use of the word "inductee," recalling his negative feelings about military conscription generally and the abuse of the draft which had prolonged the horrors of the war in Vietnam.

"Please return with me to the front counter," she said, and Steve once again did as he was told.

This time, Steve made eye contact with Julie as if to acknowledge that her warning look had been justified. She just half-smiled in sympathy.

The scrub nurse was back behind the counter and called them both forward. "Now, I will give you each some medication which will make you more relaxed for your journey."

Julie took the medication cup and water that was offered to her, but Steve said that he was fine and didn't need anything to help him relax.

"Mr. Sinclair, I don't think you understand. It is required that you take this medication now. If you choose not to do so, I will call you a taxi."

By now, Steve found himself somewhat irritated by what he perceived as callous treatment on the part of the nurse, and he said, "Well then, maybe you'd better do just that. You really think I'm going to take some unknown medication just for an airplane ride?"

The nurse picked up the handset of a phone on the desk and began entering a number on the keypad.

Julie stepped into the conversation and said to the nurse, "Please, wait a minute." Then, turning to Sinclair, she said, "Steve, right?"

Steve nodded.

"It's apparent by now that we are here for the same reason. Are you really going to give up everything you've worked for, everything you've done to get to this point, just over a couple of pills? Come on, I took them and they didn't hurt me."

Steve looked at Julie and thought about what she had said to him. Shrugging his shoulders, he grumbled, "Okay, maybe you're right after all." He took the medication cup from the nurse and used the water to wash the pills down.

The nurse replaced the handset on its cradle and then proceeded to have each of them stick their tongue out as she peered inside their mouths to insure that they had swallowed the medicine and not cheeked it to be disposed of later. "Please have a seat over there," pointing to an old brown leatherette couch along the wall that had definitely seen better days. "Your transportation will be arriving shortly. Thank you for flying Clark Aviation."

She disappeared into the back of the building, leaving Steve and Julie to look at each other in disbelief. They might have started a conversation at this point, except that they both heard the sound of a plane landing at the same time. They took their bags and stepped outside just in time to see a Gulfstream G650 business jet beginning to taxi from the main runway over to the building from which they had just exited. The jet parked, its engines went quiet, and a moment later, the door fell open.

Much to their surprise, scrub nurse came out of the building and said, "Let's go." Another look of disbelief was exchanged between them, but they followed her up the steps and into the aircraft, which had a beautifully appointed passenger cabin with about twelve seats. Oddly though, the "windows" were completely opaque.

"Take any seat you like, I think you'll find them very comfortable. There are bottles of cold water here should you get thirsty. It won't surprise you to learn that I am not a flight attendant. I am in fact a nurse, and my only function during this flight is to take care of any illness or injury that may arise. But we don't expect any problems of that kind, do we?"

Both Steve and Julie shook their heads in agreement, and that was the last thing they remembered before waking up in Med Central at the Project.

Chapter 2: Arrival

When Steve awakened, he found himself feeling somewhat groggy and lying in a very high-tech hospital bed. Awareness came slowly and in small pieces. First there was the fact that he had an IV line firmly attached to his wrist. Next, that he was surrounded by more bio-medical electronics devices than he had ever seen in one place. He looked to his left and saw another hospital bed much like his own, and then he saw that Julie Reynolds was in that bed, also connected to an IV line. He tried to speak, but his voice was hoarse and weak, "Julie?" No response. A bit louder this time, "Julie?"

She slowly turned her face to him, "Yes, who are… oh, Steve, right?"

"Yes, Steve Sinclair. Do you know where we are?"

"I presume we're at the Project. This isn't exactly what I expected though."

"Yeah, really."

Just then the scrub nurse walked into the room. "Welcome to your new home. I know that you are both groggy and have about a hundred questions to ask, and for that I have both good news and bad news. Which would you like first?" and she looked back and forth between them, waiting for an answer.

Julie was the first to reply, "Oh, why don't you give us the bad news first."

Scrub nurse said, "The bad news is that I won't be answering your questions. I will just be tending to your medical needs as long as you're here."

"How long will we be here?" Steve asked.

"See what I mean about the bad news? That's just one of the questions I won't be answering. Now before you both think that I'm a total witch, I can't answer that question only because I don't know the answer. I can tell you this much: most new members remain here only for a few hours, so long as their lab tests and vital signs show no indication of infection."

"Okay, thank you for that anyway. What is the good news then?"

"The good news is that you have arrived safely at ORT, the IV lines are there just to provide you some additional hydration since you didn't take advantage of the cold water on the plane," she said with what almost appeared to be a trace of a smile. "Also, a very personable young lady from SOC will be here shortly who will answer many of your questions."

"Sosh?" Steve asked.

"Yes, our Social Science team. They are responsible for new member orientation, community morale, and a whole host of other things. Now, please remain in your beds and don't cause me any trouble." She turned to leave the room.

"Wait," Steve said quickly, "at least won't you tell us your name?"

Scrub nurse turned back to them and, with a cryptic look on her face, replied, "Sure, I am MED-49." And with that, she left the room.

Steve and Julie stared at each other with that same look of disbelief that was becoming all too familiar. Julie was the first to speak, "I guess we're not in Kansas anymore."

Steve chuckled, "No, I guess we're not. Or are we? I don't have any idea where we are. I don't remember anything after taking a seat on the plane."

"I'm sure they intended it to be that way."

"Apparently so. I don't know how long we were in the air, but I don't feel the least bit hungry."

"I think we've been fed through these IV lines."

There was a quiet knock on the door, and then another woman entered the room who was wearing normal casual clothes, not medical garb. She approached each of them and shook their hands while speaking, "Welcome to both of you. I am Mary, and I am a member of the Social Sciences team here, which we refer to as SOC. Do you both feel up to receiving the first part of your orientation now, or would you rather sleep for a bit?"

Both Steve and Julie answered at the same time, "Orientation!"

Mary grinned and continued, "I've never had anyone answer that they would rather sleep yet, and I've been doing this since the Epoch."

"The Epoch?" asked Julie.

"Yes, the date this project began. I came in with the original start-up team. First, let me formally welcome you as the newest members of The Foundation for the Study of the Origin of the Universe, more commonly known as the Origins Research Team, or just by its acronym, ORT. Next, let me explain that we are very big on the use of acronyms and duty descriptors here. For example, I am known by my position descriptor of SOC-12. It's also common for us to use first names. It's very rare for us to use last names, although it's certainly not prohibited for any reason."

Steve asked, "So how are we to be referred to?"

"Glad you asked, because that's the next item on my agenda. As you know, Steve, you have been accepted here as a member of a special team of analysts. That team is named THOT, four letters, T-H-O-T. As the name suggests, your team provides thought and analysis to information provided to you by teams from other disciplines, including MATH, ASTRO, REL, HIST, and others, and then brainstorming concepts and ideas that ultimately go to ADMIN for evaluation."

"Whoa," Steve said, "I have a doctorate in education administration, not the physical sciences."

"Actually, most of the members of THOT do not have intensive scientific backgrounds. We have a very small and special team known as TRAN which interprets the findings of the physical science groups for your team. Obviously, with your academic background, you won't need any such interpretation from the social science teams."

"Okay then, I'm officially impressed" Steve replied.

"Now, you are the 415th member of ORT, and since you're a part of the THOT team, your duty descriptor is THOT-415. I'm pleased to meet you, THOT-415!"

"Why thank you Mary, uh, SOC-12."

Mary smiled at him, "You're catching on. Your team leader is Vivian, THOT-8, and she will be meeting with you once you leave Med Central and get settled into your new quarters."

She turned to Julie, "Now, you have been accepted as part of the ADMIN team, and I understand that you'll be involved with the Personnel sub-team. You are the 414th member of the project, so your position descriptor is ADMIN-414. I'm pleased to meet you also, ADMIN-414!"

"Thank you, SOC-12, I'm glad to meet you too," Julie replied.

SOC-12 smiled and continued, "Your sub-team leader is Kerry, ADMIN-20, and he'll be meeting with you once you're settled in." Addressing both of them again, "You'll notice from that clock on the wall over there that the time right now is 1520 hours. We use 24-hour time here, and our time zone is known as Origins Research Time."

Steve asked, "Since we're here now, where are we anyway?"

SOC-12 smiled and said, "Only a very, very few people in this facility know the answer to that question. The vast majority of us arrived here in a manner very similar to your own, and we have no idea where we are located. For project security reasons, our location and some other sensitive details about the facility are classified as need-to-know only. So, I'm sorry that I can't answer that question for you, nor for all who came before you who naturally asked the very same thing."

"Wow, okay then."

"Thank you for understanding, or at least accepting if not totally understanding. Despite the less-than-ideal process by which you came here, the dizzying use of acronyms, and the completely different social structure that exists here in ORT, I know that you will find it to be a wonderful place in which to live and work. Those of us who have been here wouldn't trade it for life back on the surface for anything."

Noticing Steve's quick glance at Julie, SOC-12 said, "Yes, that much about our location is common knowledge. We're in a very secure underground facility. The conventional wisdom is that we are located in a former military installation in Cheyenne Mountain, Colorado, but of course I can't vouch for that. I am telling you this now only because you'll be hearing it soon anyway once you're out in the community.

"Okay, now here's what happens next. As soon as you're cleared by the medical staff, each of you will be escorted to your quarters. When you arrive there, you'll find the personal items that you were permitted to ship to Clark Aviation before your departure date. Your video monitors will be tuned to the ORT orientation channel. When you're ready, just press the play button on the remote control and you'll view an in-depth orientation briefing on our history, organizational structure, and so on. It lasts about an hour. Also, please feel free to take a nap for as long as you like once you're there, either before or after you watch the video. Your time is your own for a day or two until you're more comfortable in your new environment. Once you have rested and watched the video, you are free to leave your quarters and explore the facility. When you get hungry, the location of the main cafeteria is given in the orientation video. How's that for some motivation to watch it?" she said with a smile.

Steve and Julie nodded in agreement.

"Okay then, any last 'burning desire' questions before I leave you in the good hands of the medical staff?"

"I guess not," Steve replied, and Julie murmured in agreement.

"Then in that case, on behalf of everyone here at ORT, I wish you the very best for your work and new lives with us." She smiled at them again and stepped out of the room.

Chapter 3: First Week

Within an hour of SOC-12's departure, MED-49 returned and disconnected Julie from the complex system of monitoring equipment to which they each were attached by seemingly dozens of leads. Once the process was complete, she said, "Okay, ADMIN-414, you are cleared to leave and go to your quarters. If you will come with me, I'll show you to a changing area and then we'll have someone escort you to your new home. I hope your transportation and brief stay here in Med Central was as comfortable as possible for you, and that you will enjoy working at ORT."

"Wait a minute," Steve interjected, "what about me?"

MED-49 turned to him and said, "You should be cleared shortly. Please be patient and remain in bed until I come for you, okay?"

"Okay then," Steve replied.

Julie carefully swung her legs over the side of her bed away from Steve, closed her hospital gown around her, and stood up. She started to follow the nurse out of the room but then stopped and looked back at Steve. "It's been a pleasure meeting you, even though we had very little time to talk. I know we're going to be working in different areas, but maybe we could get together over lunch or dinner sometime?"

"I'd like that very much, but how will I contact you?"

"Well, since I'll be working in ADMIN, I'm sure I'll be able to locate you. I'll be in touch."

"Okay, sounds like a plan. Good luck, Julie."

"Same to you, Steve." And in another moment, Steve was alone in the semi-private bay in Med Central which had served as the first glimpse of his new home in the Origins Research Team.

For lack of anything better to do, and perhaps as a lingering effect of whatever medication he had been given, he dozed off and on for about another two hours until MED-49 walked into the room and said, "Okay, THOT-415, now it's your turn. Same drill. Please be careful getting out of bed, since you may still be weak."

Steve sat up on the edge of the bed, began to stand up as he normally would and then quickly realized that he didn't have his full strength back yet.

"Wait a minute, Steve, take it slowly. Here, let me support you."

"Julie didn't seem to have this much trouble getting up."

"No, and you've just realized that medications act differently in different people, not to mention that the two people in question are different genders and different sizes. Don't worry, you'll be back to normal in no time. Let's see how you do walking to the changing room and then we'll know whether you can safely walk to your quarters or you get to go for a ride."

Steve looked at her and smiled, "Maybe you're not such a hard case after all."

MED-49 chuckled and said, "Don't worry, I'm human. It's just that we all have different jobs to do here, and sometimes mine requires me to be a bit, uh, compliance-oriented."

"Fair enough, ma'am. Let's head to the changing area. I think getting out of this gown and into my regular clothes will help me to feel more normal."

"I'm sure you're right. Walk with me as I support you, okay?"

"Okay."

As it turned out, either changing into his regular clothes did help or the medication finally was wearing off, because by the time he was fully dressed in the clothes he had been wearing when he arrived, he began to feel human again. He stepped out of the small combination bathroom and locker room. MED-49 was waiting right there for him at the door.

"Your color is good, Steve. You look like you're feeling better."

"I am, thank you."

"Good. Now you have a real treat in store for you, since you are fortunate enough to have me as your escort to your new quarters."

Now it was Steve's turn to chuckle while nodding his head.

"As a member of the THOT team, your quarters are located here on the Analysis level. Please come with me."

She led him out of what he assumed to be the main entrance to the medical area and into a large concourse with hallways jutting off both left and right. "Okay, here's a very condensed orientation of where you are. If you were to continue straight ahead, you would come to the main cafeteria. Passing through the cafeteria at the other end, a short hallway leads to the office complex for your team and others. But if we walk down this hallway on our right, we'll find a number of apartment units, including yours. Shall we?"

"Sure."

On their way, he observed many people heading in one direction or another, and then some others just taking advantage of the comfortable-looking seating arranged here and there in small conversation pod configurations. He noticed several large flat-panel video displays on the walls of the concourse. Some displayed text messages which he assumed might be daily schedules or internal information bulletins, and some appeared to be carrying either cable or broadcast news networks from the surface.

"Wow," he said looking around.

"Pretty impressive, isn't it?"

"Yeah, that would be an understatement."

Once they turned down the corridor she had pointed out to him, he was reminded of a luxury hotel with interior corridor rooms. They stopped about three-quarters down the length of the hallway and he saw a door with an embossed sign reading "THOT-415."

"Well this must be me," Steve said.

"Indeed it is. Here is your new ID badge." Handing it to him, she continued, "You'll notice that it has several magnetic strips on the back. One of them serves to unlock the door. Go ahead, swipe it through the reader."

He did, and after figuring out which side of the card made the lock click open, he gently turned the handle and opened the door.

"You have arrived safely at your new home, so I will leave you here. Everything you need for now, including information, is inside. The lights will come on automatically once you step in. Now, the time is about 1800 hours. The cafeteria is currently serving dinner, but you may prefer to take a nap or watch the orientation video first. Food is available twenty-four hours a day, so don't worry about starving."

"Okay, I won't. Actually I'm not all that hungry right now anyway."

"Don't worry, your appetite will return soon. Your team leader will be contacting you in a few hours by video or telephone, and until then, feel free to rest, explore, and learn."

"Thank you very much for, well, just helping me here. I really feel like I should know your name though, if you know what I mean."

"I do. My name is Connie, MED-49. Good luck, Steve, and enjoy the unique opportunity you have here to interact with some of the best minds and highly-motivated people in the world." And with that, she turned and left him at the door to his new home.

———————

Steve paused for a minute, looking up and down the corridor for no particular reason other than self-orientation, and then he entered his quarters. As promised, room lighting was activated as soon as he stepped inside. Closing the door behind him, he found himself in a small foyer. Directly ahead of him was a small kitchen area. To his left was a living room, and walking to his right down a short hallway he found a small but cozy bedroom with a queen-size bed. Checking it out further, he found the bathroom and decided that this would be a good time for him to "indoctrinate" it. He was impressed to find that the commode was self-flushing when he finished. The fixtures on the sink and the shower-bath were of modern design and were obviously high quality.

Walking back into the bedroom, he noticed a large flat-screen video panel mounted on the wall across from the head of the bed, flanked by speaker systems on both sides. He saw a remote control on the bedside table which logic indicated would be used to operate this equipment. *Nice, very nice.*

He then proceeded to check out the living room. Here again, small but very comfortable looking, and also equipped with a flat-panel display and speakers. The room was furnished with a recliner chair, a side chair, and a small sofa. Another remote control was located on a table lamp beside the recliner. He sat down in the chair, picked up the remote, and without his doing anything else, the video screen came to life. A text message appeared on the screen which read, "Please press the Play button on your remote control to begin your orientation video. Use the Pause, Rewind, and Fast Forward buttons as needed."

He sat back in the chair, raised the footrest, and pressed Play to begin the orientation. He watched and listened intently as the origins, mission, and organizational structure of the project were presented to him in a very professional and high quality production. He was quickly coming to the belief that everything about this facility was absolutely first-rate. Most of the program was narrated by a female voice perfectly suited for broadcast work. Finally, after presenting a guided tour and map of the Analysis level, she concluded the majority of the program by introducing the Chief Administrator of ORT, known as ADMIN-1, for a few words of welcome. A thin dark-haired man seated at a large desk and wearing a black turtle-neck shirt appeared on the screen: "Greetings and a very warm welcome to you as one of the newest members of the Origins Research Team. I would like to personally congratulate you on accepting this once-in-a-lifetime opportunity to work with a team dedicated to uncovering the most fundamental mysteries of the universe. I believe you will find, just as I have, that working with the ORT project is one of the most deeply stimulating and intellectually fulfilling experiences possible. As you begin your new life here, please know that it is very typical to miss being out of doors, along with many other aspects of your previous life. But as you assimilate into this very unique community, you will most likely find that you wouldn't trade being here for anything.

"I know that you have already been made aware of the various facilities available to you earlier in this orientation. But please know that many other services are also available which couldn't be covered during this short presentation. Soon, your team leader will introduce him- or herself to you. This will be your primary contact person for any need you may have or issue which may arise for you in the future.

"What lies ahead of you is an opportunity unparalleled in human history. Regardless of which team you are now a part of, you will be working with dedicated colleagues and state-of-the-art equipment. No expense has been spared to provide for your comfort and safety in this facility. No doubt you have already had a brief glimpse of our cutting-edge Med Central facility. A group of outstanding physicians, nurses, specialists, and other health professionals staff this area 24/7. Please don't hesitate to call upon them should you feel the need.

"But now, your new life begins. I encourage you to make the most of it. Ask questions of anyone you see. Every team member is available to help you make the most of your life and work here. Again, welcome to ORT, and thank you for watching."

With that, the orientation program ended and the screen went black.

Chapter 4: Steve Sinclair's Journal

Having arrived at the Origins Research Team facility just three weeks earlier, Steve had been keeping a journal and, on the occasion of his three-week anniversary as an ORT member, he decided to review his entries:

DAY 1

"My name is Steve Sinclair, now also known by my position descriptor of THOT-415. I am a new member of the Foundation for the Study of the Origin of the Universe, better known as the Origins Research Team. I arrived here today after previously going through a whole series of physical and psychological exams as well as other testing to determine my eligibility to be part of the team. I filed my application about three months ago while I was an associate professor of education at the University of Florida. I really never thought (or perhaps I should say, 'THOT') that I would be accepted, but here I am.

"Ironically, I don't actually know where 'here' is, but yet, I'm very excited to be…here. I believe that we're located in a very safe and secure area somewhere in the continental United States. Rumors have it that the compound is built inside a partially hollowed-out mountain, perhaps around a former missile silo or command post, but we really don't know for certain. From shortly after the time of my arrival at the designated staging area at Clark Aviation in Maryland, I was heavily medicated until my arrival here at ORT. It seemed that we (for there was also another new member named Julie) may have traveled for hours, but here again, there's really no way for me to tell since I slept during the entire trip. Adding further to the mystery of where we are located is that our local time zone, Origins Research Time, could be totally unrelated to any other time zone in the country.

"For the benefit of anyone who one day might read my journal, I should briefly discuss the beginnings of the Origins Research Team, a notion which reminds me of the the old 'enigma wrapped in a riddle' analogy. The first thing to know about the project is how unlikely it was for it to have ever gotten off the ground. For years, the government of the United States had been deteriorating into a miasma of corruption, greed, and incompetence. Former president Harold Tate had even thrown the country into a war in the Middle East under the pretense of the threat of an imminent attack by weapons of mass destruction. It turned out that there were no weapons of mass destruction and that the whole attack had been somewhat of a feint to funnel billions of dollars to favored defense contractors and to eliminate a dictator who had once offended the president's family. Many thousands of lives had been lost, tens of thousands more had been injured, and yet the insanity continued until a new president was elected. It was that president, Jeremy Scott King, who provided the impetus and the funding for the earliest precursor of ORT.

"President King terminated the Middle East war and reversed a large number of flawed and failed policies of the previous administration. He was also a talented visionary who realized that it was imperative, in order to protect the survival of the human species, to establish a self-sustaining colony on the surface of the earth's moon. There were just too many opportunities for mankind to destroy its home planet, either by nuclear or biological weapons, or even by destroying the ecology of the planet. Think global warming, the existence of which the previous president had also denied. Anyway, by making his case directly to the people, and through them to the Congress, he was successful. Further plans were made for additional space exploration and, hopefully, future colonies even further away from earth than the moon. This was a very public effort, and it had begun with his first State of the Union Address.

"But Jeremy King, himself a Ph.D. in political science and a university professor prior to his first entry into politics, also had another major agenda. And this one was never really publicized. He believed that the primary goal of mankind, on the grandest possible scale, was to discover the origin of the universe. How did it all begin? What creative force or forces were at play? And not only how did it happen, but just as importantly, why? And of course, he realized that there may not be a 'why.' That was just part of the mystery.

"Realistically, organized religion would have made it impossible to establish and publicly fund a project such as ORT. The growing evangelical movement in the country, which largely had clung to King's predecessor as a near-Messiah, had all the answers they needed based upon their literal belief in the Old Testament. The earth and the human species had been created in a mere week. Darwin's theory of evolution was a farce. Astrophysicists and cosmologists who worked hard to increase our knowledge of the nature of our solar system, our galaxy, and the universe itself, were simply being duped by their own hubris. Carbon dating of rocks and other particulate matter showing millions of years of age was just…well, wrong. When faith alone provides all of one's answers, there is no room for compromise and absolutely no desire to be confused by the facts. Which explains why the whole concept of the Origins Research Team was kept highly secret for a very long time.

"Not that President King eschewed the value of religious thought and faith. Indeed, we have a whole section of people here whose focus is primarily the role of spirituality through the lifespan of mankind and whose task it is to seek out relevant matter that may be of importance to the project. This is the province of the REL team.

"But as for myself? I am now the most junior member of THOT, the group that has the task of taking all of the information provided by groups such as MATH, ASTRO, and the other scientific bodies, as well as REL, HIST, and others, and then brainstorming concepts and ideas that ultimately go to ADMIN for possible action. Today and tomorrow, I'll just be settling into my quarters and receiving orientations on the project's components and day-to-day operations.

"I haven't seen Julie since our arrival here, but I very much hope to soon. She impressed me as being not only very attractive but also highly intelligent. The only problem is that she's in ADMIN, the junior member of that group as ADMIN-414, and I don't know how likely it is that we will have the opportunity for much contact. Maybe this is a question that I can pose during my individual orientation with SOC, the group that's responsible for the smooth social functioning of the team members."

<hr/>

"Funding the project, not just for the start-up but into the future as well, was a major concern for President King. He knew that a future administration or Congress could easily block funds to ORT and therefore effectively terminate the effort. But King was smart, determined, and had a lot of political capital to spend, with many members of the House and the Senate who had ridden into office on his coattails. He reasoned that if 'black operations' for war had been funded in the dark and 'off-budget' for years for so-called national security reasons, so might the Origins Research project.

"King and his congressional allies had established a huge trust fund and transferred its control to an independent board of trustees. The amount of the fund was so large that the earnings from the principal alone would be enough to fund ORT long into the future.

President King definitely had a way of getting things done.

"The reason that the project has become a bit more public over the past few years, and perhaps the main reason that current or future governmental leaders are very unlikely to try to terminate our work through means of force as opposed to funding, is because of a few of the 'spin-off' benefits from our work here. The biggest example, almost without question, is the MED team's discovery of a unique compound of chemicals, now known commercially as Oncoleve, which, when injected into a person in exactly the right quantity, attacks the growth of cancer cells at the most basic protein level. This one discovery alone, coming from the medical team's work here, unfettered by market considerations, has been responsible for saving tens of thousands of lives every year.

"There have been several other discoveries of note. Our ASTRO team has access to the most powerful telescopes and radio telescopes in the world, and beyond, when you include the Hubble II in earth orbit and now the Sagan Observatory on the surface of the moon. In concert with the most powerful super-computer ever built, which is programmed and maintained by our DATA team, the project has contributed immensely to mankind's knowledge of the universe and its constituent components. For example, ASTRO and DATA were jointly responsible for the discovery of the existence of so-called 'Black Cords' in the universe, and they believe that within a few short years, this discovery will lead to the elusive Unified Field Theory so desperately sought by Einstein and his successors.

"Between our practical discoveries and our reliable source of funding, we feel very confident about our future existence as a project."

DAY 2

"I've been reviewing my journal entries and I think I need to clear up a possible misconception. My duty assignment as THOT-415 does not indicate that there are 415 current members of the THOT team. Rather, I am member number 415 of the whole Origins Research Team. If I were to somehow transfer in the future to DATA, for example, my duty designator would be DATA-415. We keep our numbers, in a manner of speaking.

"As to the THOT team, there are only ten of us at present. Whether or not more members will be added in the future is, I suppose, a decision for the head of the team, THOT-8, and would likely have to be approved by someone in ADMIN.

"By the way, there is one exception to the duty designator numbering process, and that occurs in ADMIN only. The Chief Administrator of ORT is always designated as ADMIN-1, and his or her senior deputy as ADMIN-2, regardless of when they joined the project.

"I have not yet met ADMIN-1. The only thing I know about him is that his first name is the same as mine."

DAY 3

"You may be wondering how someone qualifies to be a member here. As I mentioned earlier, there are many physical and psychological tests that must be completed satisfactorily. The purpose of the physical requirements is not in the least to insure that everyone here is in perfect health or free of any disability. Not at all. Rather, it is primarily to insure than an applicant is free of any communicable disease that could endanger others with whom we work in close proximity. The psychological profile must show that an individual is not prone to claustrophobia or severe depression. We work indoors and don't see the light of day, so claustrophobics or those suffering from Seasonal Affective Disorder, as just two examples, might have a very difficult time living here.

"There is more. An applicant to join the project cannot have any dependent family members whatsoever. A parent can't leave one or more children behind, nor can a husband leave a wife, or vice versa. Furthermore, I am not aware of any married couples who are part of ORT. I don't know if this is because it's prohibited due to social or psychological reasons, or whether it's just co-incidence. And then, there's the mandatory sterilization necessary because there are no provisions for children in the project.

"An applicant has to be so enthusiastic and dedicated to the mission of the project that he or she is willing to commit to remaining with ORT 'in perpetuity,' which as a practical matter, of course, means for the remainder of one's lifespan.

"Consider the circumstances of our existence here. There is no compensation for time worked, and there are no retirement benefits. On the other hand, all of our needs are provided. We have private, albeit small, apartments. Food, clothing, recreation, and medical care are all available to us at no charge. When a person joins ORT, there are no more taxes to pay. There are no payments for housing or transportation. Some might liken this system to that of a prison. They would definitely not be acceptable candidates for joining the project!

"So, what is the draw for us to be here? Well, the fact is that we are working on the most fundamental issues of our existence as human beings. No corporate entity would ever fund this work, and it's too ethereal for most foundations, even if they had the kind of funds necessary to sustain an activity such as this. Those of us who have made it here, are here because there really is nowhere else that we would rather be.

"For me, there was also a 'push' to leave the surface society. Since President King left office at the end of his second term, and then fundamentalist minister L. Davis Brasington III was inaugurated, there has been a steady turn away from science and education. This is perhaps most visibly demonstrated by the rise of the New Know Nothing Party, or the NKNs. This is a group of social and fiscal conservatives, mostly supporters of President Brasington, who, with the assistance of millions of dollars from select corporate sponsors, have been taking over school boards, state legislatures, governorships, and many seats in the U.S. House and Senate. Incredibly, for the most part, they are actually proud of their lack of formal education and profess to therefore be better able to 'solve' problems with their gut instincts. Since they have no real knowledge of world events, history, or how to constructively resolve issues among people and nations, they frequently refuse to answer any questions from the news media, and somehow…somehow, many have been elected anyway. Despite all of their real-world shortcomings, they are expert at tapping into the public's fear of any challenging situation and anger at anyone different from themselves. Different races, different lifestyles, immigrants from other parts of the world, people who don't speak the 'King's English,' a downturn in the economy…all of these and more became the fodder for the right-wing media machine. Their anger, vitriolic rhetoric, and love of firearms has even led to threats of violence against public officials with whom they disagree. Congressional district offices have been vandalized, and representatives are often shouted down at town meetings. In one tragic instance, a member of Congress was shot and critically injured while at a public meeting with constituents, not by an NKN member, but by a mentally unstable person who got caught up in the disaffection and anger often spouted by the party's leaders and media mouthpieces.

The NKNs have greatly benefited from the political upheaval they've caused. In my home state of Florida, for example, the state government has been effectively taken over completely by the NKN party, and it didn't take long for them to cut corporate taxes (of course) at the same time as they increased spending on their own pet programs. All of this came at the expense of an already overburdened public education system, which is now slowly but surely being replaced by private and church 'academies' and home-schooling. Funding for higher education is in the process of being cut dramatically, and a willing legislature has eliminated funding for research grants and even the institution of tenure, which is something I worked very hard to earn over a seven-year period of time. When I learned about the Project and had the opportunity to apply and then be accepted, I was more than ready to move on to an environment where knowledge and science are still valued commodities.

"But, you may ask, what would happen were someone to change their mind and want to return to regular society? My answer has to be that I simply don't know. We enter into a contractual arrangement when we apply to join the project. The contract defines expectations of performance and a unique relationship between the applicant and the project. There are also confidentiality clauses due to the nature of the work here. I personally have not heard of any project member wanting to leave. But however it might come about that a member were to leave here, that person would never again have the privilege of working on what could very likely be the most profound and enlightening endeavor ever attempted by the human species. And any way you cut it, that's a lot to leave behind."

DAY 4

"Since I mentioned medical care earlier, it's noteworthy that our Med Central team consists of physicians, nurses, and other trained caregivers. Yet unlike the medical profession in the outside world, there is no overt distinction made between the titles or work uniforms of the team members. MED-10 may be a doctor and MED-25 a nurse, but each is referred to either by their first name or their position descriptor. After all, there is no difference in take-home pay.

"I know that it may sound a bit morbid, but I have also been curious about the whole question of what happens here when a team member dies. I have learned that, as one would expect, there have been a few deaths since the project began. After a memorial service is or is not held, in accordance with the member's previously-expressed wishes, the body is cremated and stored in a special area. I was particularly interested to learn that no team member is ever made to suffer unnecessarily when faced with a terminal condition. After appropriate counseling and in consultation with the Med Central staff, physician-assisted suicide is available to the member upon request. I have to admit that this makes a great deal of sense to me. I could never understand the prevailing belief in Western society that animals could be relieved of their suffering when there is no hope for their recovery, but that human beings should be made to fight to the very end, against all hope and perhaps in terrible agony, basically because of a religious belief that the patient may not even share with the powers-that-be who write and enforce the laws."

"I learned a lot of interesting details about life in ORT at my individual SOC orientation today. Members are free to have intimate relationships with other consenting members, regardless of gender. There is no institution of marriage here, in part because there are no children.

"It does seem that many members have monogamous relationships with another member. Since there is no obvious indication of such a relationship other than through one's personal knowledge of who may be committed to whom, I mentioned that I could see where trying to initiate such a relationship could be a bit tricky. But then SOC-12 explained to me that they maintain a registry of exclusive relationships and that ORT members can check that registry at any time.

"There are many recreational activities available to us during our free time. There are various interest groups, social mixers, the latest movie and book releases from outside, as well as current television broadcasts. We also have a very nice exercise facility.

"Dining also provides an opportunity for meeting and interacting with others. We can prepare and have meals in our own units if we like, but there is a very pleasant dining area and the food is quite good and, I'm sure, nutritious."

DAY 8

"Well, I guess it was bound to happen to me sooner or later. I was scheduled for a routine follow-up medical exam and it was my first time to visit Med Central since my arrival. It is a huge area which is brimming with the most advanced state-of-the-art medical equipment I've ever seen. Absolutely amazing!

"My exam went fine, but I was instantly attracted to MED-11, a nurse (I believe) named Kathy, who was seeing me for this visit. She has long dark hair and the most incredible bright blue eyes, along with a great smile and a '10' body. I made the mistake of inviting her to have dinner and see a movie with me without having checked the registry first. She handled it very professionally, of course, and explained to me that she was already in an exclusive relationship. I was really embarrassed at the time, but not nearly as embarrassed as I was after I did check the registry only to find out that her partner is ADMIN-1!"

DAY 10

"The name Origins Research Team might be just slightly misleading, because although our primary focus is, in fact, the origin of life in the universe and the nature of the universe itself, we also have other areas of research. For example, a few of our groups, most notably BIO and DATA, have also been working on trying to determine what may be the next evolutionary step in life on Earth. Naturally, BIO is concentrating on known genetic mutations that have taken place that might signal a new and perhaps more intelligent human being. They've been looking at the research on savants, of course, as well as persons who seem to have intensely focused specific abilities, whether it be counting cards, intuiting events, sensing something that may be occurring a long distance away, and so on.

"But DATA is working with the notion that the next evolutionary step may not even involve human beings or any other carbon-based life form, but rather is looking at silicon-based intelligence now being created by humans in the form of (thus far) primitive robots and, of course, computers themselves. They are particularly studying artificial intelligence software, which can perform at a very high level on the powerful super-computers at ORT's disposal.

"Periodically, both of these groups present their ongoing projects and preliminary findings to our group, THOT, for the unique kind of philosophical analysis that is our specialty. I am looking forward very much to one of these presentations. But for now, I must head off to my very first formal meeting of the THOT team."

"We met at 1500 hours ORT in Conference Room 5. I am very impressed with our group leader, THOT-8, whose name is Vivian. She immediately made me feel welcome in this group of very accomplished and able peers. As I mentioned earlier, there are ten of us in THOT now, and I fully realize that I am the most junior member. In situations like this, I've always found it prudent to do a lot more listening than speaking, and I followed that course today. Vivian said that she is planning another meeting within a week for the purpose of summarizing for me, as well as the rest of the group, the material with which the group has been working during the past months. I understand that much of it has come from ASTRO and has been presented to our group by TRAN. Apparently those scientists who regularly work with high order mathematics and physics don't typically make the best communicators of this information to non-physical science types such as those of us in THOT. Therefore, the three members of TRAN, who are fortunate enough to possess both the science and math skills to understand ASTRO's findings, as well as the unique ability to explain them in plain English to others, bridge the gap for us very effectively."

DAY 18

"News reports from the outside world have become very depressing and are confirming my worst fears. In the United States, since President Brasington's election nine months ago, the political and philosophical pendulum has swung back to a neo-conservative view of world affairs, and he has once again taken a 'cowboy' approach to foreign relations, ignoring the United Nations completely and instead pursuing his own ultra right-wing agenda. As a result, the world is again on the brink of chaos in the Middle East and awash with the fear of terrorism. The administration has been using fear very effectively as a tool to frighten the public into willingly giving up their civil liberties in return for the 'protection' offered by a government run rampant with cronyism, greed, and power-seeking.

"I find myself reminded of a line often stated by former President King: 'Evil comes in many denominations, the highest of which poses as the Good.'

"We at ORT wonder what effect this will have on us, but on a more important and fundamental level, we worry about the result for the outside world as a whole."

DAY 21

"It seems like it took a long time considering that we are residing in a closed community, but I finally saw Julie again, the other member who was inducted into ORT at the same time that I was. She is now serving as ADMIN-414, and we took the opportunity to join each other at dinner last evening. I believe there is the potential for a relationship between us, because we made plans to see a movie and have a 'night out' in the near future.

"Since she works in the relatively small and somewhat isolated ADMIN section, talking with her is extremely interesting on many different levels. Most basically, there is the stimulation involved in interacting with someone with whom I am sexually attracted. Neither of us is in a committed relationship and so that is certainly a possibility for us. But also, there are interesting tidbits of her work in ADMIN that she has shared with me. And perhaps equally importantly, she seems fascinated with the work that I'm doing in THOT and doesn't seem at all bored when I launch into a lecture about one position or another that has been discussed in our group meetings.

"She told me a little about ADMIN-1, a brilliant computer scientist who somehow became a close associate of President King. He was involved in highly classified work that Julie either doesn't know much about or skillfully avoids discussing with me. His partner here, Kathy, MED-11, had a very close relationship with Steve when he was involved with the government. There is a rumor in ADMIN that she was somehow responsible for saving his life, but the details on that either aren't known or aren't discussed.

"Anyway, the relationship of trust and friendship between ADMIN-1 and President King was so close that he was tapped to be the chief administrator of ORT from its outset. I asked Julie how a new chief administrator is chosen in the event that something happens to the current ADMIN-1, and all she would tell me is that 'there is a process in place for that eventuality.' I suppose it would make sense for ADMIN-2 to assume the duties of chief administrator, but then he or she would also have to be replaced. She assured me that the process covers these matters completely. She told me that if I really was interested in learning more about these ADMIN details, that once I've completed six months of service here in ORT, I could request an appointment to meet with AD-MIN-1 or ADMIN-2. She told me that ADMIN-2's name is Richard, and that he had also been a King staffer during the eight years of his administration."

Steve finished reading his journal entries and realized that he had learned a lot during his first few weeks about life in ORT, but he was possessed with seemingly insatiable curiosity and he wanted to know much, much more. He placed the journal back into the drawer of his nightstand, resolving to learn as much as he could as quickly as he could about this fascinating new environment.

Chapter 5: Maker's Mark

Steve began his fourth week of work as a member of ORT with an especially interesting THOT team meeting. He arrived in Conference Room 5 just as his nine colleagues were getting seated.

The team leader, Vivian, THOT-8, opened the meeting by announcing that a guest speaker would be joining them for today's session. Just then, a somewhat portly but distinguished looking gentleman with a beard entered the room.

Vivian gestured for him to come to the head of the table and said, "Today, we are delighted to have as a return visitor, Robert, TRAN-15, who will update us on the work being done by the DATA team. What's going on down there, Robert?"

Steve immediately picked up on the phrase "down there" and wondered where "down there" was, but he knew this was not the time to interrupt with a question of personal curiosity such as this.

Robert then addressed the group. "One of the most interesting areas that our colleagues in DATA and MATH are working on in their quest for answers about the origin of the universe…"

Steve couldn't help but feel an involuntary shiver of delight as he was so obviously reminded of the deep importance of the work that was being done here. He immediately tuned back into Robert's presentation.

"...a notion perhaps best popularized by the late Dr. Carl Sagan in his novel, *Contact.* The idea is this: if a creator were involved in the Big Bang which gave birth to the universe, he, she, or it may have left what could be viewed as a 'maker's mark' for future intelligent beings to find. Sagan used as his exemplar for such a mark the number Pi, which we know to represent the ratio of the circumference of a circle to its diameter. While Pi is commonly abbreviated as 3.14159, the fact is that the numbers to the right of the decimal point go on to infinity. Pi is known as an irrational number, which means that its value can't be expressed exactly as a fraction, where the numerator and denominator of the fraction are both integers. The term Pi comes from the first letter of the Greek word for 'periphery,' by the way."

Robert continued, "The decimal value of Pi has previously been calculated using supercomputers to a trillion, or 10 to the power of 12, digits. Now here's the thing: the decimal value of an irrational number such as Pi never ends and does not repeat. Sagan suggested that a search down the never-ending flow of decimal values of an irrational number, and by the way, there are many of them aside from Pi, might result in a sudden pattern of repeating or some other meaningful sequence of digits which could contain a message, or maker's mark, to someone with the tools and the knowledge to identify it. In Sagan's novel, scientists using a supercomputer ultimately did find a long string of only zeroes and ones, which, when arranged just right, formed a visual representation of a large circle of zeroes against a square background of ones. Now, the theory contends that the existence of a phenomenon such as this in a value like Pi, which after all represents a ratio which is burned into the physical nature of the universe itself, could only have been placed there by a creator."

Several voices from around the table expressed interest and/or amazement with this concept. Questions bubbled forth: "Are we looking for such a pattern?", "Have we found a pattern like this?"

Robert said, "Let me assure you that we are searching for patterns such as this, but let me explain why it is a very, very difficult search. First of all, as I mentioned earlier, Pi is just one example of an irrational number. There are many more irrational numbers in mathematics. A simple example is the square root of two. Certain logarithms are irrational numbers. And the list goes on. Then, when calculating their decimal values, of course, we're using a base ten number system, which is the number system we're all most familiar with. But there are an infinite number of number systems, if you will. You may be familiar with the binary system, which consists only of zeroes and ones, and the hexadecimal system, which contains sixteen digits, zero through nine and A through F. The hexadecimal system is used a great deal in computer programming and architecture, and the binary system is the basis for all computer code, since the zero represents an 'off' state and the one an 'on' state. Each digit in a binary number represents a bit, short for binary digit, and if you string eight of them together, you have a byte. The number of values that can be expressed by a byte is two to the eighth power, or 256."

Robert took a drink of water before continuing. "Anyway, the real point is that the infinite number of sets of base number systems combined with the uncountable amount of irrational numbers in the universe make for an extremely difficult search, especially when you don't know what the 'needle in the haystack' looks like. Nonetheless, DATA has the most powerful supercomputer in the world at its fingertips and some of the best mathematicians and programmer analysts using it, so they continue to search for any significant pattern that may appear somewhere far downstream in the decimal value, or binary value, hexadecimal value, and so on, of some of the more significant irrational numbers in the universe, certainly including Pi. Will they find anything? And if they do, what will it mean? That's where you members of the THOT team come into play! And I will now leave you to ponder all this as you continue your work here."

His presentation concluded to everyone's enthusiastic applause, and he excused himself to go back to his own office.

Vivian again took the floor, "I'm once again reminded of how fortunate we are to have hard scientists like Robert available to explain to us social scientists concepts such as this one." She directed her next remark to Steve, "There are three members of TRAN, Steve, and as you just observed, Robert works primarily with DATA and MATH. Other TRAN members work with ASTRO, MED, and so on. The TRAN team makes it much easier for us to do our job here in THOT."

"I can see that very clearly," Steve replied.

"Okay," Vivian continued, "that's it for right now. But what I would like each of you to do when you return to your own office is to give more T-H-O-T to Robert's presentation and come up with your own ideas as to what such a discovery might mean, if anything. How might we test it for significance? If it is deemed to be significant, what do we do with it next? And at what point in the process do we release our findings to the scientific community on the surface? Thank you for your considered, and your considerable, input."

And at that point, the meeting was adjourned.

Chapter 6: Washington

It has been a very exciting year so far for Jackson Hall, age 27, and the newly-elected Congressman from the district that includes much of Orange County, California. Known primarily as being the home of Disneyland, Knotts Berry Farm, and such mega-churches as the Crystal Cathedral and the Saddleback Church, Orange County is both affluent and reliably politically conservative. Hall had been inspired by the Brasington presidential campaign to run against a more moderate but still conservative incumbent in his party's primary, and with the money and support of citizens and corporate political action committees, he had been nominated by a small but definitive margin over the long-time member he would be replacing. The general election in the fall would prove to be *pro-forma* only, as no progressive candidate had been elected from this district in modern history. Quite literally, he owed his new seat in the U.S. House of Representatives to then President-Elect Brasington. And Jackson Hall was nothing if not committed, ambitious, and loyal.

He still remembered as if it were yesterday his first official trip to the nation's capital where he attended the freshman orientation for all newly-elected members. During this time, he had hired his staff who would then serve him both in Washington and back in his district office. He participated in the traditional process of selecting an office complex from some of the least desirable offices, which were the only ones available to new members, regardless of their political affiliation.

Then the day arrived early in January when the new Congress was gaveled into session and members were sworn in by the new Speaker of the House. This was followed by a heady series of events including committee assignments, the enjoyment of an obvious special status in Washington reserved for those holding positions of power, and an invitation to the White House following the inauguration of President Brasington on January 20, 2017.

Naturally, he developed many relationships with colleagues and House staffers. But he was particularly pleased with his new-found friend, Charles Pearce, counselor to the President and deputy White House chief of staff. Hall had cultivated this relationship for all of the obvious political reasons, but also because he genuinely liked Pearce. Over time, they had visited each other's offices, but the Rayburn House Office Building, for all of its rich history, was no comparison to the heady atmosphere of power at the White House and in the Eisenhower Executive Office Building, for it was there that the levers of power were truly located.

Jackson Hall was also a patient man, especially for someone of his young age. But soon, very soon, he would be asking a very special favor of his new friend in the White House.

Chapter 7: Washington

Freshman Congressman Jackson Hall had reason to be proud of many things, including his academic success in the University of California system, which had led not only to his undergraduate degree in history but also to his admission to law school. Always with the goal of building a career in politics, Hall knew very well the advantages of holding a law degree. As an attorney, it's easy to socialize with power-brokers and politicians. It is a great credential for seeking office, particularly if one has served as an assistant district attorney or in some other office which helped to provide name recognition through frequent media exposure. And if one runs for office and doesn't win the election, one always has his or her law degree to provide an income until the next opportunity comes along.

But Brasington's presidential run had the effect of accelerating Jackson's plans. Adopted as an infant, Hall's father was a pastor at one of the smaller but still influential evangelical Christian churches in Anaheim. Jackson Hall grew up in a household steeped in a belief in the Bible. Daily rituals of prayer and saying grace before meals, along with at least twice-weekly attendance at his father's church, as well as Bible School each summer when he was young, helped to mold him into the deeply religious person he had now become. It was sometimes difficult for him to reconcile his religious beliefs with many of his colleagues in the House, but his faith was unwavering, and no friendship or political deal-making would get in the way of what he saw as the path of righteousness.

His father was also an avid hunter, and he had instructed Jackson from a very young age in the virtues and handling of firearms, everything from a small handgun to a double-barrel shotgun. Reverend Hall had no religious qualms about hunting, whether it be for sport or for food. He also enthusiastically kept a variety of firearms in the family home for defensive purposes. When teaching his young son about the use of weapons in defense of life or property, he had only two admonitions: Never aim your gun at someone unless you intend to shoot, and aim for the heart, the head, and the groin, not necessarily in that order. And so Jackson had learned at an early age about God and Guns. He would learn all of the evils of "the Gay" at a somewhat more mature age.

But as close as Jackson was to his adoptive parents, he had developed a burning desire to know more about his biological parents as he had transitioned from child to adolescent and then to young adult. As a youth, he would look at himself in the bathroom mirror, and his red hair and green eyes were obviously not related to the dark brown hair and blue eyes possessed by both the mother and father he did know. In his teens, he had broached the issue with them. They kindly and patiently explained to him that while it was true that they had adopted him as an infant, God had placed him in their home just as surely as if he had been born there.

But Jackson wanted to know more. What could he have done so early in his life to cause his birth mother, and perhaps his biological father as well, to have cast him out of their home by putting him up for adoption? Or was he not at fault at all? He had to know the answers to these questions that went to the very fiber of his being. Reverend and Mrs. Hall tried to tell him that his adoption records were sealed for his own well-being, and that there was simply no way to get more information. They themselves had never had any contact with his biological parents, having dealt exclusively with the adoption agency.

When Jackson turned twenty-one years of age, while others of his cohort celebrated by buying alcoholic beverages legally for the first time ever in their young lives, Jackson visited the adoption agency in Los Angeles after prying the information about its location from Reverend Hall. The visit did not go well. After giving him the same explanation about court-sealed records as he had received from his adoptive parents so many years before, Jackson had loudly demanded to see his file. This led to security being called to escort him out of the building, along with a stern warning that if he ever returned, it would be the police rather than security who would be removing him from the facility. Jackson got the message, but he was furious over his helplessness to learn about his own life.

He then went to meet with an attorney, who patiently gave him the same repetitive explanation about adoption law in California and the court action which had sealed his records. He further added that Jackson should be proud and thankful to have been adopted into such a fine home in the community. To his credit, the attorney didn't even charge him for the consultation.

But Jackson's adoptive parents, the adoption agency, and the attorney all had one thing in common: they had failed to recognize that Jackson was absolutely driven to learn about his real parents. And he had a plan for doing so that was perfectly in keeping with his career objectives.

Becoming an attorney himself was just the first step. Becoming elected as a member of the U.S. House of Representatives was the second step. And he was now about to take what he hoped and believed would be the final step necessary to accomplish his goals. He quickly stepped out of the House Rayburn Office Building into the brisk winter air and found the limousine he had hired waiting for him.

Chapter 8: The White House

The Capitol Hill limousine delivered Jackson Hall to the main entrance of the White House. He checked in at the uniformed Secret Service guard station and advised them of his meeting with White House deputy chief of staff Charles Pearce. The agents checked his Congressional identification card, entered his name into their computer system, and since no danger flags were elicited, they called Pearce's office and notified his secretary that his appointment had arrived. Hall was permitted to proceed from the main gate to the visitor's entrance of the mansion itself, where he was once again detained until Pearce arrived to escort him to his West Wing office.

"Jackson, I can't tell you how nice it is to see you again. How are things going for you on the Hill?"

"Pretty fair, Chuck, thanks. And for you here in the White House?"

"The usual growing pains of a fresh new administration. Hell, I'm still trying to find my own way around this maze of offices."

Arriving at his office, he introduced Hall to his secretary and took him into his own small but utilitarian inner sanctum. "As a new member of Congress, I know you've already had the grand tour and met the president. As you can see, my own digs here are far more modest than those of the chief of staff himself."

"Ah, but that doesn't negate the real power that exists within these walls, does it now?"

"I suppose not. So tell me Mr. Congressman, what can this lowly servant of the President of the United States do for you today?"

"Chuck, I hope you consider me to be a friend as well as a political colleague?"

"Of course I do. And as I told you when we first met, we have some great plans for you as a new member of the 'Lower Body.' Not the least of which is to support and perhaps even co-sponsor some very important legislative initiatives that will soon be forthcoming."

"That sounds good to me."

"Okay. Now, you told me on the phone that you had something important you wanted to discuss with me?"

"Yes, especially since we're now officially friends," he said with his charming grin.

"Lay it on me then."

"Chuck, I need a favor, a personal favor."

"Indeed? Knowing you as a man of good character, I'm sure it's nothing unethical or illegal, so how can we help?"

"You wouldn't know this about me, and there's really no reason that you would, but I was adopted as an infant. And I'm very fortunate that my adoptive parents provided me a great upbringing, so I'm certainly not complaining about my lot in life or anything."

Pearce smiled at him and said, "Well I hope not. Let's see, your father is the pastor of a very influential church in your home city. You've had the benefit of the finest education that the Great State of California has to offer, all the way from pre-kindergarten to a law degree, and you're a newly-elected Member of the United States House of Representatives. So far no obvious reason for pity, is there?"

"Indeed not. Look Chuck, here's the thing. I suppose that many of us have mysteries in our lives, things that we desperately either need to know, or want to know, about ourselves. In my case, I must know more about my biological mother and the circumstances surrounding her giving me up for adoption. Unfortunately, the family court judge that handled my adoption used a provision of the California Statutes to seal the proceedings of my case, so despite my best efforts, including, by the way, getting myself physically removed from the downtown Los Angeles Adoption agency, I am still totally in the dark."

"I see, but Jackson, how can I possibly help you with this?"

Holding his hands up in an expansive gesture, Jackson replied, "Because this is the White House."

Pearce looked quietly at his new friend for a minute and then said, "Look, maybe if you were on staff here there might be some way, and I emphasize the word 'might,' but you're not, you're a Member of Congress. I can't see any way that we can go nosing around in court-sealed records from your past without risking the wrath of state or local officials and even worse, possibly, the news media if word got out. You see that don't you?"

"I do, and yet...and yet, this is the White House, and you do work for the President of the United States, don't you?"

Pearce paused for a moment, and then said, "This is really important to you, isn't it?"

"Uh, yeah, do you think?" Jackson replied emphatically.

"Tell you what, give me a few days to think about this. And maybe check with my boss about it. And I don't mean the president, you understand?"

"Of course I understand."

"Okay then, let me see what is and isn't possible, alright?"

"Yes, and I would definitely appreciate anything you can do."

Pearce looked at his watch and saw that it was noon. "Hey Jackson, how about joining me in the White House Mess for lunch?"

"Now that's an offer I really can't refuse, thank you."

And thus the two newly-minted federal officials, one from the legislative branch and one from the executive branch, walked side-by-side out of the West Wing office and down a hallway to one of the most exclusive lunch hang-outs in the nation's capital.

Chapter 9: Capitol Hill

Three days after meeting with his new friend in the White House, Annie Delacourt, Hall's administrative assistant, knocked and entered his office. "Sir, the Chairman of the House Select Committee on Intelligence is on the phone for you."

"What? I'm only a freshman member. What would he want with me?"

"I don't know, but he wants to speak with you now."

"Of course then, put him through."

A moment later his multi-line phone signaled for his attention.

He answered the way he always did, regardless of the caller. "Jackson Hall, how may I help you?"

The seasoned voice on the other end of the connection said, "This is Chairman Findlay. How about coming over to my office this afternoon at three o'clock?"

"Of course sir, I'll clear my schedule and be there at three."

"Very good. See you then."

As the call was disconnected, newly-elected Congressman Jackson Hall was left with a very puzzled look on his face.

Jackson arrived at the chairman's office promptly for his appointment and was greeted by one of the committee staff in an outer office. A few minutes later, Chairman Jack Findlay emerged from his own office, spotted Jackson, and walked over to him, offering his hand. "Jackson Hall, I presume?"

"Yes sir."

"I'm Jack Findlay. Come on back here with me, son, we've got some business to discuss." As Jackson began walking beside and slightly behind the chairman, Findlay put his arm around his shoulder and asked, "What do you think of this place after just a few months?"

"I'm enjoying it very much, sir, still trying to learn the ropes."

"Well, that's one of the reasons I wanted to see you today. I think you have a bright future here in the House, and I want to see that you get a good start."

"Thank you sir, I appreciate that very much."

Entering the chairman's beautifully decorated office, he gestured Jackson to have a seat. The chairman sat down behind his huge desk and offered Jackson a cigar from a decorated wooden box.

"Thank you sir, but I don't smoke."

"Good for you, it's a terrible habit. Hope you don't mind if I do?"

"No sir, of course not."

Chairman Findlay selected a huge cigar from the box and took his time to carefully prepare it for use. Finally he used an ornamental military lighter, puffed on the cigar a few times, and said, "You know, the Cubans really do make the best cigars in the world."

"That's what I hear sir."

"And you hear right."

A moment went by while he enjoyed his cigar and then carefully placed it in an ashtray on his desk, aromatic smoke curling up into the air between them.

"Here's the thing, son. Totally out of the blue, I find myself getting a call from the chief of staff over at the White House suggesting that I should appoint you to one of my Intelligence subcommittees. Now that's a mighty peculiar thing to happen, especially coming from the White House, and especially considering that you're still wet behind the ears. Know what I mean?"

"Yes sir, I do," Jackson replied carefully.

"Now on the one hand, I really don't like the executive branch messing around in my committee's business. But on the other hand, the election of President Brasington and the new members of our party who were elected to the House had the effect of elevating me from being the ranking member of this committee to being the chairman, and I have no desire to offend our new president, or his staff, without good reason. Now, do you happen to know anything about this?"

"Sir, I visited Charles Pearce, a friend of mine on the White House staff the other day. I may have mentioned to him in passing my interest in the intelligence community. That's the only thing I can think of."

The chairman picked up his cigar and puffed on it a few times, clouding the air between them with smoke. "Uh huh. Hell of a coincidence, wouldn't you say? Well, this is damned unusual, but I've heard some good things about you, and I'm inclined to cooperate with this suggestion. And it certainly would be a very good thing for your new career now, wouldn't it? You think you could take my Dutch Uncle's advice in handling your new committee assignment on matters with which you may not be totally familiar?"

"I know it would be a great career boost, sir, and I can assure you that I will serve in whatever capacity you deem appropriate, and yes, that I will follow your lead very closely when it comes to any votes that will be cast."

"I'm glad to hear you say that. Makes me think you might make a good politician in the long haul."

"Thank you, sir."

"You do realize, don't you, that to serve on any sub-committee on Intelligence, it would require a complete background check by the FBI. And I do mean a complete background check, do you understand?"

"Yes sir, I have nothing to hide."

"I hope you're right. We'll soon know for sure. I've got a few consent documents here for you to sign and then we'll get the ball rolling. I strongly suggest that you say nothing about this to anyone until you've been cleared. That includes your staff and your family back home. If any of this leaks out at all, Jackson, in any way, the offer is withdrawn immediately and, between you and me, your goose is totally cooked. Is that clear?"

"Crystal, sir."

The meeting came to a close, and Jackson Hall walked out of the chairman's office and back to his own with a very slight smile on his face, thinking over and over of the phrase, "wheels within wheels."

Chapter 10: Capitol Hill

And so it was that two weeks after his meeting with Chairman Findlay, Jackson was appointed as a provisional member of the House Select Committee on Intelligence, subcommittee on ELINT, or electronic intelligence. Because his background check was not yet complete and he wasn't cleared for top secret intelligence briefings, he was temporarily not permitted to attend subcommittee meetings. But two weeks later, his clearance was approved by the Director of National Intelligence and he was seated as a full member of the subcommittee.

This was all well and fine, but not nearly as important to him as when a courier from the White House delivered to him personally a large brown envelope. He immediately knew that this would be a copy of his background investigation. Jackson told his assistant to hold his calls as he sat back in his chair and removed the file from the envelope.

Here, at last, was the information he had so desperately wanted to see for as long as he could remember. His hands actually trembled as he opened the file folder, read the summary clearance statement, and then found the true copy of his adoption record. His biological mother was identified as Constance Marie Scarcia, born in 1974 in Los Angeles. His father was listed as "not known." That didn't sound good at all. His mother would only have been sixteen years old when she gave birth to him, and she may well have been sexually promiscuous.

This answered a few questions for him, but he needed more. Somehow he would have to locate his biological mother, but how? He couldn't use his government connections, that much was for certain. And he definitely couldn't go flying all over the country trying to find her during his freshman year in the Congress. He realized that he would have to engage a private investigator, and one who could be totally relied upon to keep his mouth shut about his client's business. He opened up the Yellow Pages in the Washington Metro telephone directory, carefully selected a few potential firms, and then made the telephone call that he hoped would finally lead him to his biological mother and the answers to his remaining questions.

The next afternoon, he welcomed into his office one Derrick Gabriel, licensed private investigator. He already knew from the telephone interview he had conducted that Gabriel had a law enforcement background and then had founded a very successful business of his own.

"Mr. Gabriel, I want to again emphasize how important it is that this investigation, should I hire you, be kept totally confidential between the two of us."

"That's not a problem, I assure you that most of my clients demand exactly that."

"Yes, but I'm a government official now, and I'm very sensitive to keeping this out of the public eye."

"Of course, Congressman. How can I help you?"

"I want you to locate my biological mother. Hall is my adoptive name. All I know about her is when and where she was born and her full name. Can you do this?"

"Mr. Hall, if she can be found, I can find her. But I want you to know that it could prove to be very expensive. I'll do as much as I can from my office here in DC, but it's often necessary to travel here or there to nail down something concrete. Let's see now, you are representing Orange County, California. Is that where your adoption took place?"

"Not quite. Los Angeles, which is also my mother's birthplace."

"Well now that's interesting, isn't it?"

"That she was born in Los Angeles?"

"No, the fact that you were adopted in California where these kinds of records are usually sealed by the court system. Has she tried to contact you?"

"No she hasn't."

"Uh huh. I see."

Hall leaned forward in his chair and said, "I can see that you're good at what you do. I think you understand the sensitive nature of this information. Now if you can do that well at locating her for me…?"

"It shouldn't be a problem. Is this time sensitive?"

"Just to the extent that I've been waiting for 27 years to find her."

"Okay then, let me get started. For this type of case, my initial retainer is $2,500, but please keep in mind that it could go much higher with travel expenses and if it takes more time than I expect."

Hall wrote out a personal check and handed it to Gabriel. "Keep me updated."

"I certainly will, and thank you for this opportunity to be of service."

Chapter 11: Washington

Derrick Gabriel began working on his new case as soon as he returned to his office. He had built a very successful firm since leaving his law enforcement career, but it wasn't every day that a private investigator acquired a Member of Congress as a client. He would handle this case personally, both because of his own interest and the obvious need for a high degree of confidentiality.

It didn't take him very long to locate the basic record information on Constance Marie Scarcia, born in Los Angeles County, California, on the exact date that the congressman had provided to him. He was even able to retrieve a copy of the Record of Live Birth issued for an unnamed child which matched Hall's birthdate. Obviously the baby had been given over for adoption right after birth.

He then checked the California Criminal Records System and found that Scarcia had experienced one brush with the law as a juvenile on a drug possession charge. She then entered a rehab facility for thirty days as part of a plea bargain. Apparently the rehab program had worked, because after completing her stay there, she quickly qualified for her G.E.D. high school equivalency diploma, went to work for two years as a Certified Nursing Assistant, and then succeeded in gaining admission to a Registered Nursing school affiliated with a major Los Angeles hospital system. Upon graduation from the program three years later, she went to work for the same hospital. And that was where his line of inquiry from the comfort of his office reached a hurdle that couldn't be overcome without a personal visit to the Human Relations department at the hospital, since they refused to provide any information to him over the telephone. He booked a flight to Los Angeles for the next day with an open return date.

His flight in business class seating was as pleasant as air travel could be in these days of deteriorating infrastructure, and his arrival at LAX was only fifty minutes late. He took his carry-on from the overhead bin and proceeded to his favorite rental car agency.

He had driven in Los Angeles many times before, and while he enjoyed the change of scenery from Washington, he hated driving here. Too many confusing freeways with unpredictable exit lanes on both sides of the highway. At least the small GPS unit he carried with him would help him get around to a great extent.

He approached the main building of the massive Century Palms Hospital complex and paid for valet parking. It was, after all, a billable expense. He located the Human Relations office on the third floor of the "A" wing. This was the point where he could either catch a break in his investigation or hit a stone wall, depending upon one of several factors. He approached the receptionist, quickly displayed his P.I. badge and ID card, and asked to speak with the HR director, Sylvia Fuentes. He was always somewhat surprised when this technique worked as well as it did. A civilian sees a badge and photo ID card and often doesn't really want to get a closer look. Within five minutes, he was seated across the desk from Ms. Fuentes.

Once again, he quickly displayed his badge and began speaking before she had a chance to ask any questions. "Ma'am, I'm here from Washington as part of a background investigation into one…," and even though he knew the name as well as his own, he looked inside a file folder with an impressive seal on its front cover, "… uh, Constance Scarcia. She either is or was an RN with your facility?"

In fact, Sylvia Fuentes was properly impressed with the credentials, the official-looking file folder, and the well-dressed and handsome gentleman sitting in her office. She thought for a moment, and then she realized whom he was asking about. "Oh, Connie, of course! Heavens, I never knew her as Constance. Yes, she did work here at one time. She was a great nurse and we were sorry to lose her."

"What happened to her?"

"Well, she decided to go into private duty nursing. If I remember correctly, the agency that recruited her specialized in wealthy clients who wanted essentially a live-in nurse who would be with them at all times, including when they traveled. I must say, it all sounded kind of exciting, but I certainly wasn't in a position to give up my career here and my benefits to go into something that could be fairly unstable. I mean, what if months went by with no client? How could you support yourself? What about health insurance? No, excitement or not, it wasn't for me. But Connie was young and ambitious and she jumped at the opportunity." She smiled broadly at

Derrick, feeling certain that she had contributed to an important matter.

Derrick returned her smile, as if to reassure her that she was doing a good job. "Very interesting, yes. You've been most helpful, but I wonder if you have some contact information for that agency?"

"Well, now, you wait right here and make yourself at home while I go find her personnel file in the archives. I'm afraid she left our employment a long enough time ago that her computer record would have been purged and stored. I'll be right back."

Derrick thanked her and looked around her office. He had no doubt that Sylvia Fuentes was a very competent if not overly-ambitious employee and that she had found the perfect place of employment for her career. The photos of her family and children were further evidence of his impression of her as a successful working mother. In some ways, he envied her achievement of having a wonderful-looking family and a fitting career. His own life might hold more excitement, but there was a lot to be said for stability. He thought of the old saying, "one person's rut is another person's career."

She returned to her office with a file folder of her own. "I've got it!" she said with enthusiasm.

"Indeed you do," Derrick replied. "And you have such a lovely family too."

She literally beamed. "Why thank you, I am truly blessed."

Before she could introduce all of her family members, Derrick looked quickly at his watch and then at her file folder. "So, did you find the agency?"

"Oh, I think so. It should all be here, just let me take a look-see." She shuffled through a few pages and then said, "Yes, here it is. She left us about six years ago to work with Travel Pro Nursing Service. And if you're planning to go there, I'm afraid you've got a drive ahead of you because it's located all the way on the other side of the city, and at this time of day, that could be a long trip for you."

Derrick grunted in agreement. "Oh well, you've been an enormous help. I can't tell you how much I appreciate it."

Her face lit up again. She was obviously enjoying this break from the humdrum routine of her everyday job.

Derrick stood up to leave, but Sylvia gestured for him to wait.

"Listen, Mr. Gabriel, maybe I can save you some time. I could call the agency for you and perhaps find out what you need to know. We HR types stick together, you know?"

"Oh, I can certainly imagine that you would. That's very kind of you. Would you mind putting the call on speakerphone?"

"Why of course," Sylvia said, now feeling like she was part of the investigation itself. She keyed the number into her phone and put it on speaker.

"Good afternoon, Travel Pro Nursing Service, how may I direct your call?"

Sylvia spoke in her most professional voice, "This is Sylvia Fuentes, Director of Human Relations at Century

Palms Hospital. May I speak with your director of nursing, please?"

"Of course, ma'am, please hold."

Sylvia winked and smiled at Derrick.

A moment later, a voice came on the line, "This is Barb Masters, how can I help you, Ms. Fuentes?"

"Oh, hi Barb, it's been a very long time, hasn't it?" Another wink at Derrick.

"It certainly has," the telephone voice replied with slight uncertainty. "What can I do for you today?"

"Listen Barb, I've got an old friend of Connie Scarcia sitting here in my office. He came all the way from Washington to find her. All I could tell him was what a great nurse she had been for us and that she later went to work for your agency. Is she still there?"

"No, but I wish she were. She's one of the best nurses we've ever had in our service. She worked for us for just over a year, taking care of one of our clients exclusively. When the client passed away, Connie gave us two weeks notice and went back East."

"Is that right? She sure does get around. Who made her an offer better than yours?"

"I don't really know. I don't even know whether she might have been leaving the profession, although I hope not. She's too good at it."

"Oh dear, oh my. Did she even leave any contact information with you? I hate to send this nice gentleman packing with nothing more to show for his trip."

"Let me check for you, hold on a minute." The line clicked over to a hold bridge.

"I'm trying," Sylvia said to Derrick.

"You certainly are, Ms. Fuentes, and I can't tell you how much we," and he emphasized the *we*, "appreciate your assistance."

"Hey Sylvia?" Barb Masters came back on the line.

"Yes Barb."

"Her final paycheck had yet to be issued when she left, so she gave us this forwarding address: Connie Scarcia, in care of FSOU, 120 Larkin Street, Olston, West Virginia."

Sylvia confirmed that she had copied the address correctly. "Any idea what the FSOU stands for?"

"None at all, I'm sorry. I remember that she seemed in kind of a hurry to leave the city. I hope she wasn't in any kind of trouble."

"Knowing Connie, I wouldn't worry about that," as she shrugged her shoulders at Derrick and gave a "what was I supposed to say?" look. "Thanks for everything Barb. Maybe it won't be so long until the next time."

"Yes, well if you have any more Connie Scarcia's on your staff who are looking for a change, please send them my way, okay?"

"Sure, if I absolutely can't convince them to stay with us," she said with a grin.

"I understand completely. Well, keep in touch."

"Will do, and thanks again," Sylvia said before disconnecting the call.

She handed the slip of paper with the address to Derrick. "I hope that your report will show that we have been thoroughly cooperative?"

"Absolutely, in fact, beyond the call of duty," Derrick told her convincingly. "And now, it looks like I will be heading to West Virginia." He arose from the chair and shook hands with Sylvia Fuentes. "It's been a real pleasure, ma'am."

"Oh, definitely. If I can be of any further help, don't hesitate to call or come back."

"You know, Sylvia, I can't begin to thank you enough, and just between you and me, I'm going to recommend in my report that you be designated as a 'Friend of the Agency'."

"Oh my, will you really do that?"

"I really will. You have a good day now."

And Derrick Gabriel left Sylvia Fuentes feeling that she had played a very special part in a very important investigation. And to Derrick, she had indeed.

Chapter 12: Olston, WV

Derrick had returned to Washington the next day. He then spent a day in his office both to recover from jet lag and to catch up on routine business. He scheduled himself out of the office for the following day to make the road trip to Olston, West Virginia. From what he could learn on the internet, Olston was an unincorporated small town not too far from the southern border of West Virginia. His GPS device told him that he would be driving about 380 miles each way, so he needed to allow seven hours from his departure to his arrival in Olston. He didn't really mind driving, but this was going to be a long hike through Virginia and then into southern West Virginia. At least the weather forecast was not calling for snow and much of the drive would be very scenic, especially the area around Front Royal. There were no directory listings for anything close to something named "FSOU" in or around Olston, so he had no recourse but to make the drive. He had also done an address search for 120 Larkin Street, but the only listing was for a hardware store. Derrick guessed that it might be a small strip mall or office complex. At any rate, he planned to leave his home at about 6:00 a.m. so that he would arrive at his destination during normal afternoon business hours.

Once during the long drive he found himself becoming very drowsy, so he found a small diner and enjoyed a late breakfast with lots of black coffee. Then a brief stop in the men's room and he was back on his way. He had been right about Front Royal, as the view from the mountain drive was always magnificent.

He crossed into West Virginia and his trusty GPS unit told him that he had about thirty miles to go until he reached Olston. About a half hour later, he approached a small and dusty looking town with what appeared to be just one main road stretching the length of the town. He stopped along the roadside for a moment to take a drink of water and explore his surroundings. Right in front of him was the official West Virginia "Olston, WV" sign. Below that on the same post was the town's own sign which read, "Welcome to Olston, West By God Virginia, pop. 3510." He wondered how often the population count was updated on this sign, if ever.

Driving on into the town, he found hardly any traffic whatsoever, and very few pedestrians. He thought that this was truly a sleepy old town if ever he had seen one. He noticed that the one road through the town was, in fact, Larkin Street, so he merely had to look for 120. A few blocks later, on his right, he spotted an old wooden building with an aged metal sign reading, "Dell's Hardware Store." Then he saw the "120" in metal numbers affixed next to the doorway. He parked literally right in front of the entrance. Not getting out of his car yet, he felt that something wasn't right. This was the address that Connie Scarcia had provided to her last employer before leaving California, but he couldn't find anything congruent between her occupation as a nurse, something called FSOU, and the old-time hardware store he was now parked in front of.

Alright, he thought, time to shop for a hammer and nails. He opened the door and entered the hardware store. The interior was fairly dark except for the light coming in two windows along the side of the store and a fluorescent lighting fixture over a counter in the back of the store, where a clerk, or perhaps the owner, was talking to an elderly gentleman about something. "Be with you in a minute, sir," he called out.

"No rush, take your time," Derrick replied. He hadn't seen anything like this in his life except in old movies or television shows. There seemed to be no order to the way in which any of the stock was arranged, but there was an ample selection of tools, fasteners, padlocks, doorknobs and hinges, and even bicycle tires. The combined odor of wood, metal, rubber, and lubricants was almost overwhelming. Shafts of sunlight through the windows revealed fine dust in the air. Maybe sawdust, he thought. He found himself looking too long at a display of flashlights, ready to choose one. And he would need batteries for it. Whoa, he thought, back to the business at hand.

The elderly customer passed him on his way out of the store, and the owner or clerk approached him. "Howdy stranger, can I help you to find somethin'?"

Derrick looked at the middle-aged man wearing denim overalls and said, "Hi. I'm afraid I might have a somewhat strange question for you."

The man laughed and said, "Don't worry, I get strange questions all the time. What do you need?"

Derrick thought that if any store in the Great State of West Virginia needed a boost, this was the one, and so he found that he couldn't help himself. "I was looking at this display of flashlights, and I couldn't help but notice this sort of state of the art LED model you've got here."

The clerk nodded and pointed his finger just so to indicate that Derrick had made a wise choice. "LEDs are great. They'll never burn out on you and they're real easy on batteries. Feel that baby."

Derrick removed the flashlight from the display and properly demonstrated that he appreciated its heft and balance. "Nice one, isn't it?" he said to the clerk.

"That baby'll last your whole life and then some."

"I believe that," Derrick replied. "How about ringing this up for me along with some alkaline batteries?"

"You've got it," the clerk said, heading for the counter at the back of the store.

As the clerk punched the keys on an old manual cash register, Derrick said, ""Listen, about that strange question. I'm looking for something called FSOU which is supposed to be at this very same address."

The clerk looked up from installing the batteries in Derrick's new flashlight and said, "Ain't nothin' strange about that question, although it only comes up two or three times a year."

"Really?"

"Yep, and I think you're in luck, because I believe old Wes is up there today."

"Up there?" Derrick asked.

"Yep, up those wood steps to the second floor. He's been renting a room from me for, oh gosh, a lot of years now."

Derrick completed the transaction and the clerk asked him if he wanted a poke for his purchase. Derrick had been looking at the old open set of stairs leading to the second floor in this fire-trap of a building and wondering who would ever rent space here. He nodded absently to the clerk, who put the flashlight into a brown paper bag and handed it to him.

"Thanks for your business today. You made a good purchase with this. Go ahead up there, old Wes'll be glad to see you."

"Okay, thanks." And Derrick climbed the rickety wooden steps, feeling briefly as if he had stepped into a different reality.

Chapter 13: Olston, WV

Derrick continued up the rickety wood staircase, came to a landing, made a turn, and then continued up another set of stairs to the second floor. The smell of age was thick in the air. He stepped into a dimly-lit hallway, wondering all the while whether the rough wood flooring was really safe for occupancy. The wall to his right was obviously the interior of one side of the building. On his left was a door with a translucent panel of glass, backlit by some lighting coming from within the room. The words "Foundation for the Study of the Origin of the Universe" were painted on the glass in black letters. A small hand-printed sign was affixed to the panel below the painted words. It read, "If unlocked, come on in. If locked, come back another time." He looked at the painted words again and realized that "FSOU" was undoubtedly an acronym for this name. He stood in front of the door for a moment, thinking that this had to be the most unlikely place in the world for a scientific foundation to be located. Nothing about it made sense, other than the fact that a piece of mail could logically have been forwarded to "FSOU" at this address.

He knocked lightly, turned the brass knob, and gently tried the door. He found that it was unlocked and it opened with a squeak. Inside the room were stacks and stacks of books. Renditions of the solar system and the Milky Way galaxy, along with other astronomical charts and maps lined the walls everywhere. An old wooden desk sat about half-way into the room, behind which were high shelving units containing even more books and printed matter. Just then he heard the sound of footsteps, and an elderly and stooped gray-haired man came from around the other side of the shelves and noticed Derrick.

"Why hello there, sorry, I didn't hear you come in. I'm afraid my hearing's not what it used to be. But welcome, welcome. I'm Wes, what can I do for you, Mister?" He was wearing an old white shirt and brown pants. Thick eyeglasses adorned his aged craggy face. But at least he smiled.

"Hello, my name is Derrick Gabriel," and as usual, he displayed his badge and ID card, but this time, his audience took a real interest in his credentials.

"Mind if I take a closer look at that, Mr. Gabriel? That's a nice-looking shield you've got there. Don't see many of those around these parts. We don't even have a police department here in Olston."

"Not at all," Derrick replied, handing the badge case to the old man.

"Boy, that's really something. You really a private investigator?"

"Yes sir I am, based out of Washington."

"Hah!" he replied. "You mean the District of Confusion?"

"A lot of people feel that way," Derrick admitted.

"And with good reason, too, eh?"

"Perhaps so. But I was wondering if you can help me with something?"

"Be glad to try, Mr. Gabriel. You interested in my research here?"

"Well, yes, I'm sure that must be very fascinating, but I'm really trying to locate someone."

"Well, you found me, that much is for sure."

Derrick smiled at the old gentleman. "Yes, but I'm afraid that I'm looking for someone else."

"I'm the only one here, except for the occasional visitor like yourself, of course. Who might you be looking for?"

"A woman named Connie Scarcia, who either is or was a nurse." Derrick briefly recounted his trip to Los Angeles and what he had learned there.

The old man first looked surprised and then smiled. "So it's Connie you're looking for?"

"Yes, you know her then?"

"Well I hope so, she's my niece. I'm Wes Scarcia. There's just one problem though," he sighed wistfully.

Derrick had briefly felt hopeful that he was close to finding his subject, but the sound of the man's voice and the look on his face quickly caused his hope to fade. "What's that?"

"I haven't seen or heard from her in years. I'm afraid she might have passed on."

"When did you last hear from her?"

"Oh, it's been at least five or six years. She stopped in to see me when she moved back from California, and I had a few pieces of mail that I was holding for her. We were never really very close, but I tried to help her out when she was young and foolish. Even sent her money a few times. Her Ma and Pa weren't good for much. I'm sorry to speak that way of my brother, but it's the God's honest truth. She had a tough childhood, that's for certain. But she was strong, kind of street-smart, you know? She got through it somehow and finally made something of herself. Became a nurse, and a darn good one too."

"If I may ask then, since I understand that she had a very successful career in California, why do you suppose she came back east?"

"I don't know. I think she had a bit of the wanderlust in her. She had been a private duty nurse for some old lady, even traveled around the world with her. She told me that after her patient passed on, she had gotten a really good offer somewhere back here in the east, but I don't know where. She told me that she would be very busy and that I probably wouldn't hear from her very much, but I haven't heard from her at all, and that just doesn't seem right to me."

"Nothing at all?"

"Nothing. It's as if she disappeared from the face of the Earth. That's why I'm afraid the Grim Reaper has taken her."

"I'm very sorry to hear that," Derrick said, quite honestly, although the reason for his own regret would have been much different from her uncle's. "What is it that you do here anyway?" he asked curiously.

"You saw the name on the door?" Wes asked.

"Yes I did. So this is some kind of scientific foundation?"

"Well, it's scientific, and I like to think of it as a foundation. But it's a one-man shop, and you're looking at him."

"And so, you're trying to study…what exactly?"

"Nothing less than the origin of our universe," Wes stated with considerable pride. "Look at all these books and maps and charts. These are my roadmaps, and I've been following them for years."

"You've made progress then?"

"Well of course I've made progress. You don't think I've just been twiddling my thumbs for the last eight or nine years, do you?"

"No, of course not. Can you tell me what you've learned?"

"Wish I could, young fella, but I'm getting everything ready for publication in a year or two. Tell you this though, when my research is published, them folks who have had a good laugh or two at my expense are going to be in for quite a surprise." As Wes had been speaking, his eyes had widened and his voice had risen sharply.

Derrick found himself questioning the man's sanity. It almost sounded as if he were having delusions of grandeur. "You already have a publisher for your work then?"

"No, not yet. Not time. Still too much to do. And then those prissy academic publishers all seem to want references and research notes. Why, they even want me to submit my material to a few other scientists first for evaluation before they'll even consider publishing it. Are they crazy? Do they really think I'm going to turn my findings over to someone else who can then claim all the credit for it? Not gonna happen! No, I may very well have to publish it myself."

Derrick once again found that he couldn't help himself. He was convinced that he would learn nothing more here, but he found himself either interested in or mildly entertained by the old man. He just had to ask him another question. "So, Dr. Scarcia, where did you complete your education?"

"Oh hell, I'm no doctor. I'm just a well-educated researcher, and I'm a proud alumnae of Olston Community Joint Senior High School. Got straight A's too, I'll have you know!"

Derrick felt that it was now time to leave. "Well, Mr. Scarcia, it's been a pleasure meeting you, and I wish you the best with your research and upcoming book."

Wes beamed, "My pleasure meeting you, Mr. Gabriel. Sorry I couldn't be of more help to you with Connie."

"Listen, would you do me a favor?" Derrick handed him one of his business cards. "If you should hear from her, would you be so kind as to give me a call at this number? Please feel free to reverse the charges."

"No problem, but don't hold your breath waiting for that call, you hear?"

"I won't. And again, good luck with your work." He turned and walked back out to the hallway, closing the door to the Foundation for the Study of the Origin of the Universe behind him. He walked gently down the old wood steps into the hardware store, out the front door, and got back into his car. As he contemplated the long drive home to Washington, he could only shake his head and wonder about the different things that make people tick. Well, he thought, I came a long way just to buy a new flashlight.

Wes Scarcia puttered around his office for ten or fifteen minutes and then sat down at his desk. He rubbed his chin with his fingers for another minute, and then picked up the handset of his old phone and called a number in area code 719, which happened to be assigned to a telephone company central office in southeastern Colorado.

Chapter 14: Capitol Hill

Jackson Hall was as excited as he had ever been in his life when he learned that Derrick Gabriel had called to make a follow-up appointment to meet with him. Gabriel had called and left a message with his administrative assistant earlier in the morning. Well aware of his boss's interest in whatever Gabriel was investigating for him, she rearranged the congressman's schedule to fit Gabriel in at 2:00 that afternoon. She had then sent a text message to her boss on the floor of the House. Hall texted back to thank her and to confirm the appointment.

Now sitting at his desk in his congressional office complex, Hall eagerly waited for Gabriel to arrive. He had already left instructions for his staff to escort the P.I. into the office immediately upon his arrival and then to hold all of his calls. At precisely 1:55, a soft knock on his door alerted him that his visitor had arrived. He opened the door and welcomed Gabriel in to have a seat, closing the door behind him. He noticed that Gabriel was carrying a leather briefcase.

"So, Mr. Gabriel, I can't tell you how pleased I am to see you so soon. What do you have for me?"

Derrick proceeded to recount the events surrounding first his computer records search, then his visit to the hospital complex in California, and finally his road trip to the old hardware store and his interview with Wes Scarcia in Olston, West Virginia.

"So, Congressman, unfortunately I haven't been able to locate your mother. There is no death record listed for her in any state or here in DC, for that matter. Nor is there any record of a current driver's license issued to a Constance or Connie Scarcia with her birthdate and description in any jurisdiction in the U.S."

"But how could that be?" Hall asked. "If she's not deceased, she's got to be somewhere."

"Indeed, but let me fill you in on a few other lines of inquiry that I pursued after returning from West Virginia. As a former law enforcement officer, I have some friends and former colleagues whom I can call upon to obtain information which would not otherwise be available. Before I proceed though, I want you to understand that there are issues of confidentiality and perhaps even legality involved here, so I want you to think carefully about whether you want me to continue telling you about my findings. And before you answer, please know that this information did not bear any fruit."

Hall was caught short by this revelation. He got up from his chair and faced the window behind his desk, looking out of his office onto the grounds of the Capitol complex. He had worked so hard to get elected to Congress. He was squeaky clean. There were no skeletons in his closet that someone could use to bring him down or to cast him in an unfavorable light in a future election. But now here he was, the private investigator he had hired to find his birth mother was sitting in his office with additional information that he already knew had not proven useful, but there was obviously something more to be learned. He respected Gabriel for his caution before proceeding further. He turned back to the P.I. and asked, "But anything we discuss is confidential, right?"

"Yes, it is between us, but please understand that there is no legal protection or privilege such as there is between attorney and client or therapist and patient. And certainly there is no protection against a court order or something of that nature. Were it not for the office you hold, I personally wouldn't have any concern about this, but I know that you need to be careful. So I thought I should leave it up to you."

"Yes, of course, and I appreciate that, Mr. Gabriel. Very professional and considerate of you." Hall thought for another moment and then said, "I would like to have the full picture."

"Of course. Then there are two additional pieces of information that I was able to obtain. The first is that your mother hasn't filed an income tax return since she left her employment with Travel Pro Nursing. And that is somewhat interesting because a quick calculation of her projected tax return for that year, had she filed one, shows that she would have received a significant refund from over-withholding of taxes while she was employed."

"And there is a second thing?"

"Yes, and this is most likely nothing at all. As I told you earlier, my visit to this FSOU office on the second floor of the old hardware store was pretty bizarre. I mean, here was this old guy in a one-room office in a ramshackle hardware store in a dusty and sleepy old town in West Virginia who believes he is somehow making important discoveries about the nature of the universe. I'm not sure how connected to reality he actually is. He might be suffering from some form or other of dementia. I even checked with some universities in West Virginia and Virginia to see what their departments of astronomy might know about him."

"Well?"

"They know absolutely nothing about him or his research. By his own admission he has no formal education beyond high school. He seems to have delusions of grandeur in terms of his abilities and the importance of what he's doing. In short, there is absolutely no reason to believe that he is anything other than a somewhat interesting old kook."

"Is there more?"

"Just a bit. One little thing that I found that doesn't quite fit in with everything else I've told you. I have a friend with the local telephone company, and I asked for a record of the old man's phone calls on the day that I visited him."

"Okay?"

"Wes Scarcia had no incoming calls on his line that day, and only one outgoing call was made. That call was placed about twenty minutes after I left his office, and it went to a number in area code 719."

"Where is that?"

"That would be in Colorado. And the call only lasted for forty-two seconds."

"So whom did he call?"

"That's the weird part. He apparently called nobody." Seeing that his client was about to interject with another question, Gabriel raised his hand briefly to signal that he was about to explain. "My friend in the phone company tracked down the number, and it took him some time. The number had been assigned years ago to a military trunk line that served the Cheyenne Mountain Directorate."

"The Cheyenne Mountain Directorate? What's that?"

"Well, I'm sure you know that NORAD headquarters used to be located in Cheyenne Mountain. After the primary headquarters was moved to another location, the facilities in Cheyenne Mountain were kept in a warm stand-by mode, and during that time, the facility was known as the Cheyenne Mountain Directorate. Then later, President King closed down the facility completely during his first term of office. So, as far as the phone company is concerned, it's a dead number."

"Did you happen to call the number yourself?"

"Of course." He pulled out a small digital voice recorder. "Let me play a recording of that attempt."

Hall heard the ten-digit number being keyed on a touch-tone pad, and then the line rang four times. Then a click, and what sounded like a recorded female voice said, "The number you have called is out of service."

Gabriel continued, "I tried the number several times, just out of curiosity, including calling it at exactly the same time of day that Wes Scarcia did, only to have the same result. I can only conclude that the old guy misdialed a number."

Hall nodded his head in agreement.

"In fact, I would say that there's a ninety-nine percent chance that that's exactly what happened."

Hall tilted his head slightly and asked, "Why not one-hundred percent?"

"Two reasons. The call lasted forty-two seconds. Not long enough for much of a conversation, certainly, but thirty-five seconds after the recorded message would have ended. But that could easily be explained just by the fact that he is elderly and may have been slow to replace the handset on the phone."

"And the other reason?"

"He didn't place another call after receiving the out of service message. I mean, if you misdial a number, you obviously intended to call someone and you would normally redial the call, right?"

"Yes, of course, but from what you've told me, this guy is old and not quite with it."

"Right. Which is exactly why I think the chances are ninety-nine percent that there's nothing to it. It just seems to be an odd coincidence that he dialed what had once been a military line leading to NORAD. But then again, I confirmed with my friend in the phone company that the line is out of service, and I tried it myself. It's not a working number anymore."

Hall sat silently for a moment, thinking about what he had learned. "Well, Mr. Gabriel, you've done a great job. I just wish you could have located her."

"I do too. I'd like to tell you that I have other leads to follow, and a less scrupulous investigator could probably milk you for weeks longer on a project like this. I won't do that. My gut tells me that she may have traveled overseas, maybe even for employment, given her love of travel. She could still be alive and working out of the country, but I did check with the State Department and there are no records of consular contact with her at all. If she died overseas, well, it would be very difficult to confirm that fact given the number of countries in the world. If you would like me to pursue it further, I will try the international route, but I have to tell you that I think it would be a waste of your money."

"I understand, Mr. Gabriel, and I appreciate your honesty. I'm not a wealthy man, and my congressional salary won't make me one, especially considering the cost of living in both Washington and California. So, if you would please prepare your final report for me and send me your bill, I would appreciate it. And again, thank you very much for your efforts on my behalf."

"Not at all, Congressman, it's been my pleasure to have you as a client. If I can be of further service to you in any regard, please don't hesitate to call upon me."

Gabriel stood, and after shaking hands, he turned and left the office. Then Hall sat back down at his desk, definitely discouraged with what he had learned, but also trying to think of any rock that might still remain unturned.

Chapter 15: The White House

Shortly after the private detective had left his congressional office, Jackson placed a call to his friend Chuck Pearce in the White House. The deputy chief of staff to the President was in a meeting, but his assistant responded to Jackson's request for an appointment without question. Either this was standard practice when a Member of Congress called personally, or she knew that her boss would want to meet with him because of their budding friendship. The appointment was scheduled for 4:00 the next afternoon. This was later than Jackson would have liked, but he also realized that Pearce was a very busy person and that he was lucky to have the kind of access that he did.

A Capitol Hill limo once again carried Jackson to the visitor's entrance at the White House. After clearing all of the security formalities, a uniformed Secret Service officer escorted Jackson to Pearce's office in the West Wing. Pearce got up from behind his desk and welcomed Jackson to a seat. "Jackson, it's so good to see you again. I understand that you're now a member of the House Select Committee on Intelligence. Congratulations!"

Jackson replied, "Yes, ah, I somehow think that you had something to do with that appointment, Chuck, and it has opened the door for me to acquire some of that information that we spoke about when we last met here."

"All I did was to speak with the Chief of Staff about your situation, but I'm really glad that it worked out well for you. That's a highly desired committee assignment, isn't it?"

"It certainly is, and the chances of a freshman congressman receiving such a committee assignment are normally somewhere between slim and nil. But then, this is the White House." And he smiled warmly at his influential friend.

"So tell me, Jackson, did you locate your birth mother?"

"Unfortunately, no. I hired a private investigator who appears to have done a great job, but he finally came to a dead end in a small town in West Virginia, of all places." Jackson went on to give a brief summary of the P.I.'s activities on the case. When he came to the final piece of information about the phone call made by Wes Scarcia, he lowered his voice, "Chuck, there is only one stone left unturned that I can find in any of this, and it has to do with a phone call that the old guy made shortly after the P.I. left his office. He called a number in area code 719, which is assigned to southeastern Colorado, but the weird thing is that it's a non-working number that used to be assigned to the NORAD facility at Cheyenne Mountain."

"So he obviously made a mistake then."

"Probably, but the thing that troubles me is that my investigator reported that Scarcia made no other call that day, and you would think that if he misdialed a number, he would have then made the call that he intended to make in the first place, right?"

"Well, sure, but maybe he was interrupted by something. Maybe someone else came into the office and occupied his attention. Maybe he just had to go to the bathroom and forgot all about the call. From what you've told me, he doesn't seem to be, shall we say, totally connected with reality."

"I know, I know. But still, don't you think it's kind of an interesting coincidence that this guy believes he is running a one-man research organization called the Foundation for the Study of the Origin of the Universe, and that the one and only call he placed that day was to a former NORAD line?"

Pearce shook his head back and forth slowly a few times, and then answered, "I don't know, Jackson, it seems like you might be grasping at straws right now. Did your investigator think there was something more to it?"

"He thinks that there's a ninety-nine percent chance that there's nothing more to it than an old guy dialing a wrong number and then being a bit slow to hang-up the handset."

Pearce reached over and placed his hand on his friend's shoulder as he said, "Look, I get how important this is to you, but it seems as though you've done all you can do, right? You've got so much important work to do here in DC that I hate to see you being distracted by this search."

Jackson had a strong and surprising reaction to his friend's touch. He felt somewhat flushed and warm, and he looked at Pearce more closely, noticing the fine lines of his handsome face and his trim yet buff body. He shook his head to bring himself back to the conversation.

Pearce noticed that something had affected Hall, and he asked him if he was okay.

"Yeah, yeah, sure. Sorry, I don't know what came over me. I guess it's just the aura of power in the White House. Could I have some ice water please?"

"Of course," and Pearce called for his secretary to get Hall's water.

"It's just so important to me to know for certain what happened to her, even if she is no longer alive. But I would surely have loved to meet and talk with her. I know you probably can't understand the depth of my feelings about this, but...," and his words trailed off.

"Okay Jackson, let's try this. Something brought you back here to see me. Is there some other way that you think I can help you?" His voice was kind and gentle, even caring. He noticed Jackson's eyes becoming moist with tears. Pearce empathized with his new friend from Congress.

At this point, Jackson was obviously close to crying, and he just shrugged his shoulders and moved his head back and forth. "I don't know, Chuck. I just can't let it go."

"I see that. Look, maybe there is one more thing I can do to help. Let me see if the Director of WHMO can come over and join us for a few minutes."

"WHMO, what's that?"

"The White House Military Office. It falls under the Executive Office of the President. It provides military support for the White House, including transportation, the President's personal physician, and a host of other functions. They have about a hundred staffers over in the Eisenhower Executive Office Building. The Navy even operates the White House Mess through WHMO. Anyway, maybe someone over there can shed some more light on a phone number that once belonged to NORAD at Cheyenne Mountain. What do you say?"

"Sure, Chuck, of course. Thank you so much for, well, going out of your way to indulge a freshman member of the House."

Pearce looked at him earnestly and said, "No, I'm just trying to help a friend in need that I happen to care about." He went over to his desk and made a brief phone call. Coming back over to the chair where Hall was sitting, he said, "Dwight Smith will be over here within ten minutes. He's the director of WHMO. Do you want to take a minute to make a pit stop first?"

"Yeah, thanks, that's very considerate. Just tell me how to get there."

Pearce smiled, "I can't do that, you're a visitor in the White House and so you have to be escorted everywhere you go. Come on, I'll lead the way."

———

They returned to the deputy chief of staff's office just as Dwight Smith also arrived. "Come on in, Dwight, I want you to meet my friend here. Jackson Hall is a new member of Congress and was just recently appointed to Jack Findlay's Intelligence Committee."

"Well, color me impressed. Nice to meet you, Mr. Hall."

"Please, just call me Jackson."

The three men filed into Pearce's office, with Pearce closing the door behind him.

Comfortably seated in the small conversation pod of chairs in the deputy chief of staff's office, Pearce said, "Dwight, we have a little bit of a mystery on our hands that we're wondering if you might be able to help us with."

"I'll certainly try. Lay it on me."

"We need some information on a phone number," he turned to Hall and asked, "Do you have it with you now?"

"Yes I do," and he handed a slip of paper to his friend.

Pearce looked at the number and continued speaking to Smith, "Okay, this phone number was once assigned to the NORAD facility in Cheyenne Mountain, and it now appears to be a non-working number."

The WMHO director shrugged his shoulders and said, "Okay, so that makes sense. The Long Lines division wouldn't likely reassign a number that had been used for military purposes, and I do believe that NORAD has since moved to nearby Peterson Air Force Base. Of course, they could have taken this trunkline with them, but it sounds like they didn't from what you're telling me."

"Right, right, it's just that, well, we know of a civilian who called this number recently and stayed on the phone long enough that he could have had a very brief conversation or sent some information on the line."

Smith's face reflected his confusion. "That doesn't make any sense at all, does it?"

"No, it doesn't. Now look, before we get the NSA or some other agency involved in this, it's only fair for me to tell you that the civilian is an old man who may, repeat may, have just misdialed a number."

"Now I'm even more confused, Chuck. It kind of sounds like this is a non-issue. What would you like me to do?"

"I'm not sure myself. Do you have anyone over in WHMO who might be able to tell us anything more about an abandoned trunkline that used to be assigned to NORAD?" he asked with a smile to show that he was only partially serious.

"Well, I don't know about the abandoned trunkline part, but the commander of Air Force One, Colonel Clarence Diggs, was once assigned to NORAD. If you would like to talk with him, this is your lucky day because while he is rarely in the WHMO office, since the President is in the White House and Diggs' deputy commander is over at Andrews with the fleet, he was there when I left."

"Dwight, please call over there and see if he can join us, okay?"

"Sure Chuck, no problem." Smith whipped out his secure cellphone and called his office. "Okay, he'll be right over. Jackson, prepare yourself to meet one mighty impressive Air Force officer."

———————

Colonel Diggs arrived within a few minutes and was immediately shown into Pearce's office. The tall

African-American officer could have appeared on a recruiting poster for the Air Force. Trim, with short curly black hair, Colonel Diggs was wearing his dress blue uniform complete with all of his ribbons and command pilot wings.

All three men stood up when he entered, partly to courteously greet him and shake hands, but partly as a response to the aura of command and competence that surrounded him.

Pearce gestured for Diggs to take his seat, and he brought his own chair around from behind his desk to join the others.

Dwight Smith began by saying, "Clarence, you already know Chuck, and Congressman Hall here is a new member of the House Select Committee on Intelligence, so you can speak pretty freely with them."

Diggs replied crisply, "How can I help you gentlemen?"

Pearce gave Diggs a brief summary of the events surrounding the phone call. "Colonel, Dwight tells us that you used to serve at NORAD. Do you have any idea if there could be any more to this phone call than an innocent misdial?"

"Well, I don't know anything about NORAD's trunklines or telephone service, but I was stationed at Cheyenne Mountain when NORAD's final move was made to Peterson Air Force Base. So let me tell you what I do know. Congressman, since I don't know how familiar you are with NORAD, would you like some background information?"

"Yes sir, I would, please."

"NORAD is an acronym, of course, for North American Aerospace Defense. The facility in Cheyenne Mountain began with excavation and construction in 1961 and was completed by 1964. It's creation had been spurred by the Soviet Union's success with Sputnik and a growing concern with the Soviet's ability to launch nuclear warheads mounted on intercontinental ballistic missiles. The Cheyenne Mountain Combat Operations Center became fully operational in 1966. To make a long story somewhat shorter, the Cheyenne Mountain complex continued to be modernized and expanded all through the 1980s and into the 1990s. A number of military units were housed there at any one time, including NORAD itself, the U.S. Strategic Command, and the U.S. Air Force Space Command, among others. A massive modernization and upgrade program was started in 1989, and unfortunately there were a lot of delays and cost overruns with the program over time. Also, some of the newly installed systems turned out not to work as well as the older existing systems. Anyway, the Combat Operations Center in Cheyenne Mountain continued in full service until 2006, when NORAD moved most of its operations to Peterson. The facility was then placed in a warm stand-by mode and renamed the Cheyenne Mountain Directorate. In 2010, President King ordered the facility to be evacuated and the remainder of the military's facilities were moved to Peterson. The Space Command had earlier moved to Vandenberg Air Force Base. As I indicated, I happened to be stationed at Cheyenne Mountain during the close-out. I know a great deal about what my team and I did at NORAD, but again, I really don't know anything about the trunkline issue."

The three men had been listening intently to Diggs' account of the history of Cheyenne Mountain and of his own service there. Pearce was the first to speak. "Well Colonel, thank you for that summary of events."

Pearce looked at Hall and said, "Jackson, I really think we've taken up enough of these folks' time for now, wouldn't you agree?"

Hall looked up and said, "Yes, of course, and I sincerely appreciate it."

The four men stood up to again shake hands. Pearce and Hall remained standing while the two WHMO staffers opened the office door to leave. Just as they were going out the door, Colonel Diggs turned back for a moment with a quizzical look on his face, and he said, "You know, I just happened to remember something from those hectic days when we were getting everything ready to vacate the complex. There was this crazy rumor, and I doubt that it could have been anything more than that, about some group of civilians who were going to be coming to the mountain to stay for awhile. Something about them studying the origin of the universe, whatever that means. In fact, we weren't permitted to shut down any of the life support functions of the complex or to disconnect any of the utilities. But we didn't think much about it at the time. President King's agenda wasn't always the same as the military's. My guess is that if anyone did enter Cheyenne Mountain after we left, it probably was just a clean-up crew. Good day gentlemen." The two WHMO staffers departed through the outer office.

In one of those rare moments in human history when two people say exactly the same thing in exactly the same place at exactly the same time, Pearce and Hall stood in the now otherwise empty room with the same look on both of their faces and simultaneously exclaimed, "What?!?"

Chapter 16: Meeting in ADMIN

Steve had waited patiently and had been doing his job to the best of his ability during his first six months at ORT. He had always been known to have an easy way with people, naturally leaning toward being friendly as opposed to being confrontational. Within weeks of his joining the THOT team, these qualities had led to his natural assumption of the role as the effective leader of the team. Vivian was still in charge and was responsible for the overall direction of the team's work, but Steve had become adept at "greasing the wheels" and making the team work together in a cohesive fashion. Therefore, he and Vivian synergistically complemented each other. He found himself being pleased that he could accomplish so much as the newest member of THOT. Plus, there was the nature of the work itself. He was being exposed to the thoughts and findings of the brightest minds from both the physical and the social sciences. In short, it was both intellectually stimulating and emotionally satisfying.

Then too, his relationship with Julie had slowly been growing deeper. And his desire to know more about the unique world he now occupied had been growing stronger week by week.

At Julie's suggestion, he had applied for a six-month anniversary meeting with ADMIN-1, and the day and time finally arrived. The plan was for him to meet Julie in the main cafeteria at 1500 hours. He left his small office in THOT at 1400, stopped by his quarters to freshen up and make himself look his best, and then headed to the main cafeteria fifteen minutes early.

Since this was not a scheduled mealtime, he found the cafeteria to be deserted and relatively dark, as only a few utility lights were turned on. He took a seat at a table near the entrance and waited. During his time in ORT, he had enjoyed his work a great deal, probably more than anything he had done in his life. Julie had been good about answering many of his questions, but clearly there were some things that she was not permitted to discuss. But what were these things, and why were they secret? He silently admonished himself for thinking the word "secret," when "confidential" or "need to know" might be more appropriate. "Secret" called to mind negative thoughts of conspiracies, cover-ups, government embarrassments and screw-ups. Okay, he admitted to himself, there were of course legitimate secrets involving national defense issues, but the abuses of classified information and executive privilege that had taken place during the Tate administration had been sufficient to make anyone cynical of their government. The administration of Jeremy Scott King that had followed the disastrous eight years of Harold Tate had done much to restore the public's faith in government, but wounds as deep as those caused by years of lies, misused intelligence reports, and outright intrusions on civil liberties in the name of "homeland security" were slow to heal. And now, with the election of President Brasington, it looked like those wounds were about to be carved again, even more deeply, into the nation's collective psyche.

He thought he heard a noise from a distance, which brought him back to the present. It was still fairly dark and he saw no one around him. *Probably just the sound of a freezer compressor cycling off or on.* He couldn't help feeling butterflies in his stomach about this meeting. Would his curiosity be satisfied? Would he learn more about ORT? He thought the latter was almost certain to be true. What would ADMIN-1 be like in person? He had seen him on internal video telecasts, he knew the sound and timber of his voice, but he certainly didn't know much about his personality or his character or his thought process.

This time the sound was unmistakable. Footsteps approaching the entrance to the cafeteria. He looked up and saw Julie, impeccably attired as always, high heels clicking on the tile floor. He stood up and couldn't help but smile and admire her form as she approached. Julie gave him a quick hug and gestured for him to sit back down.

"Well, Steve, are you ready for this?" she asked.

"As ready as I'll ever be," he replied. "Where do we go?"

"We've got a few minutes, be patient." And she smiled at him in the way that always disarmed him emotionally. "I want you to know something about AD-MIN-1, and I don't want you to take this the wrong way, but, well, we have a saying in ADMIN that Dr. Morefield, and yes, that's his real name, 'doesn't do dumb well'."

"So you think I'm dumb then!"

"No, I certainly don't. That's what I meant about not taking it the wrong way. The saying really has little to do with dumb *per se*. It has to do with how busy AD-MIN-1 is, the way his logical mind works, and his impatience for getting to the point. That's all. It really says more about him than it does about anyone else. The important thing is that I want you to open your mind, relax your expectations, and go with the flow once we get there, okay?" And again there was that fetching smile.

"Okay, I'll try. So…where do we go?" he said, feeling somewhat helpless that he didn't even know how to get to ADMIN.

"Come with me," and she took his hand and led him over to the entrance hallway to the cafeteria. They came to a windowless door with a small sign marked "Utility Room." Steve had passed this door virtually every day he had been in ORT and had never even taken notice of it before. Julie swiped her card key through the reader and the door's lock clicked open. She turned the knob, opened the door and gestured for him to precede her. He did, feeling like he was doing something clandestine. That feeling was enhanced by her quick entrance behind him and the door closing with a secure-sounding click of the lock falling into place.

Here too the lighting was very dim. They stepped into what appeared to be yet another short hallway. Only the hallway didn't lead anywhere except to another closed door. Julie swiped her card through its reader and the door slid open to reveal an elevator. "Get in, Steve. Haven't you been wanting to go through the looking glass?" And still that enigmatic smile. Steve stepped forward as did Julie, and he noticed a series of backlit and labeled large rectangular buttons which he could only assume represented different floors, or more accurately, levels, of the facility. He observed that they currently were on the topmost level, which was marked "ANALYSIS." Below this level were several others, among which were "PROGRAMMING," "ASTRO," and "RESEARCH." At the very bottom was a button labeled "ADMIN." Julie pushed it, and the door closed gently in front of them.

Feeling somewhat disoriented, Steve mumbled "We're going down," and then realized how it must have sounded to Julie. "Maybe you were right about the dumb thing after all." She just smiled again and shook her head. He could tell that they must be descending quite a distance because the feeling in his stomach told him that the elevator seemed to be moving fairly fast. Finally the indicator light next to ADMIN flicked on and the elevator beeped quietly. "Ready Steve?" He nodded his head. Julie pushed the Door Open button, and the door opened gently in front of them.

A brightly lit corridor lay in front of them. They exited the elevator and he followed Julie down the length of the hallway. He noticed signs on doors without windows labeled "COMMUNICATIONS," "OPERATIONS," "LOGISTICS," and "PERSONNEL." They continued down to the end of the corridor where there was a door labeled "ADMIN." Julie opened the door and they walked into a modest sized but nicely decorated reception area.

Julie introduced him to the attractive secretary sitting behind a desk with a computer monitor and a complex-looking telephone system. She was wearing a wireless headphone, presumably linked to the telephone.

Julie said, "Arianna, this is Steve, THOT-415, and he's here for a six-month meeting." Arianna shook hands with Steve and asked him to have a seat. Steve went to the couch along the opposite wall, and Julie quietly said to him, "Remember what I told you, Steve. Have a good meeting and I'll see you when you're finished." Steve couldn't help but notice that she had a slightly worried look on her face, which was quite a change from her usual smiling self. Julie walked away down the corridor through which they had come and entered one of the doors. Steve couldn't remember which of the signs he had seen matched with that particular door, but he assumed it was Personnel based on what little he knew about her duties here.

He took this opportunity to look around the room. Directly across from him was the receptionist's desk. To her left, along the same wall, was a door marked "Video Conference." Looking to the wall on his left, Steve saw that there was one door with an engraved silver sign that read, "ADMIN-2," and below that, "Deputy Administrator." Then he noticed the wall to his right. Only one door here too, with the same kind of plaque, but the wording was, "ADMIN-1," then "Chief Administrator." He involuntarily swallowed and became aware of how tense he was about this meeting. He had been in ORT over six months and had never even known that this area existed.

The digital clock on the wall above the receptionist indicated that it was now 1500 hours exactly. Arianna was typing away on her keyboard and paid him no attention whatsoever. As the minutes went by and nothing else happened, his thoughts turned to question his purpose in asking for this meeting. He had to admit to himself that it was curiosity more than anything else. He wanted to know more about this unique facility, this place where presumably he would spend the rest of his life. He kept checking the clock, more frequently than he would have liked. 1515 hours. He had been waiting now for about twenty minutes since Julie brought him here. Well, he thought, that's not unreasonable considering that ADMIN-1 would be a very busy person. By 1530 hours, he was beginning to regret his decision to schedule the meeting, feeling that he would be taking up time with the Chief Administrator for no better reason than his own quest for information.

He told himself that if he weren't called in for his meeting by 1545, he would excuse himself and try to find Julie or make his way back to the Analysis level. The digital clock glowed 1545, and Steve stood up to approach Arianna. Just then, he heard a small signal tone, and saw Arianna flip a key on her telephone console. Arianna said, "Yes sir," looked up at Steve and said to him, "ADMIN-2 will see you now." Steve looked confused and said, "But my meeting is with ADMIN-1." Arianna came from behind her desk and led Steve to the Deputy Administrator's door, which she opened and he walked in. She left and closed the door behind her.

ADMIN-2 was seated behind a much larger desk than the receptionist's. He was intent on examining some spreadsheets laid out before him and paid no attention to Steve. His hair was iron gray and he was husky without being overweight. Steve cleared his throat gently to make his presence known.

"Take a seat," ADMIN-2 grunted. Steve sat down.

Several minutes went by before he spoke again. Looking up at Steve with an irritated expression on his face, he said to Steve, "In case you don't already know, my name is Dick." Thoughts of how appropriately the name seemed to fit the person danced through Steve's mind, but he didn't let it show. Dick continued in a gruff voice, "So, why do you want to leave our little paradise?"

Looking as confused as he sounded, Steve replied, "Leave? I never said anything about wanting to leave."

"Oh come on now, that's the only reason anyone ever schedules one of these meetings. Maybe you don't even realize it yet. But you're either homesick or you don't like living underground. Or you have a personality conflict with your team leader. Or maybe it's a romance gone bad. There's always some excuse."

"Sir, I mean, Dick. That isn't why I'm here at all. I'm enjoying my time here very much, the work is fascinating and stimulating, and I have no romantic problems."

Dick's steely blue eyes pierced into Steve's soul for a beat, and then he said, "Bullshit! Hell, I ought to toss your ass out of here personally."

Steve felt his body stiffen and his anger rising. "Look, you don't have to believe me, but that's not why I'm here at all. To be honest, I came for this appointment because I understood that I was entitled to it, and because I wanted to learn more about this place. Don't you think I have a right to know as much as possible about the place that's to be my home for the rest of my life?"

Dick relaxed a bit. "Maybe you do, if you're being honest with me, as well as yourself, about your motives."

"Well, how do I convince you of that, Dick? Why don't you check my evaluations from Vivian? You could talk to some of my colleagues in THOT. How about Julie, the person who brought me here? She's right here in ADMIN!"

"What if I told you I've already done all those things? Then what would you say?"

"I would say that if what you learned from them led you to believe that I am less than fully committed to this research and to this place, then either you misunderstood what you read and heard completely, or else I really shouldn't be here." Steve took a breath and waited. "And by the way, my meeting was supposed to be with ADMIN-1. Why am I meeting with you anyway?"

Dick glared at him and said, "Because I'm the son of a bitch you have to convince that your having such a meeting with ADMIN-1 would be productive."

Steve felt his heart sink. How would he tell Julie that he had never met with ADMIN-1? How would this discouragement affect his future work in THOT? Would he ever be able to feel the same sense of enthusiasm about being a member of ORT?

"As it happens, though, ADMIN-1 does want to meet you this afternoon," Dick said with a slight grin.

"What? After all this?"

"Even more so because of all this." Dick arose, and Steve followed suit. "Come with me."

He led Steve to another closed door that Steve hadn't noticed before, but he suspected that it would open into the video conference area given its location and what he remembered from the reception area. Dick opened the door and gestured for Steve to go through. Steve found himself in a space-age equipped conference room with a large flat screen video monitor on one of the end walls of the room, and a huge boat-shaped conference table, where every seat at the table was equipped with a microphone and a small video display. The head of the table had a built-in control panel with a multitude of knobs, slide switches, and LED indicator lights. A few of them were illuminated or blinking in various colors as he walked past. If nothing else, this room was a terrific playground of high-tech equipment, but he knew that there was a lot more to it than that.

They had walked the length of the room and had come to a door at the end of the wall to his right. Steve was oriented to space sufficiently to know that this must lead into ADMIN-1's office.

Dick said to him, "Look, I'm sorry I had to rough you up a little. It was kind of the final part of a battery of tests you've been taking since before you ever arrived here." Steve looked at him with a puzzled expression. "Go ahead in for your meeting with ADMIN-1 now. You have a lot to learn ahead of you." Dick knocked on the door gently and opened it. Seeing that the office was vacant, he told Steve to step inside and to make himself comfortable.

Steve walked into the office and his jaw dropped in awe.

———— ◆ ————

To begin with, ADMIN-1's office was huge in comparison with other workspaces Steve had seen since coming to ORT. It was furnished with a beautiful mahogany desk, credenza, and matching chairs. There was also a smaller version of the conference table he had just passed by on his way in. The walls were adorned with framed diplomas, along with some photographs of the man he recognized from his orientation video as ADMIN-1, along with some other people. He hoped that he could perhaps take more time to look at them later. Directly in front of him, on the wall that would be to the left of the person seated at the desk, was a floor-to-ceiling window looking out upon a majestic mountain with snow caps and several waterfalls snaking down the sides to a river below. It was this view, causing cognitive dissonance with his belief that he was far below ground, that had startled him so when he walked in the office. He listened closely, and aside from the low background sound of a computer's hard drive and cooling fan in operation, he could actually hear the sound of the water flowing outside. *How could this be? How could any of this possibly be?*

Just then, he heard the sound of a door opening, a door he hadn't immediately noticed before, part of the wall behind the desk. ADMIN-1 stepped into the room quickly, saw Steve, and walked over to him to shake hands. Steve immediately recognized him as the tall, thin, almost lanky person he had been seeing from time to time on the internal video broadcasts at ORT. "Steve, I'm ADMIN-1, my name is Steve also, and I'm very pleased to meet you."

Steve shook his hand and, still in awe over what he was seeing and the fact that he was finally meeting the person who, more than anyone else, personified this whole facility, let himself be invited to have a seat in a chair across from ADMIN-1's desk.

"Fascinating, isn't it?" ADMIN-1 said with a gesture to the outside view.

"Yes, but I really don't understand. We've got to be hundreds if not thousands of feet underground. Aren't we?" ADMIN-1 smiled and nodded his head.

"Indeed we are. This is, in fact, the deepest level of occupancy here at ORT. And what you're seeing over there comes to us thanks to some very high technology and to the generosity of those who made this research center possible. The window is not real, of course. It's the state of the art in organic LED flat screen monitors coupled with an audio feed at a level that is nearly identical to what you would hear if we were located on the surface. The view itself is real, and it's actually located not far from the surface above us."

"Wow," Steve said, as he nodded his understanding. "Very impressive!"

"Thank you. People visiting here for the first time tend to find it disconcerting, just as you probably did, but then more and more natural as time goes by."

Now sitting across from ADMIN-1, Steve said, "It's an honor to meet you, sir. I didn't really think I would be meeting you after my 'chat' with your deputy."

"I apologize for what you undoubtedly, and correctly, perceived as rudeness on his part. He was supposed to speak with you exactly as he did, and he makes a terrific bad guy, don't you think? Actually, that was a large part of his job before he came here to work with us." Seeing Steve's puzzled look, he continued, "You don't recognize him? His name is Dick Henry, and he was President King's White House chief of staff during the eight years of his presidency."

The revelations were coming at him so quickly now that Steve's awe was growing exponentially. He stared at ADMIN-1's face for a few seconds, tendrils of *deja vu* tugging at his memory. "I've seen you before coming to ORT, haven't I?" Steve asked.

"It's possible. I did some specialized work for President King, but mostly behind the scenes. You may have seen me on a few public broadcasts near the end of his administration."

Steve thought back. He had been so totally absorbed in his work at the university at the time that he had really paid very little attention to politics, but there was something…then it came to him. "I remember now, you were his national security advisor on computer science, and you helped to completely rewrite some programs for the Defense Department. In fact it was for

DARPA, wasn't it?" he asked, referring to the Defense Advanced Research Projects Agency.

ADMIN-1 allowed a small grin and a nod. "That's exactly right, Steve. That's precisely what you should know about me, if you were to have known anything about me at all."

Steve sensed that there was much more to ADMIN-1's history with the King Administration than he would ever know, and he knew better than to ask. He noticed that one of the larger framed photographs on the wall behind ADMIN-1 showed him with the president and several other people he remembered as being cabinet officers in the administration. Damn, he thought, this guy was really connected when King was president! His attention returned to ADMIN-1 as he abruptly changed the subject.

"I'm very pleased that you requested this meeting. It demonstrates the curiosity and interest that we believed would exist in you when we recruited you."

Steve felt it again, that sense of his world spinning out of control, and yet he had the irresistible urge to know more. "Recruited? Sir, I became aware of the research you were doing here through a notice in an academic publication, and I contacted you."

"Steve, first of all, there's no need to call me sir. Please, just ADMIN-1, or Steve, or if you really need to be more formal, then Dr. Morefield. Secondly, let me assure you that nobody ever contacts us out of the blue. Ever. If they did make a phone call or send a letter to the project, we would never see it here, and they would most likely receive a polite but noncommittal reply from some bureaucratic agency suggesting that they apply elsewhere. Trust me."

"I don't understand," Steve said, "I began the application process as a result of a small but impressive notice in the 'Journal of Education.' I made a phone call to the number provided, and I was asked to email a *curriculum vitae* to the project. Several weeks later, I was contacted again to report to a facility in Jacksonville for some psychological and physical tests. The rest, I suppose you could say, is history."

"Yes, we could say that. But that would be a very incomplete view of history. Let me explain. You would have received a very unique copy of the Journal that month, Steve. The notice you read wouldn't have appeared in any other copy. The recruiter who answered at the phone number you called would have given a very different response to any other caller. This is a very high value project, and we're extremely particular about whom we invite here."

"You recruited me using a fake notice?" Steve exclaimed.

"Oh it was a very real notice, but it was directed solely at you." ADMIN-1 leaned forward in his chair. "Now listen to me, Steve. I have a lot more to tell you, and some of it may shock you a bit. So, please keep your mind open and breathe deeply, okay?" He smiled broadly at Steve, who was obviously discomfited by the flow of information that was rocking his world.

"I'll try," Steve said somewhat warily.

"Good. Now, the next thing I want to tell you is that we recruited you with the goal of having you join our ADMIN team. But we always assign ADMIN candidates to another team for at least six months to see how well they cope in this unique environment."

Again, the look of surprise on Steve's face.

"First of all, we read your doctoral dissertation, 'A Redesign of the American Educational System for the Twenty-First Century.' Secondly, we watched as you played a key role in negotiating an important collective bargaining agreement between the faculty and administration at your university. The negotiations had been completely stalled, hadn't they? Discord among the parties was rampant, the situation was becoming ugly, and a paralyzing strike was imminent, yes?"

Steve nodded in agreement.

"Then someone on the faculty side had the good sense to replace the previous lead negotiator with you. And, wonder of wonders, a new contract was signed within three days. Three days, Steve! I would ask how you accomplished that feat, but of course we already know the diplomacy and common sense that you managed to use at the bargaining table. Neither party wanted a strike. Neither party wanted the uncomfortably antagonistic and adversarial atmosphere that was becoming more and more pervasive. All you had to do was get the two parties to realize those facts and admit them to each other. It was almost easy for you, wasn't it?"

"I don't know that I would call it easy," Steve replied, "but that does capture the essence of what I knew I had to do once I was called upon."

"Yes, and yet, why do you suppose your predecessor didn't realize the same thing?" He hesitated for a few seconds and then continued, "Well, no matter really. You're here and he isn't." ADMIN-1 picked up a tabbed file folder and read through a few paragraphs. "Your team leader in THOT loves you, Steve. Not in the romantic sense, but she loves working with you and having you as a member of her team. I'm afraid we're going to really disappoint her when we take you away from her." He dropped the folder a few inches to the desktop. "But that's not your problem. However, you'd better brace yourself for what comes next."

Chapter 17: Invitation

"Steve, when we recruit someone new for this project, everything is meticulously planned, from how they learn about the project, to what happens when the new candidate contacts us, to the extensive background investigation we perform, the physical and psychological testing necessary to determine whether someone will be able to thrive in this unique environment, and finally, if the recruit is accepted, their transportation here itself."

"Yes, of course, the special plane with the blacked-out windows and the medication that I assume made me sleep for most of the trip."

ADMIN-1 looked at him with a surprisingly gentle expression on his face. "Steve, what I want you to understand right now is that we don't transport people here alone. In addition to the nurse who takes care of any medical needs, a new recruit is always escorted in by an existing team member."

"Well not in my case," Steve replied, "maybe because another recruit came in with me. In fact, she's right here…in…ADMIN. Wait! Are you telling me that Julie was not a recruit at all?!? That she faked being a recruit while she was watching over me on the way here?" Steve could feel a cold sweat breaking out. This wasn't possible, because if it were true, it would make a lie of their whole relationship.

"Hold on Steve. Take a breath. I know that you and Julie have developed a closer relationship than what we would have expected. She was doing her job when she brought you here, and she does it extremely well. Right now, you feel stunned and hurt; I can see it on your face. But what you need to know is that while Julie was playing a role as part of her duty assignment when you came here, and maybe even for a short while after your arrival, she became genuinely fond of you, and I can assure you that there is nothing artificial about the relationship you now have with her. Julie has been expressly prohibited from discussing any of this with you, and it has been very uncomfortable for her, to say the least. She is probably even more concerned about how the truth may affect your relationship than you are."

Now the brief display of worry on Julie's face when she brought him to the reception area, and her request for him to keep an open mind and, in effect, to expect the unexpected, fell into place.

"What happens to your relationship now is completely a matter between the two of you," ADMIN-1 continued. "You and Julie are free to be friends, lovers, both, or neither. But if you're going to join us in ADMIN, you had to know the truth, and it cannot be allowed to interfere with the two of you working together when necessary. Do you understand?"

"Yes, I hear what you're saying. Julie has been very special to me during the past six months. I'm just hoping that we can work through this and continue to...," and his voice trailed off as he noticed ADMIN-1 watching him closely. Feeling that it was best to detour away from his personal feelings and move on to a more objective plane, he said, "Wait. Julie is ADMIN-414, just one member number away from my own. That doesn't make sense given what you're telling me."

"Julie's real ORT number is much lower. She just assumed that identity temporarily. If she were to go out to transport a new recruit in the future, she would temporarily adopt a new number that would coincide sequentially with the new recruit's number. She might be ADMIN-501 for a few days, for example. Julie has other duties here in ADMIN, and I don't even know if she'll go on another transport mission, but that's the way it works. I'm sorry if this hurts you in any way, but you wanted to know more. And the stark reality is that you have to know these things if you're going to work in ADMIN."

Steve sat quietly for a moment, absorbing all that he had learned. And he realized that he still had other questions. "How did you become ADMIN-1? How is the leadership determined here anyway?"

ADMIN-1 sat back in his chair and began what must have been an explanation that he had given many times in the past. "We all live here in a very special closed community. Our facility and our work is funded and supported by a foundation established just for that purpose. I am the first chief administrator. I was appointed to my position by an oversight board. This is not a democracy, and leaders are not elected. Think of it more as an academic institution with a board of trustees. The board appoints the chief administrator, and then the chief administrator appoints his or her deputy as well as the leaders of each team in ORT. ADMIN-2 and the team leaders effectively function as the chief administrator's cabinet."

"Okay, I get that. But can you answer a question I've wondered about since before I came here?"

"I will if I can," ADMIN-1 said with a small grin.

"What happens if, despite all the testing and precautions, someone just doesn't fit in here, or for some reason just wants to leave ORT?"

"Ah, that is one of several questions which are inevitably asked. You've been here a little over six months. Have you met anyone who is unhappy or who clearly would rather not be here? How about you, Steve? Are you happy to be here?"

"Yes, I am. I admit that I've had my foundation shaken a bit this afternoon, but...yes, I am happy to be here. And to answer your other question, no, I haven't met anyone who didn't seem to really want to be here."

"Good. So you see that our screening and testing process is extremely effective."

"Yes, I'll give you that. But still, out of, what, five hundred people or so in round numbers, surely somebody at sometime must have...,"

ADMIN-1 finished his question, "wanted to or needed to leave? Yes, it has happened on rare occasion."

"And?" Steve prompted.

"What do you think? Do you think we terminated them in the cold war intelligence community sense of the word 'terminate'?" ADMIN-1 relaxed his shoulders and continued in a gentle tone of voice, "No, that's not what happens. That's not what we're about here. We are about life, in the most fundamental sense possible, not death. I would also remind you that this project was founded by President King, not his predecessor. If a team member feels that they need to leave the project, they go through a counseling process first. This is done to help the team member be certain of their desire to leave, because there is always the possibility that there is something else going on with them with which we can help. The other reason we do this is to refine our own selection and testing process, to see whether we may have made a mistake and if so, how we can avoid making it in the future. If the person still wants to leave, we have them spend some time with a very skilled psychiatrist who, with pharmacologically-enhanced hypnotism, makes the person's experience here seem more like a dream than reality. Then we use as much care in returning them to the surface as we did in bringing them here. It also takes some significant arranging on the surface to safely reintegrate them into civilian life. It's not easy. When you came here, you pretty much ceased to exist above. Your pay stopped, your retirement contributions ended, your driver's license wouldn't have been renewed, and a thousand other details and minutia that go along with living in a complex society were no longer being tended to. We invited you here, and you came here, with the intention of remaining for the rest of your life. That's a huge commitment, isn't it? And you went through a lot before you ever arrived here. The testing. The mandatory sterilization, because we have no facilities for children here. But, at the end of the day, if someone needs to leave, we do our best to make it as graceful as possible for them to re-enter life above ground. Does that answer your question?"

"Yes it does, completely. And I sincerely thank you for that, and for your candor."

"Anything else on your mind, Steve?"

"Well, you want me to come to work in ADMIN? What do you have in mind for me?"

"Yes, we're interested in having you move down to ADMIN." ADMIN-1 smiled at the incongruity but literal truth of the phrase. "But, before we proceed any further, I want you to take some time to think about it, to sort things out with Julie one way or another, and then come back to see me in about a week. You can confirm a time with Arianna on your way out. Also, just so you're not taken by surprise…you've probably had your fill of that today…Julie will be waiting for you out there," as he gestured toward the door to the reception area.

———

And she was. As Steve first made eye contact with her from across the reception room, she silently mouthed the words, "I'm sorry." They approached and gave each other a long and meaningful hug. Through subtle touches and movements, facial expressions and a few tears, they both knew that their relationship would withstand the truth that Steve had just learned. After a minute or two, Steve noticed Arianna watching them with a kind smile. He asked Julie to wait while he made his follow-up appointment with ADMIN-1. Then, still without speaking aloud, Julie took his hand and led him back to the corridor which had, just a few hours before, brought him to one of the most profound and enlightening experiences of his life.

Chapter 18: Return to THOT

Steve gestured toward the door labeled "PERSON-NEL" as they passed by it on their way back to the elevator and asked Julie, "Is that where you work, when you're not escorting some new recruit into ORT?" His grin told Julie that he was being light-hearted and not sarcastic.

"Why yes it is. I would offer to take you in and introduce you to my colleagues, but you haven't officially joined ADMIN yet."

"I know," said Steve. "ADMIN-1 wants to see me again in a week. He wants me to think about it and let him know what I want to do at that time. He was particularly concerned about how well we could work together if I come down here."

"Yes, of course. Well, hopefully you'll know the answer to that long before your next meeting." She gave him a sly look and said, "I was thinking that we might get together for dinner this evening and then watch a movie…in your quarters."

Steve caught the meaning in her words and her voice. "Why madam, are you planning to seduce me?"

"Perhaps, if you play your cards right," Julie replied, again giving Steve the Delphic smile that always made him wonder what she was thinking.

The elevator doors opened and they stepped in. Steve looked more closely at the level buttons this time. He remembered noticing that his level, ANALYSIS, was the top button. He pressed it, then asked Julie, "How do you get to the surface anyway? For some reason, I can't even remember arriving here or taking an elevator down."

"That's part of the magic of some of the medication you were given, Steve. It acts as a temporary amnesiac. You wouldn't remember, and that's deliberate. To answer your question, to the extent that I can...", and she drew out the word "can" in her most conspiratorial and mysterious voice, "there is another means of reaching the surface. You know, we're not recruiting too much anymore, and so the necessity, or opportunity, however you want to look at it, to go up to the surface is becoming more and more infrequent."

"Indeed?" Steve replied. "Listen, I've got a question for you, and this has never really occurred to me before. You know where I live in this facility, but I have no idea where you live, do I?"

"No sir, you don't. I was wondering how long it would take for you to ask, inasmuch as you are such a curious being. How about waiting a week and asking me again?"

"You and your secrets, Julie. Will I ever get to know you completely?"

"I hope not," she said as the elevator doors opened into the dimly lit hallway that Steve remembered now all too well. "This is your stop, Steve. I have to go back to work, but I'll see you later at, oh, about 1900-ish?"

Steve smiled his agreement and gave her a quick kiss before leaving the elevator.

"How terribly inappropriate," she said seductively as the doors closed between them.

Steve thought how lucky he was to be here, to have met Julie, to have had the experience of this day. He turned toward the closed door leading back out to the entrance foyer to the cafeteria and hoped that the door would open from this side without swiping a key card. He tried the lever and it turned freely. Steve walked out to the familiar environment of the main cafeteria and headed back to his quarters. He needed some time to absorb and think about all that he had learned. He sat down on top of his bed and gradually laid back on his pillows. He realized that he was in a reflective state of mind, and he thought back to the series of macro-events in the country that had brought him to this place. Having been presented with still more evidence today of what an effective and insightful leader President King had been, led him inevitably to the sadness felt by the nation as a whole when, just weeks after leaving office, King had been killed in a tragic car accident. King enjoyed nothing more than driving one of his prized sports cars, and he had been deprived of that particular pleasure for the eight years he had served as president. But his renewed enjoyment came to a sudden end when a tractor-trailer lost control on the Pennsylvania Turnpike, crushing King's small car and ending the life of the man who more than anyone else had been responsible for making this facility possible.

Steve made it a point to keep up with the news from the world he had left behind, and it wasn't a pretty picture. Under King's successor, President Brasington, the United States seemed to be regressing in scientific thought and research. The political and economic climate was obviously deteriorating, and everyone in ORT was concerned that the nation would again become involved in some military conflict that would cost billions of dollars and the precious blood of the soldiers, sailors, and marines who would then be sent off to some alien desert or jungle to fight an ill-defined conflict with no real purpose and typically no exit strategy. It could be Harold Tate's middle-east war all over again, if not worse.

Steve wondered what it was about the American electorate that could lead to the same kinds of mistakes over and over again. Surely people could learn such an important lesson that it really does matter whom they elect for their leaders, and particularly for the presidency. How could essentially the same nation of people elect a Harold Tate, suffer terribly through his administration, then elect a progressive populist like King, enjoy eight years of relative peace and prosperity, as well as the benefits of advances in science and technology, and then turn right around and elect another Tate in the guise of a fundamentalist minister who offered nothing but neoconservative dogma, another crackdown on civil liberties, and warmongering brinkmanship with other nations? He didn't think that he would ever understand it. And if Americans kept making these mistakes, despite all the lessons that should have been learned, what kind of future could the nation expect to have? Indeed, what kind of future did it deserve?

It was a depressing line of thought, and he turned his now drowsy mind back to Julie, ADMIN-414, or whatever her number might really be.

Chapter 19: Seduction

Steve napped peacefully and may have slept the whole night through were it not for the muted but insistent electronic chime of his doorbell. He sat up quickly in bed, looked at his clock, and realized that it would be Julie at his door and that he hadn't even tidied up his apartment, or himself, for that matter. He said loudly, "Be right there." His mouth tasted like the bottom of a birdcage, so he quickly rinsed with some mouthwash and ran a brush through his hair. His rumpled overall appearance would just have to do for now.

Opening the door, he found Julie wearing a short skirt, tight white blouse, and shiny black knee-high boots. She was carrying a small black duffel bag in addition to her usual purse. She was, to put it mildly, a vision. He couldn't help but stand there and take in the whole picture.

"Well, aren't you going to invite me in, Steve? Are you going to have me stand out here all evening?" And this with a smile so seductive that all he could do was gesture for her to come in. She closed the door behind her. "You look like you just got out of bed. You weren't starting without me, were you, Steve? Or perhaps some other woman was here with you?"

The sight of her, the husky sound of her voice, and her slightly-perfumed scent had him reeling. He didn't know how to respond to her, and it really didn't matter at all. She had obviously come prepared to lead during their time together this evening, and he was enjoying it too much to offer the least objection. She opened the black duffel bag and pulled out a pair of handcuffs that were obviously real and not a toy. "Take off your clothes...all of them," as she impatiently pushed one of the cuff's ratchets through its pawl. And he complied, all the while aware that he was obviously stimulated by all that was happening.

Soon he stood naked before her. "Now, hands behind your back." Steve hesitated but realized that in his present unclothed state, Julie already had the upper hand. Julie moved to him quickly, took his right wrist and closed the handcuff over it. She then pulled his other arm behind his back and affixed the remaining cuff to his left wrist.

"You didn't know that I was a police officer before coming to ORT, did you Steve?"

For the first time, Steve noticed how buff her arm muscles were. She very obviously worked out regularly. "You were really a police officer?" Steve asked.

"Oh yes, and I've had to deal with many unruly guys who thought they could get away with something. Now I took a lot of time getting myself ready for our evening together, but look at you. Took a nap, didn't you? You didn't take the time to dress up for me, did you? Sounds like disrespect to me, Steve, and police officers don't take well to disrespect. What do you think we should do about that, hmm?" she purred.

Steve was feeling very self-conscious now, especially with his hands cuffed behind his back. "Julie, I'm sorry that I didn't..." He was interrupted when she lightly slapped the side of his face.

"Is that the way you address a police officer? More disrespect!"

"I'm sorry ma'am," Steve mumbled, looking down humbly.

"Better. Much better. Now show me this bedroom that you spend so much time in!"

And he did, only to find out that she had a number of other interesting implements in her bag of tricks, and then to enjoy the most erotic encounter of his life, brought to him by Julie, ADMIN-whatever, former police officer turned personnel specialist and for this night at least, seductress extraordinaire.

Chapter 20: Back to Work

The morning came all too soon. After their play time ended, Julie stayed with Steve the rest of the night. He reveled in her warmth and comfort. He had been with many women in his life before ORT, but none like her. With his head still buried in his pillow, Steve opened one eye to confirm that the early morning mood lighting had come on. Given the lack of the normal day-night cycle provided by nature, lighting throughout ORT adjusted its tone and intensity to simulate morning, afternoon, evening, and night. All quite ingenious, he thought. He turned over gently and found Julie looking at him tenderly.

"How do you feel, Steve?"

"Wonderful, uh, may I call you Julie now?" he smiled.

"Yes, of course. Did you enjoy my little surprise?"

"That would be a massive understatement!"

Julie smiled and said, "Good!"

"Okay, so I have to ask you again, were you really a police officer?"

Julie quickly slipped out of bed, went to her purse, and brought back to the bed a black leather ID case. She opened it for him, and inside, he saw the gold shield of a Los Angeles police detective as well as the photo ID card that went with it. "Believe me now?" she asked.

"Oh yes. I did anyway just by the way you took control and handled yourself last night, but I had to ask. Is that why you've had the job of escorting new recruits here?"

"It helps, for everyone's protection."

"Were you armed when you escorted me here?"

"What do you think?"

"I'm guessing you were."

"And you're guessing correctly."

"Wow." It was all he could think of to say.

"You're too funny, Steve."

"Oh yes, I'm a regular laugh sensation, aren't I? Wait a minute, wait a minute, this just occurred to me. How were you going to protect me during the trip here when you were as medicated as I was? Or, were you?"

"I'm sorry, but of course I wasn't really medicated. And what's worse, from a deception standpoint, is that while you were waiting for me to be searched back at Clark Aviation, the nurse, whose name is Connie, and I were just having a nice conversation in the examining room. I feel especially badly about this deception now since we have a close personal relationship, but it's the way it's always been done, and it really works to help the new recruit be a little more comfortable while also being totally compliant with the pre-flight formalities. Connie, who believe me is really a very nice person, provides the impulse for compliance, and I, as your supposed co-recruit, help you to be more comfortable and not to feel alone. I was just doing my job to the best of my ability, and you did arrive here safe and well. Will you forgive me?" she asked with the expression of a little girl who's been caught with her hand in the cookie jar.

"Yes, I think we're past that now. Just don't let it happen again," he said with mock sternness.

"Yes sir," she replied and put her hand up in a gesture of salute.

Steve chuckled, "Listen, madam, I don't know what your work hours are, but I just barely have time to get ready and head to the office."

"I'll tell you what, Steve. You go ahead and get showered and dressed, and I'll make you breakfast."

"Now that's an offer I can't refuse," he said.

"You've had a lot of those in the past eight hours, haven't you?" she said with a grin so broad that Steve couldn't help but kiss her one last time before hauling himself out of bed.

Returning to the kitchen about twenty minutes later, he found Julie fully dressed and the smoky odor of bacon in the air. He thought that Julie is a real keeper, if anyone were in fact capable of keeping her.

With breakfast over and a lull in their small talk, he looked at his clock and said that he should be headed out.

"Me too, Steve. But I'll see you soon. If you want," she added.

"Oh, I very much want. And the sooner the better."

And they both left his quarters, Julie presumably heading for the elevator to take her down to ADMIN, and Steve for his small office in the THOT team area.

Chapter 21: Washington

Colonel Diggs' last-minute recollection set off a flurry of activity in the White House, beginning with Chuck Pearce going to see his boss, Jeb White, the chief of staff. Anything having to do with science and the government, particularly if it hadn't been approved by the Brasington administration, was subject to intense scrutiny. Add to the mix the notion of studying the origin of the universe and the level of scrutiny became obsessive-compulsive. Every agency of the executive branch that might have had anything whatsoever to do with such a project was directed to turn over any and all documents relating to same within forty-eight hours.

It turned out that the National Science Foundation was able to provide most of what little information seemed to be available. Clearly, former President King had done his best to conceal the work of the project from future administrations. Making things even more difficult, before King left office, the project had been transferred from the sponsorship of the federal government to a private foundation, about which almost nothing was known. Both White and the president himself were enraged to learn of this infamy, but not the least bit surprised that it emanated from the King administration, which was viewed as blatantly evil by the current occupant of the White House.

All of this would have been more than sufficient for the president to order the project to be shut down. The fact that it was located on, or more accurately, inside real estate still technically owned by the government would make issuing such an order relatively painless.

But as useful as the information from the National Science Foundation was in sealing the fate of the Origin Project, it was nothing compared to the one piece of enlightenment provided by the National Institutes of Health. The president learned for the first time that the anti-cancer medication, Oncoleve, had been developed by the medical researchers who were part of the Origin Project, and more significantly, that they had done so using embryonic stem cell research. This, of course, was an outright abomination that had to be stopped and stopped immediately.

It was against this background that Hall and Pearce met for dinner at a tony upscale Georgetown restaurant one week following their meeting with the WHMO director and Colonel Diggs in Pearce's office. Hall arrived first and got seating for the two of them with no problem whatsoever considering that a reservation had been made for a sitting member of Congress and the White House deputy chief of staff. Chuck Pearce arrived about ten minutes later and took his seat with Jackson.

As they perused their menus, Jackson said, "So give me the latest. What's happening over at 1600?"

"Well one thing I can tell you for certain, and please treat this as confidential until the news breaks, is that the president is going to issue an executive order banning the sale and use of Oncoleve. He'll be directing the FDA to issue a recall for all outstanding stockpiles."

"My God, Chuck, has he thought through all the ramifications of doing that? Oncoleve has proven to be the miracle drug to fight the scourge of cancer. People all over the world have been using it for what, at least two years now? You take this drug off the market and we go back to chemotherapy and radiation treatments. I mean, don't you think there's going to be a real backlash?"

"Well, first of all, the White House sees this drug as the fruit of a poison tree, to put it in legal terms. It was developed by an outfit that is committing blasphemy in its approach to science, and this particular discovery is the result of stem cell research. That's all the president needs to know, my man. There's no stopping him now."

Jackson slowly shook his head, saying, "Listen, I was brought up by a fundamentalist minister whose views are probably very much the same as the president's, and I can understand his line of thinking about this. But still, Chuck, we're talking about a medicine that is the cure for cancer, and it's on the market now, cheaply available to a public desperately in need of it. Plus, consider the fact that Oncoleve has been distributed all over the world. All the president can do is ban its use in the United States. Don't you think that those who can afford to do so will travel somewhere else to get it? And that those who can't will be more than a little resentful and angry?"

"I think everything you've just said is true, and I also know that it doesn't make the least bit of difference to the president. He views himself as having been elected to restore morality to a nation that has suffered under eight years of evil liberalism. This isn't something he would even think twice about. Look, Jackson, people will adapt. We'll come up with some reason to make it more palatable. Maybe there are long-term effects that weren't known when the drug was first released to the medical community."

"Uh, Chuck, I don't know that a concern for these possible long-term effects is going to have much of an impact on someone with terminal cancer, do you?"

"No, probably not. I'm just the messenger. And frankly, I'm glad that I'm not the public messenger on this one. I don't envy the press secretary his job at this point."

Their meals arrived and they dined in relative quiet. A rainstorm was raging outside with lightning flashing and thunder booming loudly.

"You know, Chuck, I can't help but think that this weather is a metaphor for what we're going to be facing in the next few weeks over this Oncoleve thing. I really think it's not going to go down well at all. Put yourself in the position of someone who needs this drug to save their life, or someone in their family."

Pearce hesitated and then said, "Okay, I'm not supposed to discuss this with anyone outside the senior staff at the White House, but since you're my friend and you're obviously very concerned, then just between us I can 'let it slip' that it will just be a temporary thing, not having an anti-cancer drug available."

"What does that mean? And what's temporary?"

"The fact is that we've got the medication. It's the research that led to it that is the crux of the problem as far as the president is concerned. There's another thing. You know that his campaign was heavily supported by the pharmaceutical industry, right?"

"Yes, I know that."

"Well, how much money are the pharmaceutical companies making on this medication? Practically none, that's how much. The licensing agreement that came with the right to manufacture and distribute Oncoleve only allows for them to recover their actual costs. It's been a huge thorn in their side."

"So?"

"And so now, one or two of these companies will use Oncoleve to manufacture a close substitute for it, with no additional research using stem cells. Of course, it will doubtless be a very expensive medication in the future when it's released under some other name, but it will be worth it, you've said so yourself. I'm no expert in this area, but I've heard speculation that this should all happen within a year or two."

"Chuck, that's a year or two of thousands of deaths and who knows how much suffering and how many outdated treatments laden with many bad side effects. I mean, I guess it's better than not having it at all, but my gut tells me that these firms had better rush something to market quickly, and that it had better be every bit as effective as Oncoleve."

The rain was coming down in torrents now and visibility was just about zero. Chuck asked Jackson, "Where are you parked anyway?"

"I'm in a parking garage about three blocks from here. It wasn't raining when I walked over here."

"I'm parked right outside in front of the restaurant. How about we finish up here and you come along home with me? I've got a beautiful apartment in the Watergate Complex that I'd love to show you. Also I've got a spare bedroom, and I'll bring you back to the garage to pick up your car in the morning. What do you say?"

The wine he had been drinking with dinner left him with a pleasant buzz, and he was feeling very mellow. Plus, contrary to his deepest religious beliefs, he had found himself becoming very attracted to Chuck Pearce during their meetings at the White House and now this evening.

"I'd like that, I'd like that very much," Jackson replied.

The two men paid the check, put on their coats, and walked out into the driving rain.

Chapter 22: The White House Calls

ADMIN-1 pushed the speed-dial button on his telephone for ADMIN-2, who answered immediately. "Join me in the conference room in five minutes, Dick. President Brasington's chief of staff wants to speak with us."

Within a few minutes, ADMIN-1 and ADMIN-2 were seated in the videoconference room, along with Arianna, who would be setting up the link and video recording the call. Only ADMIN-1 would appear in the video feed going to the White House.

Arianna spoke, counting down to the feed going live. "Five, four, three, two, live."

As ADMIN-1 watched, the video feed from the chief of staff's office appeared and Jeb White, Brasington's chief of staff, seated himself with a grunt. He spoke first in his distinctive Southern accent. "Hello? Ah you Mohfield?"

"I am Steve Morefield, and I am the administrator of this facility. What can I do for you today, Mr. White?"

White said, "Well now listen heah, President Brasington, blessed be his name, has been asking me to get some more information on what you fellas are doing down there, you heah? We've been havin' a devil of a time tryin' to figuh out how to contact you folks. He wants to be sure that you all ah on the right track, so to speak, that yoah playing on the right team, you undah-stand?"

ADMIN-1 replied, "First of all, may I congratulate the President on his election and convey the best wishes of everyone here in the project to him for a very success-ful administration."

"Oh nevah feah about that, Mohfield, we are cehtainly on the road to an enlightened and successful administration, have no doubts about that. Now what the Sam Hill ah you fellas up to anyway?"

"Sir, as you are no doubt aware, we are function-ing as a private foundation which was established un-der the King administration for the purpose of scien-tific research. While we have accomplished a number of things, including the discovery of the anti-cancer drug Oncoleve, our primary mission is to try to understand the origins of the universe itself."

"What's that you say now? The ohigins of the uni-verse? Seems to me that we've already determined that without any degree of doubt, so you fellas may want to pack up your belongins' and join the rest of civilization heah on the suhface."

"Well, sir, I wasn't aware that the origins of the uni-verse had been pinned down by another group. Could you please enlighten me?"

"Sounds like you need some enlightenment, Mo-hfield. The Bible tells us everything we need to know about such things like that. A man of your intelligence must know that! Now looky heah, President Brasington, blessed be his name, isn't going to be pleased at all, not at all, if that's the sum and substance of what I can tell him."

"Sir, I don't know what else to tell you other than the truth. That is our established mission, and in the process of working with some of the best scientific minds of our age, we have been fortunate enough to have developed some practical spin-off knowledge, not the least of which has been responsible for curing tens if not hundreds of thousands of people from the scourge of cancer."

"Cansuh, yes, a terrible thing it is too. And yet God made it along with us, didn't He? And who ah we to question His decision? I dunno Mohfield, but it sounds to me like you all should just return to the suhface and find more meaningful wohk to occupy youh time."

"Let me just be clear, Mr. White. You say more meaningful work than researching the origins of universe and life itself? More meaningful than discovering a cure for cancer? Is that what you're saying sir?"

"Ah you hahd of heahing, Mohfield? Of couhse that's what I said. Intelligent people like them that you've supposedly got down there could put themselves to good use doing the Lord's wohk here on the suhface, just as He intended. We ah doin' impohtant things here too, you know. We've got a tehhible situation with un-educated people trying to find work in a battehed econ-omy. Not to mention the evil hohdes creatin' a menace to good Amehicans all over the wohld."

"Yes, I can certainly understand the problems be-ing faced as a result of uneducated people. That's truly a tragedy. And these evil hordes you speak of, Mr. White, who would they be?"

"Oh, Mohfield, them folks in the Middle East, China, Korea, Russia, the former Soviet republics, you name it. And quite frankly, between me and you, Mohfield, we've got a batch of scientists heah and in other countries who just insist upon wastin' their time and energy on pointless puhsuits that do nuthin' but create dissension and unrest. Honestly, Mohfield, I don't know how President Brasington, blessed be his name, deals with it all."

"I can see that he has his hands full. And since we're not part of the government and no longer funded by any governmental agency, it seems to me that the best thing we can do is just to continue our work here and not bother the president with our petty issues."

"Well now uh don't rightly know about that, Mohfield, uh don't rightly know about that at all. It's up to the president, of couhse, not to a mere functionahy such as mahself, you unduhstand."

"As you say, Mr. White, although it's very clear that you are far more than a mere functionary. You are obviously an important member of the president's team and as such, I'm sure your input is very important to him."

"Well puhhaps it is, Mohfield, puhhaps it is. Ahl git back to you after I've had a chance to speak to him about all this. He's a very busy man, Mohfield, with many things on his mind, so it may be a week or so."

"That's not a problem, sir, we will stand by to hear from you at your convenience."

"Mighty glad to heah it, Mohfield." And the feed was disconnected.

ADMIN-1 sat back and looked at his deputy. "That man has the job you used to have, Dick."

"That man hasn't emerged from the cave yet, Steve."

"Now that's where you're wrong, my friend. It's not that he hasn't emerged from the cave; rather, it's that he's heading right back into it."

Chapter 23: Transfer

The first thing Steve noticed when he entered his office was a new ID badge lying in the center of his desk. Confused as to why a duplicate name badge would have found its way there, he picked it up only to see that it read "ADMIN-415." He had no sooner put the badge back down on the desk when his door chime sounded. He opened the door to see his THOT team leader, Vivian. "Steve, come on over to the conference room. Hurry!"

Steve followed her down the hallway and then into the room. In the conference room, he was surprised to find the entire THOT team assembled and a large cake sitting on the center of the table. People started applauding as he approached the cake and saw that it was inscribed, "Congratulations ADMIN-415!" Once again he realized that the past twenty-four hours had been a whirlwind full of a volley of surprises, most of them pleasant.

"But I haven't even officially accepted the offer yet," Steve protested mildly.

Vivian spoke for the group, "Steve, sincere congratulations from all of us. Your work here has been exemplary. I can't tell you how much we're going to miss your helpful suggestions, your thoughtful input, and your smiling countenance. Please don't be a stranger and come back to see us from time to time"

"But…," Steve began to say.

"There are no buts, Steve, and we both know it. When ADMIN-1 calls, we answer."

"I don't know what to say. Honestly, I didn't ask for this transfer, and it has nothing to do with me not being happy working with you all."

"We know that, Steve. Remember, we've all been here a bit longer than you have. This happens from time to time. And it couldn't happen to a better person. We're just jealous that you'll be heading to the rarified atmosphere of ADMIN!" she said.

"Well…well…thank you, everyone. I am still not quite believing any of this."

"Of course. But rather than talk any more about it for now, how about cutting the cake, ADMIN-415?"

And cut the cake he did, but he couldn't remember a more poignant celebration in all of his life.

———————

About forty-five minutes later, after the cake was eaten and he had shaken hands or exchanged hugs with his former team members, he headed back to his office, feeling a bit giddy about his promotion (and there really was no doubt in his mind that it was a promotion), but also somewhat lonely for the group of colleagues with whom he had enjoyed working so much during the past six months.

This time when he entered his office, there was a flashing message light on his phone. He pressed the appropriate key to retrieve the message; it was from Arianna, and it asked him to go to his quarters immediately upon receiving it.

He arrived at his quarters and found everything gone! His personal items, his clothes, his music collection, any evidence that he had ever inhabited this space were...gone. He looked at the phone in his living room and saw the flashing red light again. Beginning to feel as though he were in a scavenger hunt, he picked up the handset and retrieved the message. This time it was from Julie, "Wait for me. I'll be there shortly."

Chapter 24: Dinner in ADMIN

Steve waited in his now-abandoned quarters until Julie arrived about ten minutes later. "What's going on here?" he asked her.

"Steve, I'm sorry for what must have come as yet another shock to you. I didn't know about it myself until I met with ADMIN-1 earlier this morning. All he wanted to know was whether the two of us were okay and would be able to work together. I told him I believed that we would be fine working together." At that point she grinned at the memory of the events of the last evening. "He said that was all he needed to know, and that you were to be transferred down to ADMIN without delay. I didn't fully realize that his idea of 'without delay' meant that some team members from maintenance would be pressed into service moving your personal items to your new quarters in ADMIN right away. Anyway, as soon as Arianna told me what was happening, I left you a voice message and made my way here as quickly as I could. And, here I am."

"Well, that explains why a new ID badge was waiting for me in my office and why my team members had a going-away event for me a while ago. He really doesn't waste time making things happen, does he?"

"No, he doesn't. And there's another thing. This evening you're invited to a dinner with some senior staff members of ADMIN as well as all of the team leaders, so Vivian will be there too."

"What? A formal dinner? Julie, this is all a little over the top, you know?"

"It may seem like that, but it's a tradition whenever someone new joins ADMIN. Now, all of your things will be in your new quarters down in ADMIN. The staff will have tried to make the move as seamless as possible for you, but since the living spaces are not quite identical in furnishings, you may have to look for some of your things for a day or two." Seeing the somewhat wide-eyed look on his face, she continued, "Don't get the wrong idea, Steve. You're not moving into a new luxurious suite or anything. It will be similar in size to this unit, maybe a little larger and with a few more goodies, but that's all. Now come with me and I'll show you to your new home."

They both headed for the now-familiar "Utilities Room" door in the main cafeteria foyer. Julie told Steve to swipe his new ID badge through the reader. He did, and the lock clicked open. They went inside and he repeated the procedure for the elevator. In a few seconds, the doors opened. He pressed the button for ADMIN and the doors closed. He said to Julie, "This is all a bit unreal."

She replied, "I know it is Steve. Just hang in there through all the transition. I think you'll really enjoy working in ADMIN."

"I really enjoyed working in THOT. I'm going to miss all of that intellectual stimulation."

"You think so?" she smiled. "I think you're going to be too busy with other kinds of intellectual stimulation to miss the academic life too much."

They arrived at the ADMIN level, but this time the elevator doors opened behind them, revealing a large public area that he hadn't seen during his last visit here. "Yet another surprise," he said.

"Might as well get used to it Steve. That's life in ADMIN." She patted his back and they exited the elevator. "This is part of your new home, Steve. This area is used for some meetings, for socializing, for work space when you feel like a change, and for recreational activities in the evenings." She led him along the left side of the large room to a corridor into which they turned. It looked a lot like a hallway in a very nice hotel, with individual doors with numbers on both sides. They arrived at the furthermost door to the left, and he saw an embossed plastic plate that read "ADMIN-415."

"Use your card and check out your new digs, Steve."

He swiped his card and the lock clicked open. She opened the door and held it for him. Steve walked inside. A few lights were turned on, so he could immediately see that they were standing in a living room just a little larger than the one in his previous unit. There was a very nice flat-screen television mounted on the wall across from a comfortable-looking sofa. They toured the small kitchen, bath, and bedroom that were almost identical to the rooms in THOT. The main difference was the addition of a door to another room leading from the bedroom. "Go ahead," Julie said, "check it out."

Steve opened the door and stepped in. Indirect lighting came on by itself as he entered. He saw a very nicely-appointed small office, complete with desk, chair, and a sophisticated looking computer and keyboard. He noticed that the computer monitor was equipped with a small camera and microphone. There was also a multi-line telephone and what he assumed was a directory sitting next to it. "What's all this for, Julie?"

"This is your new office, Steve. Here in ADMIN, our workspaces are mostly attached to our quarters. We do a lot of our work this way, using the videoconference capabilities as we need them. Of course, we still meet frequently for conferences and brainstorming. Apparently the designers of the facility believed that this arrangement would be more efficient for the things we do here." She briefly shrugged her shoulders and continued, "Personally I think both arrangements have their pros and cons, but it works fine for me."

"Okay then," Steve said, still looking around at his new living space.

"Let's grab some lunch. We have a much smaller version of the cafeteria you're used to. We don't feed nearly as many people here, but the food is good."

"Okay, sounds fine to me, but what about this dinner tonight? I don't have any formal clothes here."

"Steve, my darling, nobody has any formal clothes here, at least none that I know of."

He was about to reply to her when the phone on his desk sounded. He noticed that the caller ID display showed "Arianna, ADMIN-32." He looked at Julie then picked up the phone, answering simply "THOT-, I mean, ADMIN-415."

Arianna's calm and professional voice said, "Hello Steve. Welcome to ADMIN. Please come to the video-conference room off the main reception area at 1900 hours this evening for dinner, where you will meet with ADMIN-1 and -2 along with others who want to meet you. May I give ADMIN-1 your RSVP?"

"Uh, yes, of course, and please thank him for me."

"I will certainly do that. See you at 1900 then." And the line clicked off to a normal dial tone.

Steve saw that Julie was watching him. "What?" he asked.

"I'm just trying to make sure that you're okay. A lot has changed for you during the past twenty-four hours. I mean, you've even had a run-in with the police!" and she grinned while she winked at him.

"Indeed I did. Do you think that same police officer is still in the area?"

"I wouldn't be the least bit surprised," she said.

———

After a short but enjoyable lunch together, Julie suggested that Steve go back to his new quarters, locate his belongings, and maybe even catch a nap before dinner. "And Steve, this time set an alarm. I don't want to have the police coming here to fetch you for dinner. Understand?"

He couldn't help but smile as he told her that he understood completely.

Before she left him, she showed him the foyer that bridged the common area with the hallway and offices that he had seen during his first visit. Once he saw that, he knew exactly where to find the videoconference room. He thought that the high-tech area he had seen was a strange place to serve dinner, but he was now beginning, just beginning, to expect the unexpected.

Steve returned to his quarters and began to make himself at home. He found all of his personal items, and his clothes were already hanging in his bedroom closet or folded neatly in his dresser drawers. He was extremely impressed. Someone, or more accurately, some people, had gone to a lot of trouble to ease his move here. Spotting a high-end audio system in his bedroom, he couldn't resist playing one of his favorite CDs as he laid down on his bed for the nap that Julie had suggested. He did feel uncharacteristically tired, so he made certain to set the alarm clock beside his bed for 1800 hours. That would give him a full hour to get himself ready for his dinner date with ADMIN-1 and whomever else would be there.

He went to sleep to the sweet sounds of "The Mamas and the Papas" and soon was dreaming about other times and other places, long ago friends and once-familiar faces. Yet oddly, Julie was there in his dreams too. Sweet, sweet Julie, always full of surprises. He felt comforted by her presence in his dream world, and then he gently drifted into an even deeper sleep. The audio system, aware that he was no longer actively listening, slowly faded the sound level of the music to total quiet, and Steve slept uninterrupted until his alarm sounded at 1800.

———————

He awakened to the gentle but insistent tone of the alarm clock, and once he began to sit up in bed, the room lighting ascended from darkness to a pleasant indirect light level suitable for seeing the room and his surroundings but not much more. As he got out of bed, the light increased to a normal brilliance. He sat back down on the bed to see what would happen, but the lighting system wasn't fooled. It ignored him and maintained its present level. Okay, Steve thought, I'm impressed again.

He decided to take a quick shower and then shaved again. He put on the nicest clean clothes that he had in his wardrobe and, at about 1845, headed to the reception area where Julie had taken him just yesterday, and yet somehow it seemed like weeks ago. He saw several other people in the common area, but they either paid little attention to him or briefly said hello or waved to him. He entered the corridor leading to the reception room and felt butterflies in his stomach just as he had the day before. Ridiculous, he told himself, and entered the reception room.

Arianna was there and greeted him, "Hello Steve, please come with me." She opened the door that led directly into the videoconference room and motioned him in. He walked into the room, but to his great surprise, the huge conference table had been turned into an elegant dining table, complete with linen tablecloth, crystal glasses, and a pattern of fine tableware that he recognized as Lenox. He had a moment alone in the room, and he noticed that there were small place cards on the table. He found his in the center of one side of the table. ADMIN-1 was at what appeared to be the head of the table, and ADMIN-2 was at the other end. He only had time to see a few others, MED-11 around the corner from ADMIN-1, his THOT team leader Vivian was on his one side, and thankfully, Julie was on his other. He hadn't even known if she would be here this evening as she hadn't mentioned it. He looked at her card more closely and saw that under her name, her designator was displayed as "ADMIN-54." Wow, he thought, that indicated that she had been at ORT from nearly its beginning, if not since its beginning, a time which he knew was referred to as the Epoch.

A few people filed into the room, but initially nobody that he recognized. Everyone seemed to recognize him, though, and they all came over to him, shook hands, and greeted him warmly. Then more people came in through the door from reception, including Vivian and Julie. Dick, ADMIN-2, entered the room through the door from his office and took his place at the foot of the table. A few minutes later, ADMIN-1 entered from his own office, stopped to shake hands with Steve, and then stepped to the head of the table. "Everyone, please take your seat." And they did, all conversation and other miscellaneous sounds coming to a halt.

ADMIN-1 continued, "This evening we have the pleasure of welcoming Steve, formerly THOT-415, to our merry band of thieves. Vivian, would you be kind enough to make the introductions?"

She did, introducing Steve to the heads of each of the specialty teams at ORT, as well as Kathy, MED-11, whom Steve remembered very well from his first routine visit to MED Central after joining ORT. He realized that she was likely here tonight because she was partnered with ADMIN-1. As soon as Vivian was finished, servers came into the room in white uniforms bringing with them a delicious turkey dinner with all of the side dishes. "Please, enjoy," ADMIN-1 said, and the meal began. Steve enjoyed the food, the fine wine that was served, as well as the company. But he enjoyed nothing more than he did having Julie at his side.

After dessert had been served and the small talk began to die down, ADMIN-1 tapped his knife on the side of his glass. To the group assembled, he said, "Now that I'm sure you will agree that we've all been well fed and have enjoyed warm and stimulating conversation, I'm afraid that I must ruin the atmosphere and inform you about a very serious problem." And the room suddenly became deathly quiet.

Chapter 25: Bad News

ADMIN-1 had everyone's undivided attention as he proceeded to address the group. "As some of you are no doubt aware, even though there is a new and very different administration in Washington now, we still have some people in high civil service positions who are friendly to our work and mission here. What we're hearing from all of them is uniformly bad." ADMIN-1 paused while members of the group reacted to what they had heard so far. "One very distressing piece of information that I became aware of just a few days ago is that our new and 'enlightened' President has come to the belief that since ORT is engaged in what he refers to as an 'ungodly' pursuit of knowledge, then everything that comes from us must be considered the fruit of a poisonous tree. I'm not particularly surprised that he regards our mission with disapproval, but he also is on the verge of outlawing the use of Oncoleve within the United States."

Startled disbelief was apparent in every person at the table. Steve stole a quick glance at ADMIN-2 at the other end of the table, where he was sitting with his head in his hands. He was the living manifestation of doom and gloom.

ADMIN-1 continued, "If the government outlaws the use of Oncoleve, we believe that it will lead to widespread protests and most likely violence. There are many people in the U.S. currently in need of the drug, and many others who have been healed by it, who will not take quietly to this turn of events. Of course, there are also those true believers who will take President Brasington's pronouncement as Gospel and will be more than ready to take up arms on the other side. And these people, particularly, are likely to have access to weapons. Not just handguns, but assault rifles and more."

Steve remembered that Brasington had reversed the previous King administration's ban on assault weapons, and some of the individual states, now led by conservative legislators and governors, had even gone so far as to require families to have firearms in their homes. Unfortunately, his home state of Florida had been one of the first of these.

"In short, we should anticipate the possibility of civil unrest on an almost unprecedented scale. Furthermore, we can definitely expect the administration to begin some degree of effort to shut us down completely."

If the faces of the members of the group had previously registered startled disbelief, then what Steve both felt and observed now was akin to anger and, perhaps, fear. People spoke at the same time: "How dare they!", "What are we going to do?", "Does this mean that we're finished?"

ADMIN-1 held up a hand, and the room again went quiet. "I want to remind you that an eventuality such as this was foreseen by President King and our board, and although nobody thought it would come to pass so soon, and some felt it would never happen, precautions were taken."

Again voices from around the table: "What precautions?", "How can we be safe if they decide to attack us with force?", "Please, can you tell us more?"

"For the security of all of us and our work, I can't go into detail right now, but for the moment, we are safe. And I will keep you updated as new developments occur." ADMIN-1 looked around the table and continued, "Now, we can expect that Brasington's views, and any actions he may decide to take, will soon be making news on the commercial news channels to which we all have access. That access will not be curtailed in any way. I want each of you team leaders to meet with your respective groups no later than tomorrow and brief them on our discussion. They're going to be seeing and hearing about this soon enough, and we don't want self-destructive rumors to interfere with our lives and our work here. What we're doing is far too important for that. And we have some amount of time to prepare due to the foresight and thoughtful planning of our founders. I want to reiterate that we are perfectly safe for the time being. We will be working with our sources in the government to try to stay at least one step ahead of whatever the administration is planning. Now, I really do apologize for the necessity of somewhat ruining the celebratory atmosphere that we normally enjoy when we welcome a new member to ADMIN, but we all must immediately begin operating in a far more defensive posture than any of us would have liked."

ADMIN-1 then excused himself and went back into his office, and it was clear that the dinner was concluded. People started to mill around and make their way back out to the reception area, but Steve and Julie remained in their seats, finally looking at each other and shaking their heads in disbelief. "Well," Steve said, "that's one way of starting to work in a new job."

Julie looked at him sympathetically and said, "I had no idea that the political climate on the surface was becoming so hostile so quickly."

Steve thought back to his earlier ruminations about the stark differences between an administration like Jeremy King's and one like that of the current president. He thought of how different things could have been had people only learned from history and might have had the insight and intelligence to have elected Celia Wright, King's vice-president, instead of the Reverend Brasington. It had been a close election, but there can only be one winner, and the die had then been irreversibly cast for what was now to come.

Chapter 26: Julie

Apart from the worrisome news imparted at its conclusion, Steve's welcoming dinner to ADMIN had been wonderful. But more wonderful yet was Julie's invitation for him to visit her quarters and to "stay the night." Her unit proved to be located in a hallway shooting out from the other side of the ADMIN concourse than his own. They arrived at the door marked "ADMIN-54" and Julie swiped her ID card through the reader to unlock it. She held the door for him and dialed up the lighting as he entered. While her quarters were laid out similar to his, the decor reflected her own feminine tastes.

"This is really very nice, Julie, you've done a lot with the place," he joked.

"I've been here years longer than you have, Steve, so I've had more time to make the place my own. Plus, I recognize that this is my home for virtually the rest of my life, so I might as well make it as attractive and comfortable as possible, don't you think?"

"Of course. You know, it's weird. I've only been in ORT for a little over six months, and I haven't missed the outside world too terribly much, but when you talk about being here for the rest of your life, it brings up a touch of melancholy in me, you know?"

"I do know. It happens to all of us. Then, in time, there comes an acceptance that this is truly home, that things here are really much more pleasant than on the surface. Still, I must admit that when I walk into ADMIN-1's office and see that beautiful video scene transmitted from above, I still miss it for a while too. But as you and I both know, life is a series of compromises from the virtual ideal world that we all have in our minds, and I'm more than satisfied with my choice to be here."

Seated beside each other now on her living room sofa, each with drink in hand, Steve decided to broach a subject about which he had been wondering from the time of his arrival. "Julie, where is here?" He noticed her body visibly tense for an instant.

"Steve, that's something I absolutely cannot discuss with you or anyone else who doesn't have an official need to know. I know we've all been exposed to the abuse of secrecy based on the term 'national security' from the government above, but this really is a matter of project security."

"I see," replied Steve.

"Do you really? I wonder. Steve, I think you're a terrific guy and you're going to be a great addition to AD-MIN. You and I together have been building a relationship that I hope will grow even deeper, but I really need you to understand that there are certain things, certain confidential pieces of information, that my particular duty assignment here has required me to become familiar with. The same thing may happen with you with other bits of information. We need to be able to live with each other, and to have confidence in our love and caring for each other, despite the fact that there exists duty-related information which cannot be shared between us. It isn't easy, and I can tell you that several other couples here have been torn apart by it. I think that it's tougher in ADMIN than in any other section because this is the repository of so much fundamental knowledge about the project."

Steve carefully considered everything Julie had been telling him. "Yes, when you put it like that, I do understand." He smiled, "I might not like it, but I understand. Things are different here. Although, I imagine that it's something like the scenario where someone on the surface has a government job with access to classified information and isn't permitted to share it with his or her significant other."

"Yes, something like that. Look, I don't mind you asking me questions as long as you can accept that there are questions which I can't answer. Sometimes because I'm not permitted to discuss something, and at other times because I may not know the answer myself."

"Somehow it's hard for me to imagine that there is much going on here that you don't know about."

"Why? Because I've been here for years?"

"That, and because you just seem to know so much, to be so comfortable here..."

She interjected, "You mean, like I'm a fixture here?"

"Well, I wouldn't use the term 'fixture,' and I mean it in a good way. You just seem to fit in perfectly, you're extremely competent, and you're very accepting of the rules and regulations that go along with being here."

"Okay, I can see that," she said, placing her empty glass on the coffee table. "Maybe you have some other question that I can answer though?"

"Can you tell me more about ADMIN-1; he's certainly a fascinating guy?"

"Hmm, perhaps a little that you don't already know. First of all, you may be aware that ADMIN-1 holds a doctoral degree in computer science. Under the Tate administration, he had worked on some top-secret government project with the Defense Advanced Research Projects Agency, before leaving Washington to go home to a small town in rural Pennsylvania to take care of his father, who was terminal with Chronic Obstructive Pulmonary Disease and a heart condition. His mom had passed away years before, and as an only-child, he and his father had been exceptionally close. When his dad died, Steve suffered some kind of a breakdown, and that's where my knowledge of the situation becomes fuzzy. All I really know is that the then newly-elected President King wanted him back in the government in the worst way. Amongst all that, somehow Steve met Kathy Carver, who at the time was an Air Force nurse, and who is now with us here as MED-11, and she was assigned to nurse him back to health before he resumed his duties. I understand that you've met Kathy?"

"Uh, yes I did, Julie, very early on, and I will admit to you that I made the mistake of asking her out for an evening without checking the register, so I didn't know that she was partnered with ADMIN-1! What a way to start a new job, especially in a small society like this one."

"Oh yes, I know all about that."

"You do?"

"Of course. Kathy and I are very best friends." Julie grinned.

"Oh Lord save me."

"Now Kathy is another fascinating individual," Julie continued.

"Aside from her being drop-dead gorgeous, second only to you, of course," Steve quickly added. "Why is she fascinating?"

"Well first of all, she's holds a Bachelor of Science degree in nursing. Then, she went on to receive her Master's in mental health counseling, and she's top flight at both careers. She and ADMIN-1 may be the only previously-married couple who are here in ORT."

"Oh really? Wow, I didn't know that. Now I feel even more embarrassed about my early *faux pas* with her."

"Well don't. She thought it was cute, and it's happened to her more than once."

"Cute eh?" Steve said with a sigh.

"Mmm hmm. Maybe you'll get to see more of her now that you're here in ADMIN."

"You're the only one I want to see more of, Julie."

"Skillfully put, Steve. You dodged a bullet on that one."

"And considering that you have real bullets, good for me."

Julie grinned, "The other thing about Kathy is that she has a real quirky, sort of kinky streak. When we get together, she provides the spice for our conversations."

"Indeed? Tell me more."

"Oh right! The only thing I'll tell you is that it was her suggestion that I play the role of police officer when I came to see you last night."

Steve sat back in the couch, unsure of what to say. He finally decided on, "Okay then. It seemed to work pretty well, didn't it?"

"I thought so, yes." Julie looked at him without blinking.

Steve wondered again about this woman, perhaps one day to be his woman, at least to the extent possible in ORT. "What is your duty assignment here anyway, if I may ask that question?"

"As you know, I work out of the Personnel section of ADMIN, but my primary assignment is security."

"Security?!?"

"Yes. It's not that we have need for much of a security presence here, although there have been a few cases over the years of someone drinking too much and causing a disturbance. It's more of a security function for new recruits coming here, just as I escorted you here six months ago." She smiled at him.

"Indeed, without my knowing it either."

"Yes, without your knowing it."

Steve felt himself again becoming aroused by the power and mystery of Julie, with whom he was sitting so closely. "So, when you're performing your security function within ORT, do you wear a uniform or anything?"

"Oh Steve, my darling, I can read you like a book at times. No, I don't wear a uniform either inside or outside of the facility." Noting the slight look of disappointment on his face, she continued, "But I still have my uniform from the LAPD before I was promoted to detective. Would you like to see it?" she asked coyly.

"I'd like to see you in it," he replied.

"Give me a few minutes and I'll see what I can do for you."

And he did.

And she did.

Chapter 27: Ultimatum

It had been two weeks since the White House Chief of Staff contacted ORT, and now a White House underling notified them to expect his follow-up call on this day and at what would be 1400 hours ORT. Once again, ADMIN-1, ADMIN-2, and Arianna gathered around the huge table in the videoconference room. The discreet signal on Arianna's console sounded at about fifteen minutes past the appointed time. ADMIN-1 told her to make the connection, and the audio/video feed came alive, only to show the chief of staff's desk in his otherwise unoccupied office. Another five minutes went by before the bulky form of Jeb White entered the room and seated himself behind his desk.

"You theah, Mohfield?" An unnecessary question since ADMIN-1 was clearly displayed upon his video monitor.

"Indeed I am, Mr. White, what can we do for you today?"

"Well now looky heah son, I spoke to President Brasington, blessed be his name, just as soon as I could, and I've got some good news for y'all down there."

"That's terrific, sir, what might that be?"

"Well the president has been vehy busy, you undahstand, what with all he's got on his plate. Mind you, the situation up heah is faw from the peace and quiet y'all might be used to down there. But to get to the point,

Mohfield, he has asked me to convey to you and youh team that theah is no longah any reason for y'all to be isolated away from the rest of the wohld. I'm sure you know that we had to take youh cansuh medicine off the market, and so theah's really no point in y'all staying down theah to make any moh of it, is theh? Of couhse not, and especially not when theah's so much impohtant wohk y'all can be doin' back heah in civilization. So he wants you all back in nohmal society within ten days. And heah's the really great news, Mohfield. President Brasington, blessed be his name, is going to meet with you and your senior staff pehsonally heah at the White House at his eahliest convenience to discuss the ways in which y'all can help youh guvenment in the future. Now what d'ya think about that?"

"That is certainly quite an honor, sir. But with all due respect, we feel that we can accomplish a great deal more here in the peace and quiet that you just alluded to. The development of Oncoleve was really a spin-off of our work here, although it turned out to be quite an important one. And it makes me wonder, with so many people in need of this medication to fight a very serious disease, do you really think that it's in the best interest of the country to have pulled it from the market?"

"Oh absolutely, Mohfield, theh's no doubt about that. Not only does it run countah to our fundamental religious teachings, but it hasn't even gone through the nohmal couhse of approval by the Food and Drug Administration. We cehtainly can't have a substance like that on the mahket. Now y'all shouldn't take it pehsonally, because we've had to pull a large numbuh of other medications from the shelves too. You wouldn't believe how many so-called miracle drugs had been developed during the last eight or nine yeahs as a result of un-Godly experimentation with stem cells and such. It's absolutely frightening, I kin tell ya. So much so that it had to be the president's first ohduh of business to get these devil drugs off the mahket. They was like poison circulating through the body of humanity, Mohfield. And make no mistake, the devil is a vehy clevuh felluh. Of couhse these potions became desihable because they seemed to provide some short-term relief from ailments and diseases, but at what cost to society? I can't begin to tell you how lucky we all ah that President Brasington, blessed be his name, came into office just in the nick of time to save humanity from this devilish business. And so the meah fact that he is willing to welcome y'all back into the tenduh embrace of God is ahmost a miracle in and of itself, isn't it? What bettuh news could theah be?"

"Sir, again with all due respect, I'm afraid that we are not in a position to leave our facility at this time. We have been tasked with important work, not only by the president's immediate predecessor, President King, but by the private foundation that has since taken over our direction and funding."

During ADMIN-1's response, the chief of staff had been becoming visibly enraged. "I don't think you un-duhstand, Mohfield, I don't think you unduhstand at all. The President of the United States and the Com-manduh in Chief has given a direct ohduh that your little project be shut down immediately and that y'all return to the suhface. And please don't even mention that devilish weasel King to me. His administration was an abomination. An abomination, you heah me?!?" His face was now red with anger.

"I do indeed hear you, Mr. White, and as it appears that we have nothing further to constructively discuss, may I suggest that we end this communication?"

"Why you little pipsqueak of a cocksucker, we'll send the whole goddamn cavalry in there to haul you all out bodily!" Oddly, his accent had mostly disappeared when his temper flared. "Don't fuck with us, my friend, or you'll all die in the process, do you hear me? You'll all die! Do you hear me?" he screamed. And with that, the connection went dead.

Arianna sat frozen in place, mouth open, unable to say anything. ADMIN-1 looked at her and then at ADMIN-2 and calmly asked his two colleagues, "Do you think it was something I said?"

Chapter 28: Alert

Colonel John Dillon, United States Army, came from a long line of career military men. His grandfather, his father, and his older brother had all been Army officers. His brother had been killed by an IED in Iraq, and Dillon had never fully recovered from his loss. As was common with many of his fellow officers from career military families, Dillon considered himself a patriot and a supporter of conservative values. As such, he had voted for President Brasington instead of then Vice President Celia Wright.

Dillon was a graduate of the U.S. Military Academy at West Point with a BS in mechanical engineering. Much of his coursework had been based in mathematics, chemistry, physics, and his engineering concentration. A very bright and career-oriented man, he felt a tingle of discomfort at some of the recent activities and policies of the Brasington administration. He was particularly concerned about the current blurring of the separation of church and state. Brasington had been a fundamentalist minister before being elected to the presidency, and he still conducted services from time to time. White House staff members had been increasingly inserting the phrase "blessed be his name" when referring to the president.

Then there was the venerable tradition of designating any aircraft that was carrying the president as

Air Force One. The White House had now changed that designation to Angel One.

Far more distressing still was the whole matter of the Patriot Amendment to the Constitution, which Brasington had proposed, and which a willing and largely rubber-stamp Congress had passed. Now in the hands of the various states for ratification, the amendment would accomplish the right-wing conservative coalition's wish-list of new laws all in one fell swoop. If ratified, the Constitution would be amended to: (1) ban flag-burning, (2) outlaw all abortion procedures anywhere in the United States, (3) totally prohibit all stem-cell research, (4) invalidate existing and prohibit future same-sex unions, (5) remove the Founders' prohibition against state-supported religion, (6) dramatically restrict the ability of federal courts to issue Writs of *Habeas Corpus*, (7) allow searches and seizures without warrant, (8) authorize indefinite detention of "terrorism suspects" without access to legal counsel, and last but not least, (9) specifically authorize "enhanced" interrogation techniques to assist in preventing acts of terror in the Homeland.

Along with Brasington's election, a host of extreme right-wing Christian Conservatives had won a majority in the U.S. House of Representatives, so there had been little doubt that the proposed amendment would sail through the House, as indeed it had. The Senate had proved to be a bit more of a thorny matter, but even there, a whirlwind public relations blitz on television and right-wing radio talk shows had brought sufficient public pressure to bear on senate members to give the amendment the necessary votes to be sent to the states for ratification. After all, said the senators, the states would have the final say, not the senate. And the new president had threatened reluctant senators with pulling spending projects from their states and then naming their "lack of courage in the face of ever-declining moral values" as the cause. Much better to let the states themselves handle it. And now, somewhat incredibly to the likes of Colonel John Dillon, the amendment was within a few states' votes of being ratified.

But now there was more. Much more. Dillon was serving as commander of the 10th Special Forces Group based at Fort Carson, Colorado, just a stone's throw away from Cheyenne Mountain, the former home of the North American Aerospace Defense Command. While most functions of NORAD had been moved to other bases in 2006, it had remained officially designated as the Cheyenne Mountain Directorate in "warm standby" mode until finally being decommissioned by President King.

Now, he had just received orders from the Pentagon that his unit was to be on alert, along with the 71st Ordnance Group and units of the 759th Military Police Battalion, also based at Fort Carson, for the purpose of mounting an armed assault on the Cheyenne Mountain complex. Who and what were they supposed to be assaulting? As far as he or anyone else in authority at Fort Carson knew, Cheyenne Mountain had been abandoned years ago. While it was true that, upon rare occasions, one or two vehicles had been spotted near the entrance of the complex, it had been chalked up to mere civilian curiosity. It was quite possible for anyone to approach the tunnel entrance because there was no longer any security force present to prevent it.

But, as a good soldier and an equally good officer, he began studying the supporting materials that were transmitted along with the alert order.

During Cheyenne Mountain's construction, a main tunnel had been bored nearly a mile through the solid granite of the mountain from one side to the other. It had been cleverly designed to allow the main force of a nuclear explosion's shock wave to go past the two 25-ton blast doors situated along one side wall and out the other end of the tunnel. The complex had been designed to withstand a 30 megaton blast within two kilometers distance. It was self-sufficient and, at its zenith, had housed some 200 military personnel fully 2,000 feet inside the mountain.

Behind the twin blast doors was a steel building complex with fifteen structures spread over a 4.5 acre chamber. Most of these structures were three stories high. Huge springs supporting the complex were designed to absorb the energy from a nuclear blast, or, for that matter, an earthquake. At one time, the complex had contained dining and medical facilities as well as office and living space for its inhabitants.

And now, he thought, we're on standby to assault a facility that had originally been designed to withstand a nuclear explosion and which long since had been abandoned. He shook his head in utter disbelief.

Chapter 29: Another Alert

Julie arrived promptly for her scheduled meeting with ADMIN-1. She was a firm believer that you didn't make the boss wait for you. Arianna showed her in to the chief administrator's office.

"Julie, come on in," ADMIN-1 said. "Please have a seat. How are things going with you and ADMIN-415?"

"Very well, sir, thank you for asking."

"You're 'sirring' me too, Julie? Must be something in the water," he said smiling at her.

"Force of habit from the LAPD Academy. You're lucky you don't get two sirs with every reply, one in front and one at the end. Anyway, you wanted to see me, sir?" She smiled, realizing that she'd said it again.

"Yes I did. Julie, I want you to prepare yourself for another trip to the surface. I'm not sure of the timeframe, but it won't be long now."

"Okay, another recruit coming in?"

"Yes, in a manner of speaking. But Julie, there's going to be something very different about this mission."

"What would that be, sir?"

"I will be going to the surface myself."

"What?!? No sir, I mean, I'm sorry sir, but as head of security, I cannot permit that under any circumstances, particularly given the state of affairs with the current administration."

"Julie?"

"Sir?"

"I see that your duty designator is ADMIN-54. Surely I don't need to remind you that mine is ADMIN-1?"

"No sir, of course not. But this is unprecedented. There's no way that I can guarantee your safety outside of the facility. Therefore, you can't go."

ADMIN-1 allowed a little smile before replying, "ADMIN-54, I will be going, with or without you. The only issue for you to decide is whether you want to be the one to accompany me."

"Sir, I can't physically stop you from going. But if you persist in this crazy notion, I will personally notify the Board!"

ADMIN-1 picked up the handset from his telephone console and handed it to her. "Would you like me to connect you?"

She had the sinking feeling that this mission was of a need to know nature, and that the need to know was "above her pay grade." "They already know about it, don't they?"

"Yes, Julie. In fact, the Board requested it."

"Oh, I see."

"Now, are you going to go with me or should I find someone else?"

"Of course I'll go, sir. I'm sorry, it just startled me to think about it."

"I understand, and I appreciate your concern for my safety. Precautions will be taken. I will be somewhat disguised."

Julie noticed the slight growth of beard on his face that was normally clean-shaven.

"And you will be armed, as usual. Also, no one other than ADMIN-2 will know when we are going. That includes your friend Steve, understand?"

She bristled. "Of course, sir. I never discuss classified information with Steve or anyone else."

"I know that, Julie. I just wanted to reinforce in your mind that this mission is most highly classified."

"Care to tell me what we'll be doing?"

"Sure, just what you said. Bringing in a new recruit."

ADMIN-1 stood up, indicating that the meeting was concluded.

Chapter 30: New Recruit

Julie and Steve were fast asleep in her bed when, in the early morning hours, her phone chimed. Julie woke quickly as was her custom. She glanced briefly at the caller ID, saw that the call was coming from ADMIN-1, and then answered, "Yes sir, what's up?"

"How about meeting me in my office as quickly as possible?"

"Of course, sir, I'll be there within ten minutes."

"Thank you, Julie," and the call disconnected.

Julie turned to Steve, now also rousing from his sleep, and said, "I've got to meet ADMIN-1, Steve. I'm not sure what's happening, but I may be away for a day or more."

"What? A day or more? Where are you going?"

"This is one of those times when you can't ask questions, my darling. Don't worry, I'll be fine." She quickly got dressed and patted the firearm in her shoulder holster.

"But, what can you possibly be doing? It's 0100 hours!"

Julie returned and sat down on the bed beside him. "Really, Steve, just trust me. Tell you what. Go back to sleep and dream some nice dreams." She smiled seductively and purred, "When I return, maybe I'll show you some more equipment from my days with the LAPD."

"Mmm, sounds interesting," Steve murmured in reply.

"Okay, I have to go now. Don't worry about me."

She left her apartment and quickly went down the corridor to the large public area and then through the concourse to the ADMIN reception room, which seemed unfamiliar in the dim night lighting and with Arianna not sitting behind her desk. She knocked on ADMIN-1's office door, opened it and went in. ADMIN-1 wasn't there yet, so she took a seat and enjoyed the moonlit mountain scene transmitted to the wall display from somewhere above. It was so quiet in the room that if she listened very carefully, she could hear the far-off sounds of nocturnal animals moving through their world. A cloud drifted across the bright full moon in the scene just as ADMIN-1 entered the office from his private quarters behind them.

"Sorry for the early morning wake-up call, but it's time for us to go now."

"I thought that might be the case, so I came prepared." She opened her jacket to show him that she was armed.

"Of course. Let's go."

They left his office via the reception area, went down the ADMIN corridor until they reached a large double door. ADMIN-1 swiped his card through the reader and the doors opened to reveal a freight elevator. They stepped in, and Julie pressed the button marked 'SURFACE.' The only other button was labeled 'ADMIN.' The elevator provided an express ride up from the lowest level of ORT, yet it still took several minutes due to the depth of the shaft they were ascending. She couldn't help but notice that ADMIN-1 seemed unusually quiet and subdued. She had been to the surface for the purpose of escorting new recruits into ORT several times.

"Sir, how long has it been since you've been up here?"

"Since the Epoch," he replied with a slight smile.

"Really? That means that…"

He interrupted. "I haven't been to the surface since before the day you joined us."

"Wow, sir, so what's going on that's causing you to make the trip now? I mean, things are very unsettled, and this may not be the best time for you to do this."

"It may not be, yet do it I must."

The doors opened before them into a dimly lit but very large vault-like cavern. They reached the heavy metal doors to the outside, and Julie slid her card through the reader. When the massive doors opened, she asked ADMIN-1 to wait for a moment while she checked the surroundings. "Sir, as far as I can tell, the coast is clear, but I want to urge you one more time to reconsider doing this. It's impossible for me to guarantee your safety."

"I know that, but you'll do your best if necessary. Come on, we're going to take the Range Rover. Would you mind driving? It's been years since I've been behind the wheel, and I've never driven this particular vehicle."

"Of course, sir." They walked for several minutes before reaching the bright red vehicle. They climbed into the SUV and Julie used her key to start the engine. "Where to, sir?"

"Take me to the train station please."

"The train station? It's going to take almost five hours! The airstrip is only minutes away."

ADMIN-1 smiled at her, "You are a delight, Julie, your friend is a very lucky man. But yes, our new recruit is coming to us on the train, and we just have time to get there…?" indicating that he wanted to get going.

She put the vehicle in gear and headed down a small dirt road into the moonlit night. "Any chance of your telling me more about this recruit, sir?"

"No chance at all, because I don't know who it is."

"What?!? You don't know who it is? How will we look for…, is it a him or her?"

"It's her, and she will find us. Just drive, Julie, and stop acting like a detective," he said with a smile in his voice.

"Yes sir, but there's very little chance of that happening."

"How well I know."

———

They had been traveling dark country roads for just over an hour when Julie noticed a car closing behind them. She alerted ADMIN-1 who had been lost in his own inner world during the so-far monotonous drive. The car gained on them and the driver activated the flashing red and blue strobes of a police cruiser light bar. Julie spoke, "Sir, I'm driving, so let me handle this without saying anything, please. This may be a legitimate stop or it could be something far less innocuous."

"I am obviously in your hands."

Julie pulled over to the side of the road, put her window down, and waited. The police car pulled over behind them and the officer shined his spotlight on their license plate.

"This may be a good sign, at least they're following normal procedure so far."

"Okay."

A uniformed officer approached the driver's side of the Range Rover. "Hello ma'am, may I see your license and registration please?"

"Of course, officer," and Julie slowly got into her purse and retrieved the desired documents. Conveniently, her driver's license was in the same case as her LAPD badge and ID card. She flipped it open for him.

The officer looked at the badge and ID card carefully. "You're a long way from home, detective."

"Yes I am, officer." A mutual token of respect had been exchanged between them.

"Sorry to inconvenience you. I just wanted to let you know that your driver's side taillight is out. That could be dangerous if you do much night driving on roads like these."

"It certainly could. I promise you that it will be repaired as soon as I can get a replacement bulb."

"Very good, I appreciate that. You and your friend have a safe drive now."

"Yes sir, we will." Julie wondered what the police officer would have thought if he had known that her "friend" was in fact not only her boss but undoubtedly one of the most important persons in the world right now.

The officer returned to his car, turned off his light bar, and drove away.

"Okay then. Gee, I'm beginning to sound like Steve," she remarked with a grin. "We need to have maintenance repair the taillight," Julie said.

"Indeed so. Let's get back on the road now. I would hate to be late for this train."

———

They arrived at the station at 0620. If the train was running on time, it would arrive at 0640. Julie parked their vehicle and asked ADMIN-1, "What now, sir?"

"As soon as we see the train pull into the station, you are going to remain here and I am going to meet the train." Julie immediately tensed herself to oppose what he said. "Julie, I know what you're thinking. You're a professional, and every instinct you have tells you not to let me go over to that platform by myself. I can't fault you for that, but please understand that this is something that I must do alone, because that is what our recruit is expecting. Parked where we are, you will be able to keep me in your line of sight, at least for part of the way."

Julie was deeply conflicted. She didn't like any of this. "Sir, with all due respect, this is damn irregular, and I resent being prevented from at least trying to protect you!"

"I know, but it will be okay. And you have your orders."

———

The train pulled in exactly on time. ADMIN-1 again instructed Julie to stay in the vehicle as he got out to head for the train platform in front of the station. The sky was still dark, so the only lighting came from the incandescent lamps on the platform and from the full moon overhead. ADMIN-1 stood under one of the lampposts and waited as the train slowly ground to a complete stop. His instructions were to wait for a female passenger to recognize him. He hadn't wanted to admit to Julie how eerie he also felt about this unusual arrangement.

People were disembarking in significant numbers from the several passenger cars that made up the train's consist. He watched closely for any sign of recognition but saw none. He also wondered how someone was going to recognize him without his also recognizing her. It wasn't like his face was at all well-known to the public.

A voice came from just behind him and startled him. "Stephen, it's been much too long."

He turned quickly and stared at her. Standing there with the help of a black aluminum cane, and with her snow white hair and kindly smile, she could have been anyone's grandmother. Her features were somewhat familiar and yet, in the subdued artificial lighting, he couldn't place her. Then suddenly, recognition struck him like a lightning bolt. "I don't believe it," ADMIN-1 said slowly, and the two of them hugged tightly. Had anyone else been close by, they would have seen the tears welling up in their eyes.

ADMIN-1 walked slowly with the new arrival back to the Range Rover. Before he opened the rear door for her, he said to Julie through the open window, "Julie, this is my Aunt Marian on my father's side. It turns out that she needs some special medical care that ORT is in the best position to provide for her. She is very tired from traveling and I expect that she will sleep the whole way back, so if you would be kind enough not to engage her in conversation?"

"Of course, sir. I'm just glad that our medical team can help her."

ADMIN-1 helped his aunt into the back seat and gently closed the door. Taking his own seat beside Julie, he said, "Thank you for understanding, Julie. You are a good friend as well as a colleague."

Julie had never heard ADMIN-1 say anything nearly so personal. His quiet sincerity touched her. "Thank you sir, I really appreciate that."

"Let's head back."

Julie put the vehicle in gear and got back on the main road that would lead them to ORT in about five hours, if the trip proved to be uneventful. And fortunately it did. During the drive, ADMIN-1 told Julie that for the time being, his aunt would be residing with Kathy and himself in the guest quarters of the chief administrator's suite.

In the days and weeks to come, Julie might have almost come to believe that the entire excursion had been a dream, for there was never another sighting of ADMIN-1's Aunt Marian.

Chapter 31: Assault

When the "go" orders arrived, Colonel John Dillon really couldn't believe it was happening. However, important additional information had come along with the orders to proceed. Apparently, a rogue group of scientists had taken over the former Cheyenne Mountain Complex and were conducting some kind of illegal research activities. It was extremely unlikely that the squatters were going to voluntarily open the blast doors and surrender themselves to Dillon's custody. But just in case, he had a strict protocol for the way in which the mission was to proceed. One thing that struck him as particularly strange about a whole mission that seemed odd was that he was directed to keep the scientists away from any news reporters that may appear.

Dillon only had about a year to go until his retirement date, and he found himself dearly wishing that this mission could have waited until after that time. Assaulting a group of civilian scientists holed up in a former military installation had all the makings of another disaster where civilian casualties occurred and the troops ordered to take back the facility would be blamed, if not actually prosecuted, for years to come. He sighed and made the necessary phone calls to the other units as well as to his own subordinate commanders to get the ball rolling.

ADMIN-1 had been notified within minutes of the assault orders being given by friends of the project remaining in the Pentagon. He opened his office door to the reception area and instructed Arianna to prepare a video feed to the entire facility in fifteen minutes time following Code Red protocol.

Within that very minute, an electronic chime sounded through all of the speakers in every level of the ORT complex, followed by Arianna's voice. "Attention. May I have your attention please. ADMIN-1 will address the entire facility in fifteen minutes about an issue of critical importance. Please prepare to watch this important announcement on your closest video monitor, including the monitors located in all living units. Thank you for your cooperation."

Julie had just returned from a staff meeting to her apartment, where Steve had been waiting for her. "Steve, this can't be good news. I recognize the format of the alert message. You can watch the address right here on the video. I need to go to the ADMIN conference room right now!"

Steve watched her remove her firearm from its drawer. "Julie, what's…"

"No time, Steve." She quickly breezed out the door.

While grabbing the remote to adjust the volume on the flat-screen monitor, he wondered what could possibly have happened.

It didn't take long for the units from Fort Carson to arrive at the main entrance to the Cheyenne Mountain complex. With Dillon's own Jeep in the lead, and followed by a phalanx of military police officers, munitions experts, and some of the most advanced assault equipment available to him on relatively short notice, he entered the tunnel. It would take several minutes before they arrived at the twin 25-ton blast doors.

At exactly the fifteen minute mark, ADMIN-1's familiar face and voice was transmitted from the video conference room simultaneously to every video and audio monitor in ORT.

"My dear colleagues, I am sorry to interrupt your important work or other activity, but I must report to you a matter of immediate importance. As your team leaders have previously discussed with you, the current administration in Washington has become increasingly hostile to science and scientists, preferring to let the problems of humanity rest in the hands of what it perceives as the Almighty. Recently, this resulted in the government's decision to declare Oncoleve an illegal substance and to order its removal from the pharmaceutical market.

"As we anticipated, those citizens who were in need of cancer treatment, or who had been successfully treated with Oncoleve, did not accept this turn of events peacefully. For over a week now, riots in major cities across the United States have been common. Congress has exempted the military from the *Posse Comitatus* Act, a law dating back to 1878 after the end of Reconstruction, which limited the use of the federal military for domestic law enforcement purposes. As you have no doubt seen on the various satellite news feeds, conditions on the surface have been destabilizing at an alarming rate. Local and regional fighting has broken out around the globe, and most particularly in the Middle East. So far, no tactical nuclear weapons have been deployed, but we see a high probability that this will occur sooner rather than later.

"Despite the administration's hostility toward science and its rejection of even such a proven life-saving drug as Oncoleve, we have been mostly insulated from this hostility and unrest due to the foresight and planning of our founders. Now, however, that insulation is going to be challenged. Even as I speak to you, military units from Fort Carson are about to enter Cheyenne Mountain in an attempt to shut down the Origins Research Team." Gasps and shouts of startled disbelief could be heard in every section of ORT.

"I urge you to remain calm and not to panic in the face of this adversity. Those who planned our mission and our facility hoped for the best but prepared for the worst. While I cannot promise you that everything will continue as it has in the past, I can with reasonable certainty assure your safety. All negotiations with the military forces will be handled by myself or ADMIN-2, and we will keep you informed as events develop. In addition, if and when either closed-circuit or broadcast video becomes available from the surface, this feed will be made available to you immediately.

"Please direct any specific concerns to your respective team leaders, who will be in constant contact with this office. Again, I urge you to remain calm and to continue your regular activities to the greatest extent possible. Thank you for your attention."

Dillon saw the massive blast doors for the first time and was awed by their size and obvious weight. He signaled the commander of the munitions team to have his troops stand by. As he had been directed, he was first to attempt to open the doors via a special keypad that was recessed into the side of the tunnel to the left of the blast doors. He approached the box that enclosed the keypad and gently opened the cover. Inside, he recognized the backlit 16-digit keypad consisting of the numbers zero to nine and the letters A to F. The keys were all "soft" keys, meaning that each time a key was touched on the pad, the entire pad rearranged itself into a different order but still displayed the same set of characters. He had been given the eight-digit code to open the doors, and he carefully touched the keypad slowly but deliberately. As soon as he touched the final key, a loud klaxon horn blared overhead, and the sound of heavy-duty machinery filled the tunnel around him.

ADMIN-1, ADMIN-2, Julie and Arianna were seated around the table in the videoconference room. Live video was now available from closed-circuit cameras installed many years before at Cheyenne Mountain, and it was being fed to every monitor in ORT.

Arianna asked ADMIN-1, "Shouldn't we be doing something to prepare for this?"

"We are doing something."

Arianna looked around the room questioningly as if to ask what.

"Steady, remember what I said during my broadcast."

"Sir, I believe that we only have a small arms locker with some handguns and TASERs. We're not prepared for anything like this!"

"You're right, not in that sense."

Arianna knew that asking any other questions would be fruitless. She could tell that ADMIN-1 wanted to be viewed as cool, calm, and collected, and yet the lines of stress across his forehead signaled that much more was going on within him than he was willing to share.

———

The machinery noise stopped almost as soon as it started. The klaxon sirens went silent. And the giant blast doors remained sealed tightly shut. Okay, Dillon thought, that worked about as well as he expected it to. The next step in his operational directive involved the covered box to the left of the keypad. He opened the box, saw the blue telephone handset, and since there was no dial or keypad, he simply lifted the handset from its hookswitch.

———————

Just as a ring-down tie-line is designed to function, at the precise moment that Dillon removed the handset from the box, a red light on Arianna's console in the videoconference room blinked insistently along with a muted chime sound.

"Sir?" she asked ADMIN-1.

He indicated for her to answer.

"This is the Origins Research Team, how may I help you?"

———————

The pleasant female voice on the other end of the phone was the last thing that Dillon expected to hear. He was slightly taken aback, but he proceeded according to plan.

"This is Colonel John Dillon, United States Army. I would like to speak to the person in charge immediately."

———————

Arianna had placed the call on speaker so everyone in the room heard the initial exchange. ADMIN-1 replied, "Good afternoon Colonel. This is Steve Morefield, and I am the administrator of this facility."

"Is your proper title Doctor Morefield?"

"That would be correct, Colonel. What can I do for you today?"

"Dr. Morefield, I come with orders from the president of the United States. You and your team are to prepare to leave this facility immediately. You are to open the blast doors so that we may enter peacefully, and we will then escort all of you to a safe location."

"And where would that safe location be, Colonel?"

"I'm sorry, but I don't have that information, and even if I did, I doubt that I would be permitted to tell you at this time."

"Indeed. Then may I ask how you know that the location is 'safe,' and just what it is that it might be safe from?"

"Sir, I am just following my orders. I am telling you what I have been instructed to tell you. Please believe me when I say that we have every desire to resolve this matter amicably."

"I don't doubt that you do, Colonel. For your own information, you should know that the Origins Research Team is a group of dedicated scientists and other highly-qualified personnel performing a mission that is peaceful in nature, and which was founded by former President King with the concurrence of both houses of Congress. Despite your desire to 'resolve this matter amicably,' may I safely assume that you are prepared to forcibly assault the facility if you consider it necessary?"

"That would be a correct assumption, Dr. Morefield. I'm sorry about any misunderstanding between your group and the government now in power in Washington, but my orders are clear. I am to take control of the Cheyenne Mountain Complex at all costs, and I can assure you that we have all of the necessary equipment to enter the facility whether or not you open the blast doors."

"Well, Colonel, then we definitely have a problem, because we regretfully will be unable to open those doors for you."

"Then, sir, I suggest that you prepare for the damage that will inevitably result to your equipment, along with potential injuries to your personnel, as a result of our carrying out our orders."

"So noted, Colonel. I'm very sorry that it has come to this. May I also point out that the process of getting through those blast doors will be dangerous for your own personnel as well, and since our mission is all about life and creation, and not death and destruction, we would hate to have any of your men and women injured."

Dillon hesitated for an instant, not expecting such a thoughtful remark from his adversary on the other end of the phone line. "Then sir, why not reconsider and open the doors for us now. That way I can guarantee you that no one will be harmed."

"I appreciate that, Colonel, I really do. But unfortunately I am unable to comply."

"I see," said Dillon in a resigned tone. "I can give you one hour to reconsider, and then we will begin cutting through the doors."

"I understand," said ADMIN-1, giving the signal to Arianna to disconnect the circuit.

On the surface, network television reporters who had been mysteriously alerted to the activity at Cheyenne Mountain began arriving on the scene. It fell upon Dillon's public information officer, Captain Joanne Ballard, to direct the media to a holding area outside the tunnel entrance and to explain to them that she really couldn't tell them anything about what was happening inside the mountain complex. This, of course, just fanned the flames of their curiosity, and as the news spread, their colleagues descended upon the complex by the dozens. Satellite trucks took up position, and men and women with microphones stood in front of handheld cameras, ready to inform the public about the unusual scene slowly unfolding in Colorado. Captain Ballard had never dealt with a situation such as this one, and all she could tell the eager media reporters was that she had no comment on the present activity due to reasons of national security.

"There certainly seems to be a lot of interest on the part of the news media, doesn't there?" ADMIN-1 said to the room as a whole and to no one in particular.

Julie looked directly at ADMIN-1 and said, "Sir, this is just wrong."

"I know it is, Julie, but we too have our orders."

"You could change those orders, sir."

"Perhaps, but this protocol was designed by someone far more wise and politically astute than myself."

———

An hour passed quickly but not uneventfully. Dillon had correctly assumed that the scientific cabal would not surrender itself voluntarily, so troops and equipment were put in place to begin the process of entering the complex. Blasting through the doors with explosives was out of the question since it would bring the walls of the tunnel crashing down on them before the blast doors were even close to being destroyed. They had considered using a high-power industrial laser to cut through the doors, but the space between the personnel and the doors was too limited to prevent serious damage from laser scatter. That left them with a high-energy plasma cutting torch as the device of choice. Due to safety concerns, only one person at a time could apply the super-heated plasma flame to the blast doors. And given the thickness and hardened nature of the doors, it was going to take hours before a rectangular cut could be made which would then permit them to carefully, ever so carefully, remove a huge chunk of one door. The opening would only be large enough to allow one soldier through at a time.

Dillon gave the order for the cutting to begin while he and his elite troops could do nothing but wonder about this mission and cool their booted heels.

———

Everyone's gaze focused with disbelief and horror on video displays all over the various levels of the ORT facility. The bright plasma flame from the cutting torch completely washed out the video feed from the camera hidden in the opposite wall from the blast doors, but other hidden cameras clearly indicated the number of troops nearby in the tunnel. One exterior camera provided an excellent view of the holding area to which the news media had been confined. Split screens picked up one of a number of satellite news network broadcasts, providing an eerie third-person perspective on the unusual activity at Cheyenne Mountain.

———

Dillon's communications officer rushed over to him. "Sir, the chairman of the Joint Chiefs is on the line for you."

Dillon picked up the handset from the field telephone pack and said, "Colonel Dillon here, sir."

"Dillon, this is General Green at the Pentagon."

"Yes sir!" Dillon replied.

"How is your mission proceeding, son? Give me a complete sitrep."

Dillon gave a precise and to-the-point situation report, just as he had been taught so many years before at West Point.

When he finished, Green said, "Now listen, Dillon. I've got your personnel jacket right here in front of me. You're a good man and an outstanding officer. If you're half as smart as I think you are, you already realize that this mission can easily turn into a career buster, and I see that you're only a year away from retirement. It looks like you drew the short straw, son, and it's a damned shame, but there's nothing I can do about it. To make matters worse, you've got the national news media camped outside, so to put it bluntly, if your pants fall down and your ass shows, the whole nation is going to enjoy the view. The only advice I can give you is to be extremely careful with the civilians inside. Whatever Brasington's beef is with these people, they're the ones who brought a cure for cancer to the world, and now you're being tasked with shutting them down. It stinks to high heaven, and I'm damned sorry about it. But you're a good soldier, just do your duty to the best of your ability and know that…well, we'll do our best for you when this is all over."

"Thank you, sir, I appreciate that very much."

"Good luck, son." And the connection clicked off.

———

Several hours passed while every activity within ORT came to a standstill. People watched the slow but steady progress being made by the military on the surface. Some team leaders on their own initiative went about the task of securing vital equipment to the greatest extent possible. Computer files were updated and backed up to server drives and to external media.

The personnel complement at ORT could not generally be described as having a strong religious orientation, but those few who did took time to pray. Other members looked to each other for comfort and reassurance, both of which were hard to come by.

ADMIN-1, ADMIN-2, Julie and Arianna maintained a vigil in the videoconference room. Arianna was clearly under the most stress of the four, and Julie did her best to comfort her.

———

It seemed like it would never end, but the skilled soldiers who took turns operating the plasma cutter finally shut the device off, advising their commanding officer that they had done all that they could. A continuous rectangle had been cut the whole way through one of the doors, and the only thing remaining was to somehow get the massive block of hardened steel removed from the door around it.

Dillon, of course, already had a plan to accomplish this task, and it had begun by his troops welding several small plates near the bottom of the rectangular piece before the cutting had even begun. Now, a complicated system of motorized blocks-and-tackle was set into motion and ever so slowly, the base of the monolithic chunk of heavy metal was drawn forward from the door. At the same time, two sturdy pistons held the top of the monolith in place. The intended net effect of these opposing forces was to force the monolith to lean back into the complex rather than out into the tunnel. Dillon warned his troops to engage their hearing protection. The monolith began to tilt backwards at the top while the mechanical lash-up continued pulling it out from the bottom. Within a few minutes, the tipping point was reached, and the slab fell back with a tremendously loud clang and a cloud of dust.

Soldiers took up position to deal with any hostiles that might be defending the area from the inside with firearms, but a few dim lights in the ceiling revealed nothing but a moldy-smelling empty space. Slowly, the troops entered the complex, led by their commanding officer, Colonel John Dillon.

———————

ADMIN-1, seated in his chair at the head of the table in the videoconference room, noted the progress being made by the Army. "This will soon be over."

———————

After the area had been declared clear, Dillon told his unit commanders to locate a freight elevator about one thousand feet inside, which proved to be an easy exercise. Dillon tried pressing the call button beside the elevator, but nothing happened. "Okay Captain, get your assault troops ready. We're going to have to force our way through these doors and climb down the cables to the bottom. According to my briefing book, that will be the administrative level, and that's where we begin to clear out the trespassers!"

Getting the huge freight elevator doors open proved to be easier said than done. Dillon briefly thought that they were going to have to bring the plasma cutter inside to cut through these doors also, but brute force and ordinary tools finally proved sufficient to pry the doors open, revealing the pitch black elevator shaft. Apparently the elevator sat at the bottom of the shaft.

"Bring in the field lighting equipment," Dillon ordered. Only after the lights were in place could they see the enormous depth of the shaft and the elevator car far below. "This isn't going to be easy, but let's get going."

In the videoconference room of ORT, the four occupants continued watching the advance of the troops, courtesy of the many video cameras put in place years before by the designers of the original Cheyenne Mountain Complex. Then something happened that every design precaution had been taken to prevent from happening. On every level of ORT, the power suddenly went dead. Every video display and computer, all lighting, everything that depended upon the sophisticated power system that had worked flawlessly and without fail for years, went dark. Team members gasped in surprise, just as they might have done as teenagers in a movie theater that suddenly went totally black.

"Damn it," said ADMIN-1. "This should never have happened!"

Dillon descended the long, long cable with his best assault troops. He and a few others entered the elevator itself through the trapdoor provided for that purpose in its ceiling. Once inside the elevator car, they had only to pry the doors open to gain entry into the administrative level. The small team which essentially served as his cover and bodyguard took up positions with their automatic rifles, because this is where the defense would come at them full force.

"Ready?" he said to the three men at his side. "Pry them open and be prepared to fire only if fired upon!" It took a few more minutes, but the elevator doors opened to total darkness. Until he unholstered and activated his combat light, all Dillon could see were the red laser beams from the automatic rifles of his men sweeping the area. He switched on his powerful flashlight, bright enough to temporarily blind someone looking directly at it, and proceeded to walk down the narrow hallway lit only by the beam of his light.

As he approached the end of the hallway, Dillon said, "Cover me." A sign on the door said "ADMIN." "This is it," Dillon said. His men again took up covering positions beside and behind him as he turned the handle and pulled the door open. Still in darkness except for the flashlight, he walked into the room beyond the door. He saw what appeared to be a receptionist's desk and then looked closer at something sitting on the desktop. His lips slowly curled into a smile, and soon his laughter filled the room while his men could only look on in wonderment.

Chapter 32: Power Failure

ADMIN-1 and his three companions in the video-conference room were completely enveloped in darkness following the total power failure. He told everyone to remain in their seats and wait. Less than a minute later, the door from the reception area burst open and a man with a bright flashlight entered.

Colonel Dillon shouted at his soldiers, "Check every level of this facility. Check every damn room!" Then, as much to himself as to anyone, he said, "But you're not going to find anyone." He turned and went back to the freight elevator.

His lead NCO, Master Sergeant Griff Ellis, watched in disbelief as his commanding officer left the area. He approached the reception desk where his boss had been standing and noticed the professionally printed sign placed on an easel facing them. It read:

"Gone fishin'
No one home."

"What the hell...?" he muttered. This mission had been jinxed from the get-go. Whatever was going on here was nothing even close to what they had expected, that much was for certain.

The man with the flashlight saw the chief administrator, his deputy, and the two women seated around the conference table in the beam of his light. "Sorry sir, the chief engineer is looking into the problem as we speak. Hopefully we'll have the power restored shortly."

"That would be nice," ADMIN-1 replied testily.

"Yes sir, here's a lantern for you to use until we get things squared away." He gently placed an LED light fount on the table in front of him.

———————

Dillon was no longer laughing. Indeed, he was as angry as he had ever been in his life. First, his commander-in-chief had sent him on a mission to shut down some kind of cancer research facility that had been established by his predecessor, and now it was becoming evident that there were no scientists or research team even contained within this one-time government mountain fortress. And to top that off, a whole bevy of news reporters were waiting for him to brief them on the mission as soon as he returned to the surface. Oh yes, this had definitely been a career-buster. *Thank you, President Brasington. Thank you, General Green.*

———————

It took nearly thirty minutes before power was restored to the ORT complex. The chief engineer, MAINT-22, sheepishly stepped into the open door of the videoconference room from the reception area. "I'm very sorry for the inconvenience, sir."

"What happened anyway?" ADMIN-1 asked.

"Sir, as you know, we have what is perhaps the most sophisticated power backup system in the world right here in ORT. We have a huge bank of nano lithium titanate batteries that are kept constantly charged by our main power source. Normally, if we experience a power interruption or brown-out, those batteries and the associated electrical equipment pick up the entire facility's power load without even a detectable delay. That's why we don't have individual backup power supplies on our computers and so on."

"And...?" said ADMIN-1.

"And everything has worked perfectly for all the years that we've been here until today, when both a primary and a secondary relay panel failed almost simultaneously. The odds against that happening are astronomical, sir."

"And yet today, at a very critical time, the odds for us were one hundred percent. Absolutely amazing. I'm sorry I snapped at you, chief. But let's try to make sure it doesn't happen again, eh?"

"Yes sir!" and the engineer hurried back to his electrical room.

"Okay, let's take inventory. Are you all okay? Dick? Julie? Arianna?"

Arianna was visibly shaken, and Julie had been doing her best to comfort her.

"Arianna, I'm sorry, but I need you to set up an audio/video feed to all monitors immediately."

Arianna turned her attention back to her own console at the table and did as she was told. "Feed ready in five, four, three, two, live."

ADMIN-1's familiar face and voice now appeared on all displays on every level of ORT. "My fellow colleagues, I am very sorry that we lost all power at a very crucial time today. As those of you who have been with us from the Epoch know, this has never happened before. Our chief engineer has advised me that we experienced a highly unlikely, but we now know definitely not impossible, simultaneous failure of both a primary and a secondary power transfer device. I deeply regret the panic that must have spread through the facility since the timing of the power outage precisely coincided with the military assault of the Cheyenne Mountain Complex. As you are now no doubt fully aware, the Origins Research Team facility is not located in Cheyenne Mountain!"

ADMIN-1's face reflected the importance of what he was about to say. "The most important project secret that we must always guard tightly is our true location. You have seen an all too vivid demonstration of the reason for this today. The unfortunate result of such a highly classified need-to-know shroud placed upon our location is that the vast majority of you had every reason to believe that our facility, our project goals, our way of life, and perhaps our very lives were in jeopardy today. And while that was never the case, let me explain why I couldn't tell you that and ease your minds earlier. Those wise men and women who founded this project, led by our late president, Jeremy King, had envisioned the possibility that something like this might occur at some point in time. They established a strict protocol for your chief administrator to follow should this unfortunate event come to pass.

"References had purposefully been made in a number of government documents that our facility was in fact located in the Cheyenne Mountain complex. We even had direct communication links with that facility so that it would appear to any outside force that we were located within. There were a number of reasons for the selection of Cheyenne Mountain as a decoy site. First, it was an obvious place to have been the real location of our facility due to the protection afforded by its original construction as a NORAD site. And, it had recently been decommissioned as a military installation and was under the control of the King administration at the time of our founding. But perhaps most importantly, the time that would be required for any assault force to get inside the massive blast doors at Cheyenne also provided the time necessary for certain information to be leaked to the national news media and for them to assemble broadcast crews to provide live coverage from the site.

"It was absolutely crucial to the plan laid down by our founders for the media to arrive at Cheyenne before troops could stand down and make it appear that nothing had ever happened there today. And this is why I couldn't say anything to ease your concerns. There are a small number of our project team members who have unfettered communications with the outside world, and we could take absolutely no chance whatsoever that anything might be transmitted to the surface to indicate that we either were or were not concerned about our safety in this situation. Our protocol dictated that I or my successor say nothing to the project as a whole until after the siege was completed and the plan with the news media had either worked its course or not. We will know more about that element of the plan very shortly.

"If you feel up to it, please continue with your day as if this had never happened. But if you need to take the rest of the day to relax and steady your nerves, that is also most understandable. Additionally, our MED team is standing by to assist you and will be checking in with everyone in the next few hours should you continue to be affected by the trauma from this assault.

"I will report back to you later today if and when events develop on the surface as a result of the media portion of our plan. Thank you very much for your patience and understanding in this most extraordinary of circumstances."

ADMIN-1 gave Arianna the signal and she discontinued the feed.

Chapter 33: Colonel Dillon

Colonel Dillon walked out of the hole cut through the blast doors and told his communications officer to have Captain Ballard report to him immediately. Ballard was all too happy to have an excuse to leave the press holding area and she reported to Dillon within five minutes. "Joanne, what's the mood out there?"

"Not good, sir. They somehow already have pretty accurate information about what we've been doing here, and they're accusing us of trying to perpetrate a cover-up."

"Oh Christ, what am I supposed to tell these people anyway? That our leader screwed the pooch?"

"Sir, if you want, I'll simply go back out there and repeat that our mission is classified due to national security and that we will be departing the site shortly."

"Yeah, I'm sure they'll accept that! Oh, and by the way, we've got a huge hole cut through those blast doors that anyone and their brother can just walk through at their leisure and check out the complex for themselves! We're going to have to post MPs out here on a 24/7 basis until somebody decides what they want to do about repairing that door somehow."

"It's pretty much of a mess, isn't it, sir?"

"That would be quite an understatement, Captain. Listen, I'm going to get our people out of here and set up the guard detail. If the media people give you too much of a hassle, tell them that I'll speak with them in about an hour, okay?"

"Yes, sir!" and Joanne Ballard headed back to an increasingly insistent and demanding press contingent.

———————

With the area secured and cleaned up to the greatest extent possible, Dillon then turned his attention to the huge pool of news reporters now gathered outside the tunnel entrance. He walked slowly to a point where he could overhear the questions and Joanne Ballard's professional but failing attempts to satisfy their demands for information. Within a few moments, it became clear to him that she was being eaten alive by the throng of representatives of the television and the wire news media. He had once been told as a cadet at West Point that the most difficult decisions that an officer might be faced with in his or her career were the ones that would have to be made the most quickly. Without any further delay, he strode to the makeshift podium and bundle of microphones.

"Captain Ballard, I relieve you. Thank you for your work here today."

Joanne Ballard saw the determined look on her commander's face and simply said, "Yes sir," before retreating back to her unit at the main assembly area. She couldn't help but think that she must have screwed up this assignment royally to have made Dillon angry enough to relieve her in front of the whole world. Then she wondered what he would say to the media that would be any different than her own attempts to explain to them why she couldn't tell them anything. As she walked past one of the Army field communication vehicles, she noticed that several monitors were tuned to one or more of the satellite feeds coming from the media pool. She immediately stopped to watch and listen.

Dillon turned his attention to the reporters and camera operators. Speaking directly into the boom microphones proffered to him, he began to speak clearly and distinctly. "Ladies and gentlemen of the media, and to all those watching from afar, let me begin by introducing myself." At that point, he removed his colonel's eagle rank insignia and ripped the unit shoulder patches from his uniform. "I am John Dillon, former full colonel in the United States Army and commander of the 10th Special Forces Group. What I have to say to you today would be totally inappropriate for an officer and unit commander, so I have chosen to resign my commission effective immediately."

There were gasps of surprise from the media before a hushed silence descended on the area.

———◆———

ADMIN-1 and the others in the videoconference room watched the broadcast with intense interest. As soon as he heard Dillon's first words, he said to ADMIN-2, "Dick, he's either going to kill himself or be killed by the time he's finished speaking. Do we have any friendlies around Cheyenne Mountain?"

"I'm not sure, Steve, let me make a call or two."

"Do it quickly, he doesn't have much time."

John Dillon, former full colonel, resumed speaking to the stunned journalists. "The brave men and women of my unit and the auxiliary units that were under my command were sent here today to communicate with and shut down the work of the team of scientists who, among other things, most of which I am not fully aware, ended the scourge of cancer in the world by inventing the wonder drug we have known as Oncoleve. My own sister was saved from breast cancer with this medication, and today she lives a happy and productive life with her husband and two children as a result.

"I have been a loyal soldier and officer in the United States Army since my days as a cadet at West Point, where I pledged to uphold the Constitution of the United States and to follow the orders of my commander-in-chief and those of my superior officers. This I have done during my entire career of nineteen years, which included service in Iraq, the Pentagon, and everywhere in between until my recent command of this unit.

"When I received orders to assault this site, which once served as the primary control center for the North American Aerospace Defense Command, it gave me pause, to say the least. We were to remove, by force if necessary, this group of scientists who were supposedly illegally occupying this classified facility. But any sane person would ask how they would have occupied the facility to begin with. It took my forces several hours just to cut a large enough space through the huge blast doors in this tunnel behind me to even enter the upper level. There was no sign of forcible entry on the part of these scientists, and as it turned out, they weren't inside to begin with!

"What does it say about a government that would make illegal the one substance in the world that has proven to be a miracle cure for a related group of devastating diseases? To what level of hell have we descended when our leaders can, with serious intent, declare the horrible scourge of cancer to be God's creation, and the substance which educated men and women discovered to cure it to be against God's wishes?

"Maybe it makes sense to some of you, but it has stopped making any sense to me whatsoever. Thus my decision to end the military career for which I prepared during my entire life. I can no longer serve with honor under leaders who have seemingly abandoned all reason and common sense in favor of a religious dogma which favors sickness over health, and death over life.

"To my honorable colleagues in the U.S. Armed Forces everywhere, I want to emphasize that I do not pretend to speak for you, and I sincerely apologize if I bring any dishonor to you. This is certainly not my intent.

"Now, just one last thing..." but he was interrupted in mid-speech as a loud shot rang out and he was hit squarely in the chest. Former Full Colonel John Dillon collapsed in a heap on the makeshift platform.

Joanne Ballard, watching in horror, yelled for a team of medics to attend to her downed commander.

"Damn it, damn it to hell, what a tragic waste of life," said ADMIN-1 with disgust.

ADMIN-2 looked at his boss and said, "I tried, Steve, I was able to make contact in the area, but it looks like it was too late."

"I know." He got up from his seat without another word and left the room.

———

A military ambulance pulled up to the media staging area, and two corpsmen quickly jumped out and ran to the platform. Other soldiers blocked off the area, ordering the media teams to leave under threat of force. The whole area was a pandemonium of chaotic activity, for their commander had first resigned and then been shot down. Dillon's deputy assumed command, but his only known mission was to get everyone out of the area except for the guards who were to be stationed at the entrance to the mountain compound. Dillon's body was loaded into the ambulance and driven off, presumably to the closest available medical facility.

———

The ambulance quickly departed Cheyenne Mountain, and the driver watched in the mirror the surgeon and nurse in the back attend to the fallen soldier as he drove not to the Fort Carson Medical Center, but to a little-used airstrip nearby. Once he arrived, he turned to the doctor and asked, "How did I do, sir?"

The doctor looked up from his patient briefly and said, "You couldn't have done a better job. You delivered the tranquilizer dart to exactly the right place."

"He'll be okay then, sir?"

"He's going to be unconscious for quite a while, but he should be fine. He fractured his left arm when he fell, but that couldn't be helped. Don't worry, we'll take good care of him."

And they did, waiting patiently for the private jet to arrive that would carry him off to…somewhere.

Dillon first became aware of pain on his left side, and a feeling of nausea that slowly receded. His head hurt like it had been hit by a jackhammer. He tried to open his eyes, but the light caused his head to hurt more. He couldn't even move his arms or his legs. What had happened? He tried to remember. There was the mission to take Cheyenne Mountain which had gone horribly wrong. Then he spoke to the news media. Then, nothing, until this. He lapsed back into sleep and a dream, a dream of heaven and angels. One of the angels spoke to him.

"John, John, can you hear me?"

He ignored the angel and for some reason thought of the dress parades when he had been in the Military Academy. He had served as a cadet company commander in his senior year, and he vividly recalled marching his troops past the reviewing stand, giving the order to present arms, knowing that his men and women looked their best because he had conducted his own inspection before they formed up for the parade. Those were good days. Everything seemed so simple then. He knew right from wrong, honor from dishonor. Things were black and white, good or bad, no shades of gray. The angel kept speaking to him.

"Come on, John, it's time to wake up," and she gently shook him while carefully avoiding his injured arm and shoulder.

The angel was becoming a real nuisance. She had no business interfering with this ceremony. He was afraid that one of the officers on the reviewing stand would notice, and then he would surely catch hell for it. Now it was raining, damn it, and it was cold too.

The nurse had sprinkled some drops of cold water on his face.

Slowly, he tried opening his eyes again. The pain was gone now, and he knew that he must have died and gone to heaven because the most beautiful woman he had ever seen was looking intently at him with care. A few details came into his consciousness. The angel wasn't an angel after all, but a nurse? She seemed to be wearing blue scrubs. Blue scrubs? In heaven?

"Can you hear me now, John?"

He tried to lift his hand to his head but he couldn't move his arm. "What is this? Who are you? Am I alive?"

"Welcome back, John Dillon. You are very much alive. My name is Kathy, and I am one of your nurses here."

Still unbelievably groggy, his vision was far from perfect, but he could now see that he was in a hospital bed and that there was electronic equipment all around him. "Where am I?"

"You're safe, John. That's the most important thing you need to know right now."

His instincts as a professional soldier began to return, and he attempted to position himself in a defensive posture to the extent that he could, but mostly he found that he couldn't move.

"Please calm down, John. You're perfectly safe. Look at me."

He focused his eyes on her picture-perfect face framed by glossy black hair and accented with the most incredibly bright blue eyes he had ever seen. She smiled at him, and he took the cue to relax.

"Thank you. I know that wasn't easy for you. For your own safety, you're in restraints. Can I remove them now?"

He looked at himself and noticed that his left arm was immobilized as if it were broken, and then he saw the leather cuff securing his other wrist to the bed. It felt like similar cuffs were on both of his ankles as well. He looked at her again and mumbled, "Yes, please."

She smiled again and asked, "Do you promise to be good?"

He couldn't help but return her smile. "I would give you my promise as an officer and a gentleman, but since I'm no longer an officer..."

"I'll accept your promise as a gentleman," she replied kindly.

"You have my word then, ma'am."

"It never ceases to amaze me how nicely these re-straints can tame the savage beast."

"Maybe it's you and not the restraints at all."

She smiled again, "Well, thank you. Maybe it's a combination of things. Now, I'm going to remove the cuff from your right arm first." She took a key from her pocket and unlocked the restraint, freeing his good arm. "I'm sure that feels better, doesn't it?"

"Much," he said, slowly moving his wrist and arm. "What happened to my left arm?"

"Unfortunately, you fractured it when you fell. Once you're out of isolation, one of our orthopods will set it properly for you and then it will be fine in a couple of months."

"Isolation? Where am I anyway?"

A tall thin man wearing blue jeans and a black tur-tleneck stepped forward to his bed. ADMIN-1 said, "I am Steve Morefield, the man whom you were determined to capture or kill, and you are now, at least temporarily, a guest of the Origins Research Team. And we're very relieved that you're alive and here with us."

Colonel John Dillon, former commander of the 10th Special Forces Group, found himself, for the first time in his life, totally speechless.

———

Dillon straightened himself in bed to the extent that he could since his ankles were still in restraints. "My God, man, how did you ever make this happen? Where is this place?"

ADMIN-1 smiled, "That's just about the first question everyone who comes here asks, and it's the question that we can't answer because it's a strictly need-to-know matter. Please forgive me, but I'm sure you understand given your military background."

"Yes, I guess I do. But how did you do it? Why did you do it? I was leading the assault force against you!"

"Let me take those questions in order. We did it by using some very special people who were fortunately close to Cheyenne Mountain, probably as a result of all of your efforts there. Why did we do it? My sense is that you're a good man, Colonel Dillon, you proved that by your actions after the assault was over. And we really don't like to let good people get taken down for no good reason."

"But what made you think you could trust me? What makes you think it even now?"

"Well, first of all, I'm a pretty good judge of character. Second, we knew enough about you to know that you had no life to speak of left on the surface. Your military career was over, and you were soon to be shot with a real bullet or hauled off to a federal detention facility somewhere. Third, you're still pumped fairly full of potent medications, and you're still partially restrained. And then, if all that fails, Julie is standing over there in the corner."

Dillon peered through the dimness of his vision and the low-level lighting in the room. Another very attractive and obviously physically fit young woman waved from the opposite corner of the room. She smiled at him and tapped her hand against a holstered TASER strapped to her waist.

"Okay, okay, I surrender," he said, smiling and holding his good hand in the air.

"I knew you were a smart man, Colonel. Here's what's going to happen next. Kathy is going to remove the ankle restraints, but you are going to remain in bed for several hours to get some needed rest and complete the isolation process. During this time, our medical people will be drawing some blood and running tests to make sure you're not carrying any communicable diseases. I would like you to watch an hour-long orientation video that we use when new recruits come to join us. Then, after you've rested and had time to think about things, you and I will talk again to see whether you've decided to stay here with us."

Dillon shook his head briefly, trying to clear his mind. "Dr. Morefield, please, I know how these things work. I really have no choice, do I? It's either remain here or meet the same fate as I would have on the surface."

"You don't know as much about us as you think you do, Colonel. Don't you remember me telling you on the tie-line that we're about life and creation, not death and destruction? If you decide that you would rather not be a part of our project, we will medicate you and use some very sophisticated hypnotherapeutic techniques to insure that you remember very little about your time here, and then we will return you to the surface. After that, however, there is no way that I can guarantee your safety or your future quality of life."

"I'm impressed, and I have been remiss in not thanking you sooner for going to all this trouble for someone who was, after all, trying to hunt you down."

"Not a problem, we wouldn't have done it without good reason, I assure you. Our resources on the surface are limited, and we had to pull some big strings very quickly to get you here before it was too late."

"I realize that now. Thank you, Dr. Morefield, and your staff here too."

"You're welcome. Now, before I leave you in the care of the best nurse in the facility, there is no need to address me by title. Here, we use first names or position descriptors only. You'll learn more about that from the video. You may refer to me as just Steve or AD-MIN-1. Kathy here is MED-11, and Julie over there is ADMIN-54."

"Well then, who am I?"

ADMIN-1 smiled at him and replied, "We'll talk about that soon." He turned to Julie and said, "I don't think your services will be needed here for too long, but do you mind staying for a while to assist with the Colonel's orientation?"

"Of course not, sir," she replied.

He reached for Dillon's right hand and shook it briefly, saying, "She rarely gets a chance to play with that weapon, don't give her reason to, okay?"

"Don't worry, I won't. I know when I'm outnumbered."

"Very good. Seriously, I'm very glad that you're here, and I hope you will decide to stay with us as a project member."

"Thank you, Steve, thank you very much. You saved my life and you won't regret it."

"Until later then." ADMIN-1 left the room.

Chapter 34: Dillon Decides

John Dillon had been required to remain in Med Central overnight until all of his lab tests were completed and so that an orthopedic surgeon could tend to his fractured arm the following morning. During that time, he had been closely watched by the nursing staff and he had also been treated to an intensive psychotherapy session by Kathy, MED-11, who was a trained mental health therapist as well as a registered nurse. Julie had remained as a security precaution until Kathy cleared him as safe. Kathy made full use of the monitoring equipment that was connected to Dillon as she had conducted her evaluation, which gave her the additional advantage of having real-time polygraphic information available to her when asking him several key questions.

Then too, he had been encouraged to view not only the ORT orientation video, but also live news feeds from the surface. His native high intelligence in concert with his military background made it painfully clear to him that chaos and turmoil had been unleashed on society, and that anything he may have thought of previously as normal life was now a thing of the past.

Kathy entered his room at about 1130 hours to check on him. "How are you feeling today, John?"

"I'm not sure which took more out of me, being hit by the tranquilizer dart and breaking my arm, or being grilled by you, ma'am," he answered in a good-natured tone of voice.

"Me? Little old me? Surely you jest," Kathy replied.

"Yes, somewhat. But listen, on a serious note, I can't begin to thank you all nearly enough for getting me out of what was becoming a very bad situation. I have been watching the news from above and things are looking more and more grim. How can I possibly begin to repay you?"

"Well first of all, you didn't ask for our help, but we were very glad to have been able to get you out of there in time. As for repaying us, I would encourage you to reframe that notion into 'helping the human race.' And along those lines, ADMIN-1 wants to meet with you as soon as you feel up to it to discuss your decision about staying here with us or leaving."

"Kathy, I'm in if you'll have me. I'll do whatever I can to help out, and I'm desperately sorry for everything that happened at Cheyenne Mountain."

"John, if you hadn't led that mission, someone else would have. You showed your true courage when you stood up to the administration in front of the media. That was very impressive to us here."

"You really are quite a therapist, aren't you? Is there a lucky guy in your life?"

Kathy chuckled. "You could say so, yes."

"Pity," Dillon replied. "So when do I meet with Dr. Morefield, or, uh, ADMIN-1?"

"Well, we're going to discharge you from Med Central within the hour. I can arrange that meeting whenever you are ready."

"I'm ready now."

"Very good, let me make a call."

———————

Kathy fetched some clean scrubs for John to wear when he left Med Central, and since he was still a bit weak from his trauma and bed rest, she also brought a wheelchair to his room. "Hop in, soldier, you're going for a ride."

Dillon laughed and did as he was told. Kathy wheeled him out to the main entrance of the medical facility where Julie was waiting for him. "Oh no, it's TAS-ER Woman!" he exclaimed.

"Now John, let's not dwell on the past. Just think of me as your friendly escort to the world of ADMIN."

"Fine by me." As she wheeled him through the main concourse of the Analysis level, he said, "The orientation video doesn't do this place justice. It's a lot bigger than I thought it would be."

"The Analysis level is the largest space here. It houses many of the scientific teams as well as most of the support staff for the facility." She took him to the entrance lobby of the cafeteria and used her key card to open the door that led to the elevator.

"So we're going to a different level now, obviously."

"Right, I'm taking you down to ADMIN, which occupies the lowest level of ORT. You might remember that from Cheyenne Mountain, hmm?" she teased.

"Julie, please, I'm trying to forget all about that place."

"I can understand that." She wheeled him into the elevator and touched the ADMIN button. "Down we go."

Moments later, the elevator doors opened into the corridor leading to the reception area. "My God, this does look familiar, but so much more welcoming with the lights on."

They entered Reception, and John looked for the counter that had the "Gone Fishin" sign in the Cheyenne Mountain mockup. He saw the counter, but instead of looking for the sign, his gaze immediately went to Arianna seated in her usual spot behind the desk.

"Welcome to ADMIN, Colonel," she said. "I hope you won't mind my saying that I'm glad I'm meeting you here today rather than two days ago."

"That makes two of us, ma'am. Believe me, I didn't feel good about what I was doing at Cheyenne Mountain."

She came around the counter and relieved Julie. "May I take you into ADMIN-1's office now?" she asked.

"Wait a second, please. Do you mind if I try standing? I'd rather walk into his office if I can."

"Of course. Let me help you." She held onto his good arm as he straightened his legs and put his feet on the floor. Slowly, with her support, he stood up from the chair.

"I feel a bit weak, but I think I can do it."

"I'll follow you in just in case."

Dillon stopped and looked at her before speaking again. "I can't believe how well you're all treating me considering that I was your mortal enemy just a very short time ago. It really, really, means a lot to me." And for the first time in a very long time, tears began to well up in his eyes.

"It's okay, John. We're all friends and colleagues here." Arianna handed him a tissue. "Tell me when you're ready."

"I'm ready."

Arianna knocked lightly on ADMIN-1's office door.

ADMIN-1 opened the door and welcomed Dillon with a firm handshake. "How are you feeling, Colonel?"

"Please, sir, that's a title from my past. How about just John or Dillon?"

"Okay, John, that will do...temporarily at least. Come on in and have a seat."

Dillon immediately pointed to the video wall, but before he could say anything, ADMIN-1 explained what he was seeing and hearing.

"Wow, that's impressive!"

"As you might guess, it's quite a conversation piece."

"Yeah, I guess it would be."

"So, I understand that you may want to stay here with us?"

"Yes sir, I definitely would, and as I told Kathy a short time ago, I can't begin to thank you all for what you've done."

"Good, and you're welcome."

"But how can I contribute to your project here? I'm a trained engineer and military officer. I don't have a scientific background other than that, and I earned my degree at West Point almost twenty years ago."

"I actually have something else in mind for you, John. Let me tell you about it and see what you think."

They remained in conversation for nearly two hours, and when they were finished, John Dillon found himself once again speechless.

Chapter 35: Riots

During the time it had taken for Dillon's soldiers to cut through the blast doors, the 24-hour satellite and cable news networks had been reporting live from Cheyenne Mountain with information provided from anonymous sources. The field reporters at the site, bolstered by the familiar faces and voices of the anchor men and women in New York and Washington, repeated over and over again how the government was apparently trying to do away with the "cancer research scientists" once and for all.

The public's outrage over the government's decision to take Oncoleve off the market after several years of having an effective and dependable treatment for cancer now boiled over. People left their workplaces and homes in protest of a government that seemed to be completely out of touch with reality. Within hours, the streets around the White House were jammed with protesters carrying signs calling for an end to the ban on Oncoleve specifically and to science more generally. Police and National Guard troops were called in to quell the uprising, but this only served to exacerbate an already explosive situation.

Following Colonel Dillon's dramatic address to the media reporters and the shooting that occurred before he was able to finish speaking, a violent confrontation near the White House resulted in a civilian being shot and killed by a police officer. This tragic incident was also picked up by the national media and interlaced with even more speculation about what was appropriately being perceived as the overall incompetence of the Brasington administration. The Secret Service decided to load President Brasington onto Marine Angel One and transport him to Naval Support Facility Thurmont, more popularly known as Camp David, until peace had been restored. But by the time the presidential helicopter fleet arrived at Camp David, the roads leading up the Catoctin Mountains in Frederick County, Maryland, to the presidential compound were already lined with cars and trucks full of ordinary citizens who had assumed that he would be retreating there. And since arms sales had increased dramatically under the urging of the new conservative government, and the assault weapons ban had been lifted by the president and Congress, many of these ordinary citizens were armed with assault weapons as well as shotguns and handguns. While Camp David was still believed to be totally secure, the Secret Service was in no mood to take chances. They instructed the helicopter fleet to remain in the air and take the president instead to Site R, more officially known as the Raven Rock Mountain Complex (RRMC), located about nine miles east of Waynesboro, Pennsylvania, and just six miles north-northeast of Camp David. Informally known as the Underground Pentagon, the RRMC was one of the "undisclosed locations" used by the government following previous terrorist attacks on the continental United States, to which the Tate administration had given the somewhat Orwellian appellation of the

"Homeland." The facility is completely self-contained and has extensive command, control, and communications capabilities, making it perfectly capable of directing the armed forces of the nation, including the issuance of nuclear weapons release codes if ordered by the president.

With the president now safely and very publicly transported away from the White House, the crowd focused on the Capitol Building almost exclusively. Capitol Hill police and National Guard personnel soon realized that members of the House and Senate were also vulnerable to the protesters' anger, and while they had no doubt that they could easily disperse the crowd at least temporarily with tear gas and other crowd control measures, they also knew that many of the protesters were carrying significant weaponry, and visions of the Vietnam era Kent State massacre or worse danced through their heads and caused their leaders to opt for discretion over confrontation.

Chapter 36: Capitol Hill

Following Colonel Dillon's dramatic and sponta-
neous address to the news media at Cheyenne Mountain, Congressman Jackson Hall sat with members of
his staff in his administrative assistant's office, where
the flat-screen television had been continuously tuned
to one of the cable news channels. They watched the
president being taken from the White House aboard
Marine One to an undisclosed location, which Jackson
assumed might be Camp David. They had never before
witnessed this kind of intense violence and protest in
their relatively young lives. Reading about the protests
that had occurred in the 1960s and 1970s over the Vietnam conflict was nothing compared to watching this
drama unfold live before them.

Annie, his AA, asked Jackson, "Sir, where do you
think this is heading? Will transporting the president
away from the White House defuse this mob?"

"I don't know, Annie, I honestly don't know." They
sat in front of the video display with their eyes and ears
glued to the ongoing events and commentary from the
other end of Pennsylvania Avenue. It soon became evident that with the president now safely out of reach, the
firestorm of anger in the crowd had only been further
inflamed. Scuffles among citizens and the police and
military troops grew more frequent and more severe.
Tear gas was fired, rubber bullets were shot into the

crowd, and the debilitating stored energy from TASERs stopped several people in their tracks. But the crowd grew ever larger and more menacing, like a living organism with a mind of its own, and it began moving away from the White House and toward Capitol Hill. "Uh oh, this doesn't look good at all," Jackson said quietly to Annie.

Just then, the doors to his outer office burst open and a squad of heavily armed men quickly entered and called out, "Congressman Hall!"

Too stunned to move, Jackson stared at the troops and their automatic weapons. There were two officers wearing the familiar navy blue uniforms of the U.S. Capitol Police, but the most heavily armed men wore strange mustard-color uniforms. The leader of the squad had what appeared to be a book of photographs. He peered at it briefly and then looked over at Jackson. He gave a command to his troops and they rushed into Annie's office, took Jackson by both arms, and half-dragged him to the main entrance.

"Congressman, I am Sergeant McGill of the Homeland Security Police. We were sent here by the Secretary to evacuate all members of Congress to a safe location. You will come with us now."

Jackson saw the unfamiliar insignia on the uniform and then remembered that President Brasington had established this special unit within the Department of Homeland Security for certain necessary but vague and unspecified purposes. Brasington's political detractors had criticized the unit for serving as the president's personal storm-troopers. Most such criticism was largely muted after a few of the same detractors had suffered serious accidents or other misfortune. After a few months, it had all been accepted, if not appreciated, as necessary for the protection of the Homeland from the potential attacks of terrorists, either from within the country or from foreign locations.

"Sergeant, I understand, but I prefer to stay here with my staff. We'll be fine, but thank you for your concern."

"Congressman, obviously you don't understand. You are being taken to a secure facility under the continuity of government provisions of federal law. This is not an option. Please come with us now, voluntarily, or we will use whatever force is necessary."

Without waiting for a reply, they dragged him from his office suite, took him through the hallways to a rear entrance of the House Rayburn Office Building, and shoved him onto a heavily-armored dark blue bus with the number fourteen on the side. It reminded him of a prison transport vehicle. Many of his colleagues were already on the bus, and a few more followed him. The smell of fear and panic was rampant within the group. Within minutes, they had gone from being lawmakers and part of Washington's political elite to being prisoners of their own government. More troops wearing the odd mustard-color uniforms paced back and forth inside the bus, checking off lists, verifying Congressional identification cards, and confiscating cell phones and any other communications devices from the involuntary passengers.

One senior member of the House rose from his seat in protest, stating that he needed to call his family immediately. One of the Mustards shoved the butt of his rifle into the man's chest and he fell back hard in his seat with a gasp. House Select Committee on Intelligence Chairman Jack Findlay, seated across the aisle of the bus, said, "Just a minute, officer! What the hell do you think you're doing treating a congressman like that?"

The Mustard quickly swiveled toward Chairman Findlay, pulled his handgun from its holster, and placed the muzzle against his forehead. "Not another word, do you understand?"

Findlay nodded his head slowly and crouched down low into his seat.

Jackson heard someone give an order to the driver, the doors closed, and the bus pulled away from behind the building and out onto the street, heading quickly away from Washington.

———

Once they were out of the city, the Mustard in charge keyed a microphone and addressed the passengers. "Good afternoon and apologies to all of you members of Congress for this quick and forceful evacuation. In case any of you were otherwise engaged and may not have been up on current developments, you should be aware that the past few hours have seen angry and violent protests in the nation's capital and at various locations around the country. The president has departed from the White House to a secure location. Since we have reason to believe that you and your colleagues were also about to be in harm's way, it became our duty to transport all of you to another secure location. We are headed for the Mount Weather Emergency Operations Center near Bluemont, Virginia. Mount Weather is also known as the High Point Special Facility or just 'SF.' Nominally a facility for the Federal Emergency Management Agency or FEMA, the surface complex, known as Area A, occupies over 400 acres of land. The hardened underground Area B occupies over 600,000 square feet. You will be housed in Area B until the danger has passed.

"We will be passing through or close by Arlington, Reston, and Leesburg. It should take us just over an hour to reach Bluemont, which is close to the border of Virginia and West Virginia. We are taking this action at the direction of the president and under the authority of the continuity of government provisions of Executive Order 48935. Before you ask questions unnecessarily, only the 435 members of the House, the one hundred United States Senators, and the nine justices of the Supreme Court will be housed at High Point. There is no room at the facility for family members or any other person not designated in the executive order. For your own safety and security, we have taken your cell phones. We are hopeful that you won't be staying at the facility for more than a few days as we work to restore order in Washington and around the country. Once you arrive there, you will be given a brief orientation tour of the underground facility, and we will establish a sign-up list for members wishing to make a call to their families. These calls will be monitored real-time, and you are strictly prohibited from mentioning your location or discussing how long you might be away. Be advised that I will not be entertaining any questions or comments. That is all."

The House members merely looked at each other in a daze as the bus continued on its way to Bluemont, Virginia.

———

It was a strange and quiet ride. The members of the House spoke not a word, afraid even to move after the Mustard's pointed warning to one of the most powerful members of the lower chamber. Naturally, Jackson's mind raced with questions. He hadn't been a member of the intelligence committee long enough to have received a briefing on the facility to which they were being taken, so he had no idea what to expect. He wished that he would have had the opportunity to call Chuck Pearce at the White House, if he were even still there. The past several weeks had witnessed their relationship grow from casual friends to close friends to—and he was heavily conflicted to admit it to himself—passionate lovers. He was racked with guilt over being involved in a homosexual relationship. It was totally condemned by his religious upbringing and belief system. Yet, he wondered, how could anything that felt so right, let alone so good, possibly be evil in the eyes of his Lord? He doubted that he would ever be able to reconcile the cognitive dissonance existing within him. Nonetheless, he wondered if Chuck was safe with the president at Camp David. Given Chuck's position as deputy chief of staff, he surely would have been evacuated from the White House. And, Camp David should certainly be secure, as there were many barriers to entry guarded by both U.S. Navy and Secret Service officers.

But what would happen to him and his colleagues now? He had just started running through the ramifications of the afternoon's events when the bus slowed and approached a gated and fortified entrance. First he read the large sign outside the gates: "U.S. Department of Agriculture, Field Research Station. Authorized Personnel Only." Then he noticed the elaborate fencing system that stretched as far as the eye could see. It consisted of an outer fence with razor wire, a second fence with razor wire, and then another fence with no razor wire but with a huge sign that read: "Electrified Fence Charged With Lethal Voltage." Below, another sign read: "Close Proximity Means Instant Death." More razor wire topped a fourth and final inner fence. Obviously this perimeter was designed both to keep people out as well as in. This was not a comforting realization under the present circumstances. He briefly wondered why there were two outer fences, but then he heard and saw the reason. The area between the two outer fences was being patrolled by vicious, snarling guard dogs. The dogs approached as close as they could, barking and growling loudly as the bus pulled to a stop at the gate house.

The driver showed some credentials and paperwork to one of the heavily-armed guards, the motorized gates separated, and the bus proceeded slowly into the compound.

———— ◆ ————

They drove for two or three miles to a large concrete block structure. The bus doors opened and the Mustard in charge again spoke to them over the public address system. "We have now arrived at the High Point Special Facility. You will file out of the bus one at a time and an officer will check your name on the roster. You will then proceed between the two rope lines and enter the building you see in front of you. Do not, under any circumstances, deviate from this pathway. I assure you that the result would be most undesirable. We will now begin with persons sitting in the front seats and then follow row by row. You..." and he pointed to a person sitting in the front of the bus, "go now." And the process of exiting the bus and entering Site SF began.

When Jackson's turn came, he stepped off the bus. The officers checked his House ID card and made a few marks on a form attached to a clipboard. He walked slowly behind several of his peers until they entered a large and musty smelling room. He saw the doors of what appeared to be a large elevator in front of them. More guards were stationed at the elevator doors. In a few minutes, the doors opened and the guards allowed about twenty of the House members to enter. Jackson did a quick count and, given his position in the queue, figured that he would not get on the elevator until it had made three more trips.

His turn came and the guards ushered him in. An officer in the elevator pushed the buttons to close the door and begin its descent. After about a minute, the doors opened, and Jackson's group was led down a corridor and into a very large auditorium with hundreds of theater-style seats. They were told to take a seat and remain quiet.

It took almost an hour for the last group of members to arrive in the room. Several officials in the mustard color uniforms took to the small stage in the front of the auditorium. The leader of the group stepped to a podium and addressed them through a microphone.

"Good afternoon to you all. My name is Colonel Nathan Seifert, and as the chief of the Homeland Security Police, I would like to welcome you to the High Point Special Facility. As members of the legislative branch of our government, you were brought here for your own protection as a result of civil unrest in our nation's capital and in other locations. I regret to report that the violence has only increased during the time it took for you to be transported here. My forces and other federal officials are working diligently to restore order so that you can return to your homes and congressional offices as soon as possible. However, with the increased violence and numbers of protesters, it's impossible to estimate when that might be. In a few minutes, one of my associates will give you an orientation tour of the facility and show you to your sleeping quarters. I'm sure you can appreciate that this facility is designed for efficiency in an emergency to house a large number of government officials, so please understand that the ambience is spartan compared to your normal environment.

"There is one other matter I want to speak with you about today, and that is to offer my sincere apologies specifically to two members of Congress, and also to all of the passengers on bus number fourteen, who were treated rudely at best and with totally inappropriate force." Jackson realized that the chief was referring to his bus. The Mustard continued, "I can report to you that the officer responsible for this incident is no longer a member of the Homeland Security Police. In fact, he is also no longer alive, as he was killed in an exchange of gunfire shortly after your bus departed."

Jackson looked at the members sitting to his left and right. No doubt they all wondered the same thing: who had actually fired the gun that killed the offending officer? Was it another Mustard carrying out execution orders? His attention returned to the stage.

"At this time," said the colonel, "I want to introduce to you the president's specially-appointed spokesman, Galen Gatling, who also just recently arrived here." Jackson's jaw dropped in shocked surprise as he watched the former right-wing radio talk-show host walk onto the stage, and he was also wearing one of the mustard uniforms, although absent any insignia of rank. He stood before them, a man who knew little about anything posing as an expert who knew all about everything. Without any formal education beyond high school, but through the spouting of outrageous half-truths, deliberately distorting facts, and by tapping into the reptilian anger of the frightened public at large, he had managed to convince his millions of devoted listeners that they should follow his every word.

Gatling had been instrumental in helping President Brasington to be nominated by the conservative party and then elected as president. Obviously his presence here in the shelter for high government officials was some kind of political repayment for his efforts. When he spoke into the microphone, there wasn't a person in the room who didn't recognize Gatling's pompous, self-righteous, and gravelly voice, qualities which led his detractors to describe him as a "blowhard."

"I would also like to personally welcome you here on behalf of President Brasington, blessed be his name. I will be serving as his official spokesman and liaison unless and until such time as he might also arrive here. At the present time, he is at the Underground Pentagon at Site R both praying for our salvation and tending to the needs of national defense. I will be your source for official news and announcements." With no further comment or explanation as to his presence among them, he exchanged high-fives with Colonel Seifert and walked off the stage.

Jackson felt a certain deep-seated anger growing within him. What if his friend, Chuck Pearce, had not been taken to a safe location after all, while this media hack had been brought here with elected U.S. congressmen and senators? He realized that it was better not to think about that possibility too much until he knew more about Chuck's whereabouts.

Chapter 37: Site SF

The atmosphere within Site SF had changed dramatically by the morning of the day following Jackson's arrival along with his congressional colleagues. Apparently sometime during the night, the Mustards had left the facility. Jackson assumed that they must have been needed more elsewhere than in this tightly closed community of lawmakers. As he understood it, overall supervision of the group had been left with a Committee-of-Three consisting of the Speaker of the House, the president pro tempore of the Senate, and the chief justice of the Supreme Court. They were then to delegate specific operational and managerial duties to the director of FEMA, who was also in the facility.

The self-styled "family values" vice president had been forced to resign shortly after taking office following the reporting of an illicit romantic affair which he had accomplished at taxpayer expense while he was in the Unites States Senate. The president had not had sufficient time to nominate a replacement, and so the office remained vacant.

Although they had limited communications with the outside world, they knew enough to understand that the world may well be on the verge of nuclear war. Most members of the House and Senate knew full well that there would be no winner in an all-out exchange of strategic nuclear weapons. It was the scenario developed and referred to as "Mutually Assured Destruction," or MAD, during the height of the Cold War between the U.S. and the Soviet Union. And in the very short time frame of less than one day, given this realization, along with the absence of family members, any semblance of morale had disappeared among the residents of the High Point Special Facility.

During the previous evening, each new arrival had been given the opportunity to attempt to place one telephone call. Deeply conflicted as to whether to call his parents in California or to try to reach Chuck Pearce, Jackson knew he more than owed it to his parents to call them. It was a short and sad conversation. Without his adoptive father and mother or Jackson himself saying anything to indicate it was so, they all seemed to sense that this would, in all likelihood, be their last conversation. They had five minutes to say goodbye without saying goodbye, and to communicate their love for each other. After his call was disconnected, Jackson found himself profoundly depressed. He was consumed by a deep black hole in the center of his being with no clue how to climb out of it, or even much of a desire to do so. He had only his faith left to turn to, but he even found this lacking under these circumstances. His colleagues seemed to be in the same state of shock and disbelief.

Some of them talked or played cards into the middle of the night, perhaps hoping to wake up from what was rapidly becoming the worst nightmare possible. Some took advantage of sleeping pills being dispensed by the small medical office. Jackson finally went to his assigned bed, rack five in bay seven, and after tossing and turning for what seemed like hours, mercifully went to sleep.

He awoke with a severe headache, went to the medical office for some pain pills, and made his way to what was designated as the cafeteria. It was really just a room full of tables and chairs with a small serving window. He consumed some eggs and toast while wondering just how long their food supply would last. He saw Jack Findlay at a neighboring table and asked him what he knew about it, but Findlay seemed self-absorbed and reluctant to talk about anything. Jackson left the cafeteria and went to the commons room, which was the auditorium where they had first been taken upon their arrival.

He reflected upon the past few weeks. While the White House had become almost totally preoccupied with shutting down the scientific research project that had developed Oncoleve, Jackson had put two and two together and realized that there was a small but real possibility that his birth mother might be located within that very scientific community. Her disappearance from the public grid, along with the existence of her uncle's "Foundation for the Study of the Origin of the Universe" above the hardware store in Olston, West Virginia, even as crazy and disconnected from reality as it seemed, was just too much of a coincidence.

Then there was another mystery. Wes Scarcia had completely disappeared by the time it took the FBI to become involved and to arrive in Olston to question him. He had vanished without a trace, all of his research materials still occupying the musty FSOU office, and all of his personal belongings left in his mobile home in a trailer park just outside the sleepy little town.

Jackson had disapproved of the plan to assault the Cheyenne Mountain facility, but his opinion didn't matter to the president. What was the point? Aside from the fact that his biological mother might actually be there and could easily be harmed or killed in the process, it was just a scientific research project. But, the project's stated purpose, to discover the nature of the origin of the universe, and its one known discovery, Oncoleve, both deeply offended the president's religious beliefs. And so the full might of the nation's military had been brought to bear to get inside the facility and to disband the project. But incredibly, it turned out that there was no project and there were no people, scientists or otherwise, inside the mountain stronghold. All of which caused Jackson to wonder if there even were such a project. And if there were, where was it located? It was hard for him to avoid feeling as though he was simply not destined to ever find the answers to these questions and perhaps, just perhaps, to locate his mother.

But Jackson had one last thing to try, if he could get away with it within the confines of life within Site SF.

With the Mustards gone, SF's occupants were free to roam around the facility, and it didn't take long to learn where everything was located. Jackson waited until mid-afternoon and innocently wandered over to the small but extremely high-tech communications room. He stood at the doorway until the duty communications officer noticed him and asked what he wanted.

Jackson deliberately stared wide-eyed at the many racks of high-tech equipment in the room and said, "Hi, I'm Congressman Jackson Hall, and being an Amateur Radio operator, I'm really fascinated by all of the sophisticated equipment you've got here. Any chance of getting an informal tour sometime?"

The comm officer, who was wearing a Navy uniform with chief petty officer rank insignia, walked over to Jackson and shook hands with him. "Now that's a coincidence, isn't it, because I'm a ham operator, too." The two men proceeded to exchange their FCC callsigns and chat a little about where they lived and how they had become interested in Amateur Radio. "I'm afraid the equipment and operations in this room are highly classified. I don't suppose you happen to hold a top-secret clearance, do you?"

"As a matter of fact I do," Jackson replied, "I'm a member of the House Select Committee on Intelligence."

"Alright then! I'll tell you what, we're really swamped with message traffic right now, as I'm sure you can imagine, but if you come back in a day or two during my shift at this time of day, I'll give you a cook's tour of the 'shack,' how does that sound?"

"Sounds great to me." *You'd better believe I'll be back.* Jackson finished with the universal greeting between ham radio operators from the days when they extensively used International Morse Code for communications, "73s my friend."

"73s back at you."

———————

It was just after dinner, if the small meal could even be called a dinner, when a burst of energy and activity became noticeable among the facility's staff. Shortly thereafter, Jackson saw the Committee-of-Three gather at the doors of the elevator leading to the surface. "What's going on?" Jackson asked one of the senate leaders he had met a few times in the capitol building.

"The president will be arriving here shortly. They're bringing him from Site R so that all three branches of government will be represented here. That's not a good sign about things on the surface, I'm afraid."

Jackson broke out in a cold sweat and just nodded his agreement.

Chapter 38: Armageddon

During the following hours, much of the activity occurring within the United States by the government to relocate its leaders to secure locations was reported to the world by the news media, and some less than friendly nations interpreted the massive evacuation as a sign of a pending preemptive strike. In the Middle East, already a tinderbox due to recent hostility between Israel and its neighboring countries, a high-ranking military officer in one of the warring factions either deliberately or mistakenly armed a tactical nuclear warhead and used it to "clear" a disputed area of territory currently occupied by the enemy. Even though a tactical nuclear weapon's damage is much more "surgical" and limited than that of a strategic nuclear warhead, a nuclear explosion is, after all, a nuclear explosion. Intelligence sources quickly reported this loosing of the hounds of war back to their respective governments.

In North Korea, an already unstable dictator decided that this would be the perfect time to reclaim South Korea while the United States would be otherwise occupied, and troops stormed across the 38th Parallel into the South.

Back in the Middle East, the deployment of one tactical nuclear weapon was obviously taken as an act of war, and following a volley of tactical nukes back and forth over the course of a few hours, it was clearly time to "end the carnage" with the use of a strategic nuclear weapon. This had the predictable effect of causing all of the nuclear powers in the region to use their ballistic missiles on each other until all that was left in the entire area was rubble as well as carnage.

A similar chain of events took place in Korea, with Chinese nuclear weapons being used on the South. Of course, this was more than sufficient provocation to activate SEATO, the Southeast Asia Treaty Organization, to which the United States was the most powerful signatory.

Once the use of the first tactical nuclear weapon had been detected and confirmed by U.S. Intelligence, which reported the event at about the same time as the satellite news media, the decision was quickly made to move the president from Site R to Site SF, since both executive and legislative powers would be needed for continuity of government operations, not the least of which would be fighting what was quickly becoming World War III.

Chapter 39: Site SF

In fact it was about two hours later when the elevator doors opened and President Brasington and his entourage filed into the facility. After exchanging a few words with the reassembled Committee-of-Three, he was quickly escorted to his private quarters by his Mustard guards. Apparently Brasington had eschewed the traditional Secret Service agents, instead favoring his own Homeland Security team.

Jackson scanned the group exiting the elevator, looking for Chuck Pearce. He recognized White House chief of staff Jeb White, a few members of the cabinet, including Defense Secretary Jonathan Pearl, and a few other senior advisors to the president. But to his great dismay, Chuck Pearce was not among them.

"Are there any more members of the president's party still to come down from the surface?" he asked the Speaker of the House.

The Speaker just shook his head and quickly walked away in the same direction as the president had been taken.

Get a grip, this doesn't mean that Chuck is on the surface and in harm's way. He could still be back at Site R at the Underground Pentagon or at some other safe location.

As soon as the situation permitted, he resolved to speak with Jeb White, Chuck's immediate superior, who would know for certain about Chuck's whereabouts.

With nothing else left for him to do, Jackson returned to the auditorium to see if he could learn anything more about what was going on. The room was nearly empty, and nobody there seemed to know anything more than he did.

About one hour later, newly-minted presidential spokesman Galen Gatling made an announcement via the public address system throughout the entire facility:

"Attention! May I have the attention of everyone in the facility for an extremely important announcement. All elected officials are asked to assemble in the auditorium immediately. Nuclear weapons have been unleashed around the world, and President Brasington, blessed be his name, will be acting in his capacity as commander in chief of America's armed forces to authorize retaliatory nuclear responses. He will perform the authorization protocol in your presence on this historic occasion. That is all."

Historic occasion? Jackson asked himself. *That's one way to look at it.* He was already sitting in the front of the auditorium, so he would have a close-up view of whatever was about to happen.

The president, the secretary of defense, a U.S. Navy lieutenant commander carrying a black briefcase, and Galen Gatling appeared on stage. Gatling approached the microphone while the other three men sat down in folding chairs around a small card table. Gatling, pumped full of his own self-importance at being the master of ceremonies for the "historic occasion," began a running commentary on what was happening on stage for the benefit of this very special audience.

"In the interest of history, it is very important that you fully understand what will be taking place here within a few minutes. In the United States, we have always followed the 'two-man rule' when it comes to action so drastic as releasing strategic nuclear weapons. In every missile launch control room, for example, two officers must simultaneously insert and turn their launch keys in order to release the missiles in the silos they control. On board a ballistic missile submarine, both the captain and the executive officer must concur and use their launch keys to release their missiles. And so on and so forth all the way up the chain of command to the president as commander in chief. Even with the president, the two-man rule applies. At this level, the president of the United States and the secretary of defense jointly constitute an entity known as the National Command Authorities. Both officials must agree that any order to launch nuclear weapons is necessary for the protection of the nation."

Jackson was transfixed by the horror of what was about to happen. As Gatling droned on, he noticed a few things about the president that were unnerving. His eyes were open very wide, and whenever he looked at his audience, he almost seemed to be disconnected from the gravity of the situation. His hands trembled slightly, and he had a rheumy look about him, as if he weren't physically well.

Gatling continued, "Here on the stage before you is, of course, President L. Davis Brasington III, blessed be his name, Secretary of Defense Jonathan Pearl, and Navy Lieutenant Commander Charles Odom, who has the privilege of carrying what is commonly known as the 'nuclear football' on this particular day of great significance. May I have a round of applause for these brave leaders!"

To Jackson's utter astonishment, nearly everyone in the audience stood and applauded the event that was about to begin U.S. participation in World War III. Gatling then said, "Now, I would ask that we all recite the Pledge of Allegiance." Everyone in the hall faced the flag in the front corner of the auditorium and covered their heart with their right hand. "I pledge allegiance to the flag of the United States of America, and to the republic for which it stands, one nation under God, indivisible, with liberty and justice for all."

"Please remain standing while the chaplain leads us in prayer."

An army chaplain walked onto the stage and came to the microphone. "All Mighty and most merciful Father, we humbly beseech Thee, of Thy great goodness, to bless our valiant leaders in their endeavor to save our blessed nation. Grant them the courage to perform their duties under these most difficult of circumstances. Graciously use Thy power to protect us as your soldiers so that we may destroy the Godlessness of our enemies and establish Thy will and Thy justice among all mankind and nations. Amen."

Gatling returned to the microphone. "Please be seated. At this time, Lieutenant Commander Odom will begin the formalities."

Jackson could only stare in disbelief as these events unfolded around him. It wasn't enough to authorize the use of nuclear weapons for the first time since Fat Man and Little Boy had been dropped on Japan to end World War II in the Pacific. They had to wrap the whole ceremony in the flag and then call upon God to bless the endeavor. Jackson fought a rising wave of nausea.

The naval officer unzipped a side flap on the briefcase and removed a small wireless keyboard from the compartment. Turning to Brasington, he said, "Mr. President, may I have your identification codeword please?"

Brasington stood and reached inside his breast pocket for his "biscuit," a plastic card that contained a series of code words. His shaky finger traced down the card until he found the right code for the day. He began spelling the codeword phonetically, "Bravo, Echo, Echo..."

As the president continued reading the sequence, Jackson felt light-headed. *Surely this can't be happening.*

Odom entered the code using the remote keyboard. One high-pitch beep sounded from inside the briefcase. He then replied, "Sir, I confirm your identification as the commander-in-chief." He then turned to Pearl and said, "Mr. Secretary, may I have your identification codeword please?"

Pearl already had his biscuit in his hand, replying, "Charlie, Alpha, Tango, November, India, Papa."

Odom entered the second code on the keyboard. This time, two beeps sounded from the briefcase along with a click, apparently indicating that the case was now unlocked. "Sir, I confirm your identification as the secretary of defense. Mr. President, I await your orders, sir!"

Brasington turned to his audience with an excited look on his face. "I'm the only president ever to have done this!" Then he spoke directly to Odom, "Initiate Condition Scarlet, Global, Total."

Odom asked Pearl, "Mr. Secretary, do you concur with the order to initiate Condition Scarlet, Global, Total?"

Pearl replied, "Affirmative. Send the command to initiate Condition Scarlet, Global, Total, to the chairman of the Joint Chiefs."

The naval officer now opened the briefcase. Inside was another keyboard and a small display screen, along with a red binder. Jackson noticed a short black rubber-ducky style antenna affixed to the inside of the top of the briefcase. Odom opened the red binder which contained what appeared to be computer-printed pages. Jackson watched Odom consult an index sheet and then turn to a page which he assumed corresponded to Condition Scarlet, Global, Total. Then Odom typed a coded message on the keyboard. He must have received a response immediately, because he said, "Mr. President, Mr. Secretary, the Joint Chiefs have received your orders and are now implementing them."

Jackson knew enough about the authorization process to know that a highly-encrypted signal had just been sent from the nuclear football to multiple redundant receivers that would relay it along to the National Military Command Center at the Pentagon, to the Alternate National Military Command Center at Site R, and to the general officer commanding the Boeing E-4B National Airborne Operations Center. The command center at the Pentagon, if it were surviving, or one of the others if it weren't, would now, as specified in SIOP, the Single Integrated Operational Plan, send Major Attack Options via pre-formatted Emergency Action Messages (EAM) in digital format to major commands through AUTODIN, the secure Automatic Digital Network. These EAMs would then be relayed to aircraft carrying nuclear bombs via the high frequency Global Communications System, to ballistic missile submarines via very low frequency transmitters, and to underground missile launch control centers via hardened buried cables. Department of Defense communications satellites would also relay orders around the world.

The codes contained in the EAMs would then be used to enable Permissive Action Links contained within the nuclear weapons themselves. In effect, this process served the function of removing the safety switch from the triggers of the greatest arsenal of weapons ever known to mankind. In some cases, commanders would even set "Dial-A-Yield" controls on individual weapons in accordance with their specific orders.

Jackson found himself repeating the same thought over and over in his mind: *This idiot president has just baked the perfect cake from the recipe book on How to End the World.*

Chapter 40: Site SF

Even with the help of the sleeping medicine, Jackson endured a very sleepless night in his bunk. He thought morale was bad before the president had released nuclear weapons, but now…now was much worse. Everyone in the compound knew that they would never be returning to the surface. Everyone, that is, with the exception of President Brasington, who seemed to revel in the fact that he would have a major role in creating a new and more pure God-fearing society. He believed all of this despite FEMA warnings that the radiation level on the surface would be lethal to humans for a time-span far beyond their own lifetimes.

Finally, at about 0500 hours, he got up to go to the medical office for some more pain medication. His headaches were becoming more frequent and severe. *No wonder!*

Jackson had given himself one mission for this day, and that was to speak with Jeb White about Chuck Pearce. Somewhat surprisingly, it happened almost too soon, before he had fully prepared himself for what to say. When he arrived at the cafeteria to try to eat some breakfast, he saw White sitting alone at one of the small tables in the room. He quickly put some food on his tray, not caring what he took, and walked directly to White's table.

"Mr. White, mind if I join you this morning?"

"No suh, be muh guest. Sorry I don't recognize you."

"I'm Congressman Jackson Hall from California, sir."

"Ah, Hall from California. Well son, I seriously doubt that California is any longuh in existence. Or much of the rest of the world, for that mattuh."

"Yes sir, it is a terrible tragedy. But I was wondering if you could answer a question for me?"

"Well, I'll certainly try. There aren't many secrets left to keep, are there?"

"No sir, I suppose not. Your deputy, Chuck Pearce, do you know if he might be safe in another secure location?"

White's puffy face turned more sour than usual. "Now theh's another tragedy. I gave Pearce every oppuhtunity in the world. A talented man, no doubt about it. That's why I made him my depuhty."

"So what happened to him?"

"Well, son, only the very highest senior White House staff members were taken to Site R with the president. Now heah's the tragedy. The deputy chief of staff could have been considered senior staff, and I would have liked nothing moh."

Jackson felt his neck muscles stiffen. "But he wasn't there when the president and his staff were evacuated?"

"Aw no, he was there alright, sittin' in his office, doin' his job right up 'til the end."

"But he's not here?"

"No suh, he's not. And heah's the reason. It had just come to my attention that the little cocksucker was involved in a homosexual relationship. A homosexual relationship by someone ȯn muh staff! Right theah in the centuh of powah wheah President Brasington, blessed be his name, was workin' mightily for a new world ohduh, a wohld wheah God is King of All. I tell you, son, it hurt me. It hurt me bad. So in the end, I cuhtainly couldn't give the orduh to include him in the transport, now could I? So to answuh your question, I can only assume that he has returned to his Maker, and may God have mercy on his soul."

Jackson could only stare at the man for a moment while he fully processed what he had just been told. Finally he said angrily, "Let me get this right. You learned that he was gay, and so you decided that he deserved to die in a nuclear holocaust?"

"Well now, that's puttin' it a little harshly, son, truly it is. It's not muh place to decide who might live or who might die. I just had to decide who was to be evacuated from the White House, based on their responsibilities to the president and their quality of character and upright moral standing."

Jackson was enraged. He had never been so tempted to lash out at someone as he was right now. But he had another mission to accomplish while he was in this hell-hole of a facility, and so he did one of the most difficult things he had ever done in his life: he walked away from the table without strangling Jeb White to death with his bare hands.

Hours. It took him hours of retreat back in his bunk before he could even begin to control his rage. But he knew that he had to do so, because he needed to visit the communications office again, and not just for a tour.

By mid-afternoon, when he believed that the navy chief petty officer would be on duty again, he returned to the doorway of the communications room. It was no longer a hustling beehive of activity like it had been the day before. His Amateur Radio "brother" seemed to be alone in the room.

"Hi Chief, how are you doing under the circumstances?"

The man walked over to Jackson. "Please, just call me Paul."

Jackson could see that the man had been crying. "Did you have family on the surface Paul?"

"Yeah, a wife and two kids."

"I'm so sorry for your loss."

"How did it happen? Why did it have to happen? Can you explain it to me? You're a congressman."

"I don't believe it did have to happen. But it did, nonetheless. If there are any historians left in the world, I expect they'll be pondering the whys and wherefores of all this for a long, long time. I lost my parents and a very dear friend, not to mention my own staff and others about whom I cared deeply. It's a terrible, unspeakable tragedy. I wish there were something I could say that would offer more comfort to you, but there isn't. There just isn't."

Paul nodded. "Come on in. I know you wanted a tour, and you're more than welcome to look around, but to be honest with you, I just don't have any enthusiasm left for describing how great and wonderful all of this hardware is, considering everything."

"Of course, I understand completely," Jackson said as he entered the room and the two men sat down in front of what he assumed was the main control console for all communications in and out of Site SF.

They sat quietly for a few minutes, each of them lost in his own thoughts and memories. Various color LEDs blinked off and on in front of them. Others were lit solid, and some were dark. Jackson wondered how much of this equipment was still functional given conditions on the surface. Antennas of one sort or another would be needed to send and receive signals. Could they have possibly survived intact?

"Paul, do you have any contact with the outside world at all?"

"Just some secure military facilities here and there. I've picked up some little snippets of shortwave broadcasts, but the noise level is way too high to even hear what they're saying."

"I see. Let me ask you something else. I uh, I've been searching for all of my adolescent and adult life trying to locate my biological mother. I even had a private detective working on it for a while. And then I found out something that led me to believe that she might be working in a secret scientific research station somewhere. In fact, the very one that the government thought was located in Cheyenne Mountain."

"Oh that fiasco! That really got the ball rolling right down here to SF, didn't it?"

"In a way, it did. But, my question is, do you have any kind of a directory of government facilities that might, just might, have some kind of listing for that project?"

"You mean the one that doesn't exist?"

"Well, it didn't exist in Cheyenne Mountain, that's for sure. But suppose it does exist in some other secure location? President King was a master planner, and that whole project was established by his administration. He or his team would certainly have chosen a safe place, don't you think?"

"I thought it was owned by some foundation."

"It was turned over to a private foundation before King left office. But look, we know that it actually existed at some point in time because the scientists working there discovered Oncoleve and who knows what else?"

Paul shook his head. "I don't know that much of anything could have survived the inferno up there, but…," and he reached up on a shelf and pulled down a thick three-ring binder, "…you're welcome to look through this digital network directory. If you even know what to look for. If you find something, we can enter the network address right here on this keyboard and see if we get a response."

"Thank you, Paul, thank you very much. I really appreciate this."

Jackson took the binder and saw that the entries seemed to consist mainly of military bases along with such obvious entries as the White House telecommunications office, the capitol building communications center, FEMA centers, and even state and county emergency management agencies all over the country. There were many major police departments, hospitals, and more. He immediately turned to the page where entries beginning with the letter "F" were located. He looked for anything beginning with the word "Foundation" but found nothing. *This doesn't look good.*

He resolved to search the directory from the beginning to the end. It would be much like searching through a phone book page by page, but he had to try. The directory began with numbered military units, and then started into the "A" listings. He saw many listings that under other circumstances would have fascinated him. But he continued searching, ignoring the obvious military listings. Alaska EMA. Appalachian Signal Hub. Boulder Dam Control Room. The listings continued like ants on a march. Emergency Communications Center, East, Central, and West. Great Neck Microwave Site. Montana EMA. Nevada EMA. Offutt Air Force Base. Origins Research Team. Southern Operational...wait!! Origins Research Team?!? *It couldn't possibly be this simple.*

"Paul, look! Could this be it?" He returned the binder to his friend, his hands shaking with excitement.

The chief looked at the listing and said, "Never heard of it, partner. But it can't hurt to try."

He typed the six-digit network code on his keyboard and pressed the "enter" key. For a moment nothing happened, and then, from the speaker on the console came a very pleasant female voice:

"Origins Research Team, how may I help you?"

Chapter 41: Site SF

Both men were startled to hear a live person answering their signal on the digital network. They looked at each other in amazement.

The voice repeated, "Origins Research Team, how may I help you?"

Paul reached for a microphone on the desk and pressed the push-to-talk button. "This is Chief Petty Officer Paul Gutshall calling from the Highpoint Special Facility in Virginia."

"Yes?"

Paul shrugged his shoulders and looked questioningly at Jackson, not knowing what to say next. Jackson gestured to him to pass the microphone over.

"Origins Research Team, this is Congressman Jackson Hall. May I speak with your officer in charge, please?"

"That would be Dr. Morefield, our chief administrator. He is not available right now, but if you can stand by there, I can have him return your call in about fifteen minutes."

Jackson replied with excitement in his voice, "Uh, yes, that would be great. Do you have our number?" Paul immediately nodded his head at his friend.

"Yes, it's displayed on our equipment here. If you enable your video equipment, we will signal you back in video conference mode."

"Can we do that, Paul?"

Paul again nodded.

"Yes, we will be prepared for your video call."

"Very well. This is Origins Research Team, out."

"Thank you, thank you very much, ma'am"

A slight click seemed to indicate that the connection was no longer active.

Jackson exclaimed to Paul, "Well I'll be damned."

"You already are, my friend, you're down here."

"Isn't that the truth? I can't believe that we've actually contacted them. Can you tell where they're located?"

"I'm afraid not. All we have is their network address."

Now it was Jackson's turn to nod. "Now the question is, is my birth mother even there, and will they tell me if she is?"

"I don't know, but why wouldn't they? At this point, what harm could it possibly do?"

Jackson noticed his hands slightly shaking again. The last few days had been incredibly difficult, obviously. The possibility of connecting with his mother was the only thing he had to look forward to in whatever time remained in his life.

Paul noticed his new friend's nervous tension and said, "Try to calm down, partner. When they call us back, you need to be on top of your game. Not to add to your anxiety or anything." He smiled at Jackson.

"Yeah, really, no anxiety here."

At the appointed time, an LED lit on the console and an electronic tone sounded.

Paul said, "This is your call, see the video screen?"

The video monitor showed blue text on a black field, "Origins Research Team / Digital Network Address AC34FG"

Paul pressed a key and Jackson saw a very attractive young woman on the screen. A small inset of the video they were transmitting from their own equipment also appeared. At the moment, the inset showed both Paul and Jackson.

Paul spoke first, "This is Chief Petty Officer Gutshall at Highpoint Special Facility."

The woman on the other end of the connection said, "Please stand by while I transfer your call to Dr. Morefield."

Another click and the screen momentarily went dark. A moment later it filled with the image of a thin man wearing a black turtleneck shirt sitting at a desk. "This is Steve Morefield at the Origins Research Team."

Jackson looked directly into the camera, which zoomed in on his face. "Sir, my name is Jackson Hall. I'm here at this facility because I am, well, I suppose it's more accurate to say that I used to be, a member of the House of Representatives from Orange County, California."

Morefield asked, "How are you holding up? If memory serves, Site SF is beneath the main FEMA facility in Virginia, correct?"

"Yes sir, that is correct. I can't speak for everyone here, of course, but I would have to say that we are alive and somewhat well, at least physically. Not so much emotionally."

"I can imagine. Our physicists tell me that the radiation levels on most of the surface of the U.S. are lethal and will be for over ninety years."

"That agrees with what the FEMA people are telling us too. You appear to be safe also, may I ask where you are located?"

"You may ask, but now there really is no point in discussing our most closely guarded secret, is there? I think you already know that we're not in Cheyenne Mountain."

"Yes, we became aware of that in a most unfortunate manner. Sir, may I just offer my apologies for the military assault that took place there? At least please know that I was not part of that decision-making process."

"Of course. That would have been President L. Davis Brasington III, blessed be his name."

Jackson couldn't miss the spark of anger that showed in Morefield's voice and on his face.

"I'm afraid so, sir. I don't know what to say other than how desperately sorry I am for all that has transpired in the last several days."

"So why are you calling, Congressman? I don't think we have any business left to conduct with whatever remains of the government."

"Dr. Morefield, I would just like to talk with you for a few minutes as one person to another. I am not representing the government."

"Please call me Steve."

"Fine, and I am Jackson."

"What can I do for you, Jackson?"

"Okay, please bear with me while I make a long story short." Jackson related the events surrounding his search for his mother, including his hiring of a private investigator, the trips the P.I. had made to California and to West Virginia, which then culminated in his own meetings with Chuck Pearce and Air Force Colonel Diggs from the White House Military Office.

Morefield glared at Jackson. "So then you yourself were actually responsible for focusing the White House's attention on us?"

"I'm afraid that may be true, sir, but please believe that it was never my intention to do anything but locate my birth mother. I have now lost my adoptive parents in California, a very dear friend who used to work in the White House who was just trying to help me in my search, and many others on the surface to this terrible war."

"Yes, I'm sure that's the case. It wasn't your fault, I do realize that. We know more about the chain of events leading up to this day than you probably realize."

"You do? But tell me, the crazy old man in the hardware store in West Virginia obviously had no relationship to your team, right?"

"That crazy old man in West Virginia was Dr. Wesley Scarcia, the Chairman of the Board of the Foundation for the Study of the Origin of the Universe, which is, or rather was, the parent organization of the Origins Research Team."

"But the P.I. said that the man seemed to be somewhat disconnected from reality, that he was just a high school graduate pretending to be studying the universe."

"Well, then he was a good actor as well as a good person. He did his job admirably in the end. I just regret that we didn't have time to save him."

"He supposedly made a short phone call to a non-working number that used to be assigned to a military unit at Cheyenne Mountain."

"Dr. Scarcia did place a call to a special number and entered a code on the phone's keypad that sent an early warning signal to us that trouble may be brewing. All too obviously, he was right."

"But that number was in Colorado."

"Some very special people went to a lot of trouble to make it appear that way."

"I see, okay. But Steve, about my mother?"

"What's her name?"

"Connie Scarcia, supposedly the niece of the man you've identified as Dr. Scarcia."

Morefield sat back in his chair, the fingers of both hands held in a steeple at his chin. He thought for a moment before speaking again.

"Jackson, this whole situation is highly unorthodox, and to be honest with you, I'm uncertain about what to do with you."

"Please, sir, this is all I have left in my life. I've been trying to locate her since I was a child. My adoptive parents were terrific, but I've always wanted to meet and talk with my biological mother. It's unbelievably important to me."

"I can see that. Under these most unusual of circumstances, I will break protocol and tell you that there is a Connie Scarcia in our facility, and that she is a nurse."

"She's there? She's actually there?" He couldn't keep the excitement out of his voice.

"I don't know if she's your mother, and I'm not familiar with the circumstances that might have led up to your adoption if she is. Here's what I'll do. We'll speak with her and tell her about your call. I don't want to rush it, as I can't predict how she'll handle learning about all of this. Can you be at this station twenty-four hours from now?"

Jackson looked at Paul, who nodded his head.

"Yes, yes, I'll be here."

"Someone from my team will call you at that time. Connie Scarcia may or may not join that call. That will be her decision. Do you understand?"

"Yes, I understand, but please convey to her how important this is to me."

"We will, but please know that her wishes and well-being will be considered first and foremost."

"Yes sir, and thank you very much."

"Morefield out."

The connection went dark. Jackson was now trembling, barely able to speak. "I can't believe it. After all these years, I just can't believe it."

Paul said gently, "Just remember, partner, it hasn't happened yet, but I surely hope it does for your sake."

Chapter 42: ORT

Kathy, MED-11, was restocking one of the supply rooms in Med Central when she received an alert on her pager to call ADMIN-1. She quickly picked up the closest phone and entered ADMIN-1's private code. He picked up immediately and told her about the call he had just received from Site SF.

"Kathy, is Connie on duty there right now?"

"Yes, she is. What do you want me to say to her?"

"Tell her privately everything I've just told you. I don't know what the circumstances are surrounding this Jackson Hall. But he certainly believes that Connie is his birth mother. As her friend, and with your background as a mental health counselor, I don't know anyone better to break this news to her."

"Of course."

"Okay, make sure she understands that she is under no obligation to communicate with him. As a matter of fact, we're not even going to allow her to make that call unless you clear it. That way she can proceed with her life here mostly free of guilt if she really doesn't want to speak with him. Sound like a plan?"

"Sounds like a good plan. I'll let you know how it goes in a little while."

Kathy found Connie chatting with one of the radiology technicians on duty. Thankfully, this was a very slow day in Med Central.

"Hey, Connie, can you come with me? I want to show you something."

"Sure, Kat, what is it?"

Kathy motioned for Connie to walk along with her. When they came to an unoccupied examining room, the two nurses walked in and Kathy closed the door behind them.

"What's going on, Kathy? Is everything okay?"

After they were both seated, Kathy said, "Connie, do you remember the deep-breathing and muscle relaxation exercises I showed you?"

"Yeah, of course, why?"

"Well, I want you to use some of those techniques right now. I have something to tell you that might come as a shock.

"Kathy, what's going on?"

"Steve just received a call from a continuity of government facility known as the Highpoint Special Facility, or just Site SF, located underground in Virginia."

"Okay, so?"

"The call came from a young congressman named Jackson Hall. He had been representing a district around Orange County, California." Kathy watched her friend closely for any response.

"What does any of this have to do with me?"

"Connie, apparently he has spent most of his life searching for his biological mother, and he now believes that he has found her."

"What? You mean me? How could he, I mean, it's just not possible, there's no way that..." Her voice trailed off and her eyes filled with tears. "Oh my God, oh my God."

Kathy put her arm around her and let her friend sob uncontrollably. She spoke quietly and gently, "It's okay, it's okay. I'm here for you. We're all here for you. We're family. You're not alone." She continued repeating these reassuring words for several minutes until Connie had partially regained her composure.

"It was so long ago. I've tried not to think about it. This just isn't possible."

Now she spoke in a torrent, telling Kathy the unhappy story of her youth and adolescence, things she didn't want to remember, let alone tell someone else. But Kathy was her friend and she was easy to talk with. Connie instinctively knew that if anyone in the world would refrain from judging her, it would be Kathy Carver.

Nearly an hour passed. Kathy's level of concern for Connie had increased dramatically as she listened to her story unfold. She was faced with the possibility of communicating with the son she hadn't seen since he was an infant, but whom she would never have the opportunity to meet, to touch, to hold. Plus, the nuclear holocaust that had been unleashed on the earth obviously had everyone's emotions tightly wound. Connie was typically viewed as a hard-nosed nurse with a tough shell. But now this news seemed to have completely devastated her friend. Connie repeated several times that this was more than she could handle.

"Connie, I don't want you to be alone right now. Trust me, I'm your friend. We're going to go to a private room here in Med Central and you're going to lie down for a while. I'm going to give you a sedative to help take the edge off this for you, and you're going to rest for a few hours. Then, we're going to talk some more and decide what to do next, if anything. Steve was emphatic that you're under no obligation whatsoever to speak with Jackson. We will handle it for you if you want."

"Kathy, I can't possibly lie down now. I can't relax. There are things I should say, I mean, do, I mean..."

"Connie, you know me well enough to understand that you really don't have a choice about what I'm telling you to do now, don't you?"

She briefly smiled through her tears, "Yes, I'm probably one of the very few people here who know how you and Steve Morefield first met. You pulled him through a very rough time, certainly worse than mine. Of course, you had the help of the FBI and a whole hospital full of doctors and nurses dedicated to making him well, didn't you?"

"Yes I did, not to mention a newly-elected president who took both a professional and a personal interest in his well-being. And that meant that I had a lot of latitude in treating him, including holding him in a hospital against his will."

"Don't even think about putting me in that position!"

Kathy looked at her with the same intense bright blue eyes that Steve Morefield had seen so many years ago when he awakened in a hospital bed following an aborted suicide attempt. "Connie, you are my friend and you are my colleague. I wouldn't hesitate for a minute to lock you up or do whatever I think is necessary to insure your safety and wellbeing. But I can tell by the look on your face that you already know that. So right now, you will do as I say. Understood?"

"Yes ma'am, understood," she said with a half smile.

Kathy took her friend to a patient room in Med Central, gave her some medication, and tucked her into bed.

Since Kathy had administered the sedative by injection, Connie was already feeling groggy. "You're a true friend Kathy. A true fremd. Tank you, Kat..."

Kathy left her to sleep. Knowing the exact dosage and effect of the medication she had administered, she would return to the room before Connie awakened.

She walked down the hallway to a nurse's station and called ADMIN-1.

"She's in pretty bad shape. I gave her some meds to relax her and make her sleep for a while. She told me the whole story. This is something that she has never really faced head on or resolved. In a few hours, she can make the decision about what to do next. I explained that she didn't have to do anything. But my gut tells me that when all is said and done, she'll want to talk with him. And that's probably the best thing for both of them. It's tragic that they're never going to have the opportunity to meet in person though."

ADMIN-1 thanked her and made a suggestion on how to proceed with the contact if Connie decided to do so.

"Okay Steve. She is very shaken, but I think that with our support she'll be okay. I'll see you in a few hours." Kathy disconnected the call and sat down behind the station. One of the monitor screens in front of her showed Connie sound asleep in the hospital bed. *But what will tomorrow hold for her?*

Chapter 43: Contact

When Connie awoke, Kathy was right there at her side. They talked for hours, late into the night. By the end of what had effectively been a *de facto* therapy session, Kathy was reasonably certain that Connie would get through this rough patch without further decompensating or acting out by trying to harm herself. Nonetheless, with an abundance of caution, she asked Connie to agree to a plan of care that would last at least until she had the conversation with her son. The plan called for Connie to remain at Med Central for the rest of the night, where she would be monitored by the nursing staff on duty. Then, Connie asked Kathy if she would stay with her during the course of the videoconference, with Kathy remaining out of camera range.

———

ADMIN-1 provided his office for their use, and about thirty minutes before the appointed time, the two women entered the room. Connie sat at the desk so that she would be in view of the videoconference camera, while Kathy sat discreetly off to one side.

Connie was visibly tense, and she seemed momentarily startled when the video wall switched from its normal outside mountain view to just a black field with blue text, "FEMA Special Facility / Digital Network Address

FEMASF." Arianna was setting up the call from her console at the receptionist desk, and it was agreed that she would not begin the live feed from ORT to Site SF until Connie gave the okay.

———————

Jackson arrived at the communications center nearly an hour early. He had nothing else to do and so he thought he could at least talk to Paul until it was time for the ORT facility to call.

As the digital clock ticked down to just five minutes remaining, Paul said, "Listen, I'm going to do something totally against regulations and leave you alone here during your call. The link has already been established, see?" as he pointed to the video display which once again showed the blue text on a black field coming from ORT. "All you have to do is press this key when their audio/video feed goes live, and then our feed will be transmitted to them. I'll be right outside, just let me know when you're done, okay?"

"Okay, Paul, thanks. I can't tell you how much I appreciate your doing this for me."

Paul hesitated a minute and then said, "You know, Jackson, I've been stationed here for two years now, and I've never seen all of this equipment being put to a better use than it is right now for this purpose. I hope you get to see your mother. Take your time." He left the room and quietly closed the door behind him.

Jackson turned his attention back to the video monitor and the digital clock on the console, wondering all the while whether he would finally see his mother.

Suddenly, the video feed came alive, showing the same attractive blond operator wearing a wireless headset whom he had seen during yesterday's call. Jackson stared at the screen for a beat and then remembered to press the key to begin his transmission.

The ORT operator spoke first, "Site SF, this is Origins Research Team. I see you are there, Congressman."

"Yes ma'am, I am."

Having already received Connie's signal to proceed, Arianna said, "I am connecting you with Connie Scarcia in five, four, three, two, one."

And immediately, the ORT feed switched to the chief administrator's office he had seen the day before, but this time he saw a woman with red hair and wearing medical scrubs sitting behind the huge desk.

Jackson had to clear his throat before he could utter a word.

Connie watched the ID display from Site SF on the room's massive video wall cut to a live feed. A handsome young man in his mid- to late-twenties looked at her and cleared his throat.

He appeared to compose himself and then said, "My name is Jackson Hall, and if you are Connie Scarcia, a nurse who used to work for Century Palms Hospital in Los Angeles and later for Travel Pro Nursing, then I believe you are my biological mother."

Connie felt a lump form in her throat and tears welled in her eyes. "Jackson, I am that person. May I ask if you have any birthmarks?"

Now it was Jackson's turn to show his emotions as his "professional" voice gave way to a much softer tone. "I have a large brown spot on my upper left thigh."

With tears now running freely down her face, Connie said, "Oh Jackson, you are my son. I am so very sorry. You must think that I never cared for you since I put you up for adoption." Jackson started to speak but Connie continued, "No, please hear me out before you say anything else. I was little more than a child myself when you were born. I had no money, no stable home, and no good prospects. Before I found out that I was pregnant, I had been a substance abuser. Jackson, the only good decision I ever made in my life up until that time was to try to make sure that you had a good home and loving, capable parents. Please believe that I did it for you. I just…couldn't…give you the kind of home and upbringing you deserved. I loved you so much, son, that I had to let you go. It was the hardest thing I've ever done in my life."

———

What he heard caused any semblance of fortitude to disappear as tears filled his eyes. This was it, the moment he had dreamed about, planned for, and worked toward for much of his life. And somehow, he was nearly speechless, with no idea what to say next.

He hesitated and then said, "I have been trying so hard for so long to contact you, and now…" He grabbed a tissue to wipe his eyes before continuing. "So you do care about me?"

"Oh yes, of course I do. The adoption process was double-blind, so I had no way to find you after my addiction treatment and when I got my life together. I just had to trust that you were in good hands and that you would have a chance for a decent life. And now look at you. I understand that you are a member of Congress."

"Yes, I went to college and then law school. And now, I'm sorry to say that I was successful in mounting a primary challenge to the incumbent and then winning the general election largely on the coattails of President Brasington. Even I can see what a bad choice that was for me, let alone the nation."

"Don't dwell on that now, Jackson. We all make bad decisions. I'm a living example of that. You accomplished more than most people could ever hope for. Try to take some comfort in that at least."

"There's something else, but I don't even know how to address you?"

Connie smiled kindly at him and said, "Whatever you're comfortable with. Connie, mother, mom. The important thing is that we're getting to meet each other."

"Connie…," and he shook his head, "No, I'd prefer mom. Not everything I've done would likely have your approval. One of the people I met during my brief political career was Chuck Pearce, a White House staffer.

He helped me a lot in my efforts to find you. Much to my surprise, we fell in love with each other. He's deceased now, as far as I know. But I was raised by a fundamentalist minister and his wife, and I can guarantee you that homosexuality was not on their list of approved lifestyles."

"Well, son, that doesn't matter a wit to me. Here in this project, we are very tolerant of all races and lifestyles. As long as it doesn't hurt anyone else, it's considered a private matter. You might be interested to learn that we don't even have formal marriage here, just registered partners. Gender is irrelevant. So, Jackson, if you were here, nobody would think twice about it. And by the way, the last time I heard, ten percent of the population of the United States was gay. You see?"

"So, you accept me then, just as I am?"

"Oh Jackson, dear Jackson, of course I do. But it really only matters that you accept yourself for who you are."

Jackson was having difficulty maintaining his composure, and he couldn't help but notice that his voice was somewhat weak and strained. He felt a tingling sensation along his arms and legs.

"I wish I could be there with you, Mom, but I'm afraid fate has taken that opportunity away from us."

"Yes. Well, fate and President L. Davis Brasington III, blessed be his name," Connie replied.

Her son's face flashed with anger. "Yes, my hero, President Brasington. I truly believed he was going to do good things for the country, I really did. But I was wrong. Dead wrong, as it turns out."

"Son, are you okay there where you are? Not that there's anything I can do about it now, it's just that I hope you are."

"I wish I could truthfully tell you yes, but things here are, well, conditions are deteriorating day by day. There's something wrong with the air handling system and it's much warmer than it should be. We're receiving smaller portions of food, and we can't get any answers about how long our supply will last. Do you really want to hear more?"

"Of course I do, even though it's bad, and I'm so sorry that it is."

"Well, morale is in the tank. The elected officials here know that there is no country left to govern. No people left to serve and no resources left to allocate. And, the FEMA people tell us that we won't be returning to the surface because it will be deadly radioactive for almost a hundred years. Add to that limited medical resources. We obviously have no Oncoleve in the facility to treat cancer. And we've had three suicides so far, including two of the three Homeland Security police assigned to protect the president. Of course, they both had easy access to firearms. It's not a pretty picture."

"It sounds awful. Again, I am so sorry. Will we be able to talk again?"

"I would like to, Mom, more than I can say. But I think we shouldn't plan on it. I just don't know how long…," At this point, Jackson broke down completely, covering his face with his hands to hide his tears.

"It's okay, I understand. I hope this doesn't sound patronizing to you, but despite the years and years during which we had no contact, please know that I am proud of you. I…I love you, Jackson. I always have, and I always will."

"I love you too, Mom," he said through his tears. "I guess I have to go now. The communications guy was kind enough to break all kinds of rules to let me alone in here for our talk. I should get him back in before he gets court-martialed or something. I'm, uh, going to say goodbye now, and I hope you will be able to live a full and happy life. I wish you the very best." He hesitated, and then slowly said, "Please remember me."

Connie couldn't stop herself from crying now. She knew that this was their first and last contact as two adults. "I will always remember you, son. Thank you for trying so hard to reach me. It means the world to me."

Jackson just nodded his head. "Goodbye, Mom."

"Goodbye, Jackson."

The video wall in ADMIN-1's office returned to the outside mountain view. Connie could only look mournfully at Kathy, unable to say anything.

Kathy said, "Connie, you did great. Bless your heart, you told him all of the good things and none of the bad things. That was a real gift to him."

Still crying, Connie replied, "What possible good would it have done for me to tell him that he was the child of a rapist?"

"None, sweetie, none at all. Come over here and let me hug you."

And slowly she came from behind the desk, and the two friends embraced each other tightly.

Chapter 44: Site SF

The monitor built into the console in front of Jackson went black. He cried until he felt that he had no tears left. He knew that he had to let Paul back into the room, so he composed himself as much as he could and then opened the door a crack. Paul was standing against the opposite wall, and Jackson gestured for him to come in.

"Did you get to talk with her?"

"Yes I did, thank you."

"How was she? Are you both okay with each other?"

Jackson actually managed a small smile. "Yes, it went better than I could have hoped, and we are definitely okay with each other."

"That's great, partner. I can't tell you how happy I am for you."

"I couldn't have done it without your help. I want you to know that."

Paul started to shake Jackson's hand, but Jackson put his arms around him instead.

Paul said, "It's probably the one truly moral thing I've done since I've been in this place."

Still embracing Paul in his arms, Jackson said, "You have a good heart, Paul. I'm really very sorry. Please forgive me."

"What are you talking about?"

Paul had barely gotten the last word out when Jackson drove his right knee into his friend's groin, causing him to double over in pain with a shocked gasp. Then, utilizing a technique that he had learned as a college wrestler but which he had been strictly forbidden from actually using, with his right arm he applied a lateral vascular neck restraint, also known as a sleeper hold, which compressed Paul's carotid arteries and jugular veins. Temporarily deprived of oxygenated blood, he collapsed into unconsciousness within a few seconds.

Jackson quickly laid him out on the floor, removed Paul's service handgun from its holster, and then using some surgical tape he had discreetly removed from the medical office, he securely bound Paul's hands and legs. He placed his handkerchief in his mouth and then covered his mouth with more of the tape. He didn't really know how long Paul would be incapacitated or when someone else might come to the communications room, so he knew that he had to act quickly. He tucked the handgun into his waistband and pulled his shirt over it. He slowly opened the door to the corridor and then closed it quickly behind him.

It didn't take long for him to walk to the facility's small makeshift chapel where President Brasington was conducting one of his multiple daily prayer services. Jackson entered the room quietly and took one of the many empty seats. He was pleased to see that the president's one remaining Mustard guard was not in the room. It appeared that even the guard could only stand to listen to the same sermon a finite number of times. Plus, given the present circumstances for everyone in Site SF, the need for protection was now viewed as minimal.

The president, however, had managed to find many silver linings in the otherwise dark cloud of their existence. He reasoned that this destruction of the God-less had been necessary, and that it would fall upon himself and his followers to begin a new and better society, one which would be deeply steeped in his own religious values and the teachings of the Old Testament. Indeed, he told anyone who would listen, this had been God's plan all along, and that they were the chosen few tasked with bringing about a rebirth of this new "enlightened" society.

When government officials from the FEMA contingent warned that the radiation level on the surface would be lethal to human beings for a far longer period of time than their own lifespans, Brasington told his flock to "just have faith and patience in God's will."

Jackson had heard it all before, of course. What else was left for Brasington to say? It was during the familiar line when the president was again praising the Lord for bringing forth the new world order that Jackson abruptly stood up and interrupted the proceedings.

"You fucking idiot! You horse's ass of the first order! Don't you see what you've done? Our families... are dead! Our homes are gone! Our nation, our world, is gone! There is no new world order, you incompetent blathering fool!" He took the handgun from his waistband and quickly fired three shots at Brasington. And being a very good shot, he hit him in the head, the heart, and the groin, not necessarily in that order.

Turning to his shocked colleagues, he said, "Think what might have been saved had this boob stayed in his pulpit and never sought public office!" He hesitated for a minute and then continued, "There is no honor whatsoever in what I've just done, but under the circumstances, hopefully there will be some honor in this."

He then aimed the weapon at his own head and pulled the trigger. Following the four deafening blasts of gunfire within the enclosed space, the others in the room merely sat in stunned, disbelieving silence.

Chapter 45: Assessment & Recriminations

One week after the assault at Cheyenne Mountain, ADMIN-1 and his senior staff met in the videoconference room to assess the situation in the world as well as in ORT. Generally, the major world powers had all become involved in the quickest and most devastating war the Earth had ever witnessed. All major cities and defense installations in the United States, the United Kingdom, the European Union, Russia, and China, as well as a host of smaller nations, had been virtually wiped out. Radiation sickness was spreading to those people on the surface who had survived the initial nuclear exchange. In the United States, the only remnants of government now existed at Site SF, where sporadic broadcasts were being made via shortwave radio assuring "everyone" that the "situation was under control" and that "citizens should avoid panic."

"This is unbelievable," ADMIN-1 said to his staff. "The plan we followed was designed only to bring enough public pressure on the government to discourage future attempts to find and terminate our work. Unfortunately, the new administration had been so bereft of any working diplomacy to deal with the real world, so hostile to foreign nations, and so incompetent to its core that this tragic result would have occurred with or without any provocation that we may have provided. Nonetheless, we are where we are, and our mission now will be necessarily modified to work with the colonists at Lunar One to try to insure the survival of humanity in some form or fashion.

"One significant concern that I've had, aside from the obvious devastation on the surface, is the viability of our communication link with the Lunar One colony. Our communications people are working on that as we speak. For the moment, the world-wide electromagnetic disturbance caused by the nuclear blasts has disrupted nearly all communications. But, our equipment was EMP-shielded and our antennas and satellite dishes were protected to the greatest extent possible. Once again I can't say enough about the planning and preparation that went into the design and location of this facility to protect it against even this most devastating of events.

"As you know, we have a self-contained food and water supply due to hydroponics and to the latest technology, so other than a change in diet, which is to say less, if any, meat, we should be okay. Our air supply is equally protected."

"But sir," Julie interrupted, "since we obviously can't procreate, our own work is obviously time-limited by our own useful life-spans."

"That's true, Julie, except that we will be supplying our knowledge and scientific research findings to Lunar One as quickly as possible. Additionally, there is another contingency plan to bring in a group of new recruits of both genders, fertile and of child-bearing age, to a level just above us which has previously been closed off and unused."

Gasps of surprise erupted from around the table.

"But where will this group of recruits come from?" asked Julie. "Radiation poisoning is spreading quickly, and we don't know if any areas on the surface will be spared from it."

"True again, which is why we have to work quickly once our own physicists in residence, working with the meteorology and medical teams, determine whether it is safe for us to go to the surface, and if so, for how long. Our communications team is also listening on a broad range of frequencies for any remaining commercial broadcast stations, Amateur Radio operators, and so forth. I expect that within another forty-eight hours or so, we'll know a great deal more than we do now about the state of the world." Murmurs of agreement came from all members of the staff.

Chapter 46: Lunar One

Arianna was seated as usual at the ADMIN reception station when a unique signal sounded on her communications console. She pressed the key and answered, "Origins Research Team, how may I help you?"

The pleasant male voice on the other end of the connection replied, "This is Lunar One Actual calling for Origins Actual."

Arianna understood exactly who was on the line and what she needed to do. "Sir, please give me a moment to connect you with Origins Actual."

"Of course, thank you. I'll be standing by."

Arianna placed the call on hold and pressed the key that would connect her directly to ADMIN-1 in either his office or his private quarters. He answered immediately, "Yes, Arianna, what's up?"

"Sir, I have a call for you from Lunar One Actual."

"Alright! Put it through to my office, please. Do you have video or just audio?"

"Both, sir. I'm connecting you now."

ADMIN-1 watched the video wall in his office change abruptly from the normal mountain scene to the face of his counterpart, the chief administrator of Lunar One. "Bill, I can't tell you how relieved I am to hear from you. We were concerned that our communications link with you may have been lost permanently during the war."

"You're relieved? My friend, up here we were all afraid that you and your team had been wiped out. My God, what an inferno down there! Did you survive unscathed?"

"We're okay, and you're right about the inferno. Can you believe that this has actually happened?"

"No, and yes. We were instructed, as were you, to hope for the best but to prepare for the worst. It's a damn good thing that we did!"

"Indeed it is. It looks like Lunar One now carries the primary burden for the survival of humanity. No pressure on you though, right?"

"Right! We are well equipped in terms of power and water. We have a small nuclear generator much like yours, and we're making our own water. Our food supply will now be limited to what we can produce hydroponically, of course, but we're prepared to support the entire colony with it." He hesitated for a moment and continued in a somber tone, "Of course, our plans for establishing another colony here will be on hold for a while, and we've had to scrap our dreams of moving deeper into space."

"Yes, of course. Do you have the ability to either resupply or rescue the good folks on the International Space Station?"

"We will be able to make one trip to bring them back here. The ISS will be closed down permanently, I'm afraid."

"One thing at a time, old friend, and one day at a time. How are your colonists holding up?"

"It's rough, Steve, they've virtually all lost friends and family on Earth. They're understandably traumatized, and our medical team will be busy helping them for a long time."

"Yes, I'm sure. We'll be doing the same here, although due to the nature of our personnel complement, there isn't as much loss of family for our people. Still, we've always been working to improve the lot of mankind on the surface, and it certainly won't be the same now."

"Have you had any communications from the surface? Are there survivors?"

"We've been monitoring all radio frequencies. There are survivors, and indeed there are a very few areas of Earth that, so far at least, seem to be totally untouched by radiation poisoning."

"That's terrific news. How will you proceed from here?"

"We're working on that. There is one level of our facility which was reserved for an eventuality like this, and we will be looking into the feasibility of bringing some men and women of child-bearing age down here in order to learn and reproduce and keep the project going into the future. It's important, because while we can and will transmit all of our research findings up to Lunar One for your use, we've got a very talented bunch of people here who have much, much more to offer."

"That's great, absolutely great. Our staff and colonists are going to be so happy to hear that you're all alive and well."

"Maybe it would be a good idea, once things settle down a bit, for us to put our counterpart physical scientists, engineers, and social scientists in touch with each other on a regular basis. It would be good for morale as well as for information sharing."

"Roger that. Just let us know when you're ready. I'd even like to let one of our media crew interview you for broadcast throughout the colony. That would be very helpful for morale here."

"No problem. Give us a week or two and we should have more to report to your community."

Bill looked directly through the camera at his old friend, "I guess I don't really believe that it has come to this. How could humanity have been so foolish, so reckless, so prone to believe whatever was being fed to it by the media?"

"I don't know. I'm afraid we will be wrestling with that question for many years to come." He hesitated for a moment, then said, "Listen Bill, there's something I can tell you that will definitely brighten your day."

"Please do."

As ADMIN-1 spoke, Bill's eyes widened in disbelief, and then his jaw dropped. "Does your team know about this yet, Steve?" he asked.

"Not yet, but they will soon."

"Absolutely amazing. I just can't imagine how…"

"I know. I was taken totally by surprise."

"Well, all I can say for now then is to keep up the good work, okay?"

"Of course."

"Do you remember what we used to say in the old days when it came time to part company?"

"How could I ever forget: Leave us leave."

Bill's face actually formed a small smile, and with a twinkle in his blue Irish eyes, he returned the phrase, "Leave us leave."

And the connection between Earth and Moon was terminated.

Chapter 47: Partners

In one sense, it was merely a formality. Steve and Julie had been living together in her quarters virtually from the time he had moved down to ADMIN. And with all that had been going on since the assault on Cheyenne Mountain and the onslaught on the surface caused by what had quickly become World War III, it had been a very busy time for both of them. They had both been assigned to work along with John Dillon on planning and arranging for the opening of the unused level for a new mini-colony of recruits of child-bearing age. The three of them had been coordinating closely with ADMIN-2 on this project, and despite Steve's initial misgivings about working with him, he had found Dick to be a careful planner, an excellent administrator, and that his formal education as a sociology major and his practical experience as an accomplished politician had proven to be invaluable to the task at hand.

But despite all of the work and turmoil, they had continued to make time for themselves, and their relationship continued to deepen. Steve thought it was time to "pop the question" to Julie. Following a long day at work, they sat together on the sofa in the living room of her quarters. "Julie, I've been thinking."

"That's an encouraging sign," she teased.

"Yes, well, I was thinking that, if you felt the same way, that I would like for us to register with SOC as having a committed relationship."

Julie looked at him with a slight smile. "I don't know whether to make it easy for you and tell you that I was wondering when you were going to ask me, or whether to give you a hard time and make you get down on your knees and ask, um, respectfully."

Steve returned her smile. "You know me too well, Julie Reynolds. Either way is fine with me."

Julie chuckled. "I would be pleased and honored to be your registered partner, and we'll save the kneeling and begging for another time, how's that?"

"Yes ma'am, anytime, anywhere."

"Be careful what you wish for, Steve. I am learning that I have a devious mind when it comes to you."

"Indeed you do."

"Maybe we should celebrate!"

"I like that idea too!" Steve replied.

"Of course you do, but I didn't mean in THAT way."

"Okay, what do you have in mind?"

She smiled the enigmatic smile that Steve knew meant she wasn't about to reveal her plan just yet.

"Okay then, I guess I'll wait and see, won't I?"

"Yes, you will," she replied.

―――――◆―――――

An envelope addressed to both of them arrived at Julie's quarters several days later. The nicely printed note inside invited them to ADMIN-1's residence suite the following evening for dinner in celebration of their new formal relationship.

"I'm impressed," Steve said. "This is your doing?"

"I just mentioned to Kathy that we were going to register as partners, that's all."

"Yeah right, whenever you and Kathy get together..."

"Now, now, be nice," Julie said in mock admonishment.

Steve just looked at her and shook his head. "I meant that only in the best sense."

"Of course you did."

"Well, are we supposed to RSVP?"

"It's already taken care of, my darling."

"Why am I not surprised?"

"Because you think you know me."

"Oh, I only think I know you?"

Julie just grinned. "It's really quite an honor. Do you know how many team members have seen ADMIN-1's suite? Most of the ADMIN staff have never even been there. He's a very private sort and isn't taken to entertaining on that level."

"Okay then, I understand. What should I expect?"

"What should you expect? Expect to have a good time, of course."

———

They had been asked to arrive at ADMIN-1's office at 1700 ORT, so they left Julie's quarters at about

1645. "This is not one of those times when you want to arrive fashionably late," Julie said as they walked out of the door and into the corridor.

"I thought we were going to his quarters," Steve said.

"We are. His office is the gateway to his residence area. Did you notice the door behind his desk when you were in his office?"

"Yes, in fact he entered that way when I was waiting for him during our first meeting."

"Well, that leads to his suite. I only know this because Kathy has had me over several times for a visit."

"Ah, Kathy again."

"Now hush, Kathy is my very best girlfriend, and her advice has been very helpful to me when it comes to men."

"So I've noticed," he said with a grin.

She grinned back at him.

They continued walking and arrived at the AD-MIN reception area by 1655. Arianna was there to greet them, and she ushered them first into the chief administrator's office, and then knocked lightly on the door behind his desk that Steve now realized led to ADMIN-1's quarters. Kathy opened the door and welcomed the guests inside. Dressed in a black leather catsuit, Kathy was every bit as gorgeous as Steve had remembered from his very first medical exam after he had arrived at the project. But he was quite pleased with himself that he noted this in passing only, because Julie was now the sole object of his affection. They walked through a short hallway and then into a wonderfully warm and inviting living room, much larger than any he had seen previously in ORT. There was the usual large flat-screen video monitor on one wall, framed by some very high-end speakers. A step-down conversation pit with marvelously comfortable-looking sofas and chairs dominated the center of the room.

Kathy said, "Steve, Julie has seen our suite on several occasions, but would you like a brief tour?"

"Yes, please, by all means."

She graciously showed them the kitchen, a private dining room, the master bedroom with a king-size bed and the same kind of large flat-screen video display as the one in the living room, and then the master bath with a Jacuzzi big enough to accommodate several people. She pointed in the direction of a door leading from their bedroom and said that "her Steve" was just finishing up a few things in his private office and that he would join them shortly. She also indicated that there was a guest suite attached to their quarters, but she didn't offer to give them a tour of that area.

As they came back to the living room, Steve commented that something certainly smelled delicious in the kitchen. Julie said, "Kathy is treating us to her world-famous pot roast tonight. I love it!" Kathy smiled and nodded.

"How long have you two known each other," Steve asked the two friends.

Kathy and Julie looked at each other briefly, and Kathy said, "We knew each other casually for a couple of years prior to the Epoch. We became close friends after we arrived here."

"Okay, so Julie tells me that you were in the Air Force, and I know that she was an LAPD detective. How did you happen to meet?"

Kathy turned to Julie. "Is he always this curious?"

"Always!"

Turning back to Steve, Kathy said, "I was in the Air Force and I was on TDY, that's temporary duty, with the Military Office at the White House."

"So how did that get you close to someone in the Los Angeles Police Department?"

Kathy asked Julie, "You haven't told him what you were doing between the LAPD and ORT, have you?"

"No, he already thinks he knows everything about me, so I figured he deserved a surprise or two."

"Good girl," Kathy said. "You're learning well."

Speaking directly to Steve again, Kathy said, "Well, then, you might want to know that your new partner left the LAPD in order to join the Presidential Protective Division of the U.S. Secret Service, and that's how we first met each other."

Steve's jaw dropped as he looked at Julie. "You never told me that."

She smiled. "You never asked."

"Okay, okay, I'm obviously outnumbered here. The two of you make a wonderful tag team."

Just then, ADMIN-1 came into the room. "Welcome to both of you, and congratulations!"

Almost simultaneously, Julie and Steve said, "Thank you, sir."

"Come on now, no 'sirs' this evening. This is a social gathering in celebration of your new commitment to each other. Listen, I do have a serious question for you."

Julie said, "Yes sir. I mean, sure."

ADMIN-1 chuckled and looked at Steve and said, "You're a lucky guy, because Julie is a very special lady."

"Yes sir, I know she is."

"Remember, no 'sirs' this evening, okay?"

"I'll try."

"Good. Now my question is for both of you. I happen to know that Kathy has prepared enough food to feed a small army, and yet there are only four of us here. I wondered how you would feel about inviting a few more of our colleagues to your party?"

Julie and Steve looked at each other briefly, nodded, and Julie said, "That would be great."

"Okay then," and ADMIN-1 picked up a handset. He must have been connected directly to Arianna, and he said, "Please give those other folks a call and ask them if they're available to join us this evening." He put the handset back on its cradle. "Let's see who shows up then, shall we?" he said with a grin.

Steve thought that someone would have to be dead or dying to pass up an invitation like this, even if it did come at the last minute.

The four of them made small talk for a short time, until there was a muted knock on the door. Kathy made her way to the door and came back through the hallway with ADMIN-2.

The chief administrator said, "Dick, welcome, glad you could make it on such short notice. We're celebrating Steve and Julie's decision to register their partnership."

"That's wonderful news, congratulations to both of you! But now for the important thing, is that Kathy's pot roast my nose detects?"

They all laughed, and Kathy said, "Yes, Dick, that is my pot roast you have detected." She said to everyone, "It happens to be his favorite dish."

Another knock at the door and the scene played out once more, only this time Kathy returned with John Dillon, formerly of the United States Army.

"John, come on in here," ADMIN-1 said, once again explaining the reason for the gathering.

"Well, I'm honored to be here with you all. Thank you very much for inviting me."

"We're all glad you're here too, John, and we might even work in a little business this evening if Kathy will let me get away with it."

Kathy gave "her Steve" a mock look of warning, "Have I ever been able to stop you?"

"I can think of a time or two," ADMIN-1 said with a wink.

Another muted knock on the door. ADMIN-1 said, "This should be our final guest for the evening."

Kathy came back through the hallway saying, "Julie, I think you may know this person."

"Connie!" Julie rushed over to give her friend a hug.

Looking ever so slightly askance at the new arrival, Steve said, "Ah yes, I remember you very well indeed."

"I hope you don't hold grudges, Steve, I was just doing my job."

"And you did it very well, I might add. Although I wasn't too thrilled with…"

Everyone else except for John Dillon interrupted Steve with, "the full body cavity search!"

"That would be correct," Steve said.

"I'm kind of glad I missed out on that part," Dillon said.

Connie came over to him and said, "Oh honey, I hate to tell you this, but you didn't really miss out on it, you just weren't aware of what was going on."

"Oh, okay then," Dillon replied, his face turning a light shade of red.

The women giggled at his discomfiture, and AD-MIN-1 said to Dick, Dillon, and Steve, "Come, let us gather together to speak of manly things and ban these wenches to the kitchen!"

They scurried to the conversation pit to get away from a chorus of boos and hisses from the three women.

———————

Dinner had been a huge hit, as anyone who had been treated to Kathy's hospitality before would have expected. They had just finished dessert when ADMIN-1 tapped his spoon on his glass and invited everyone to join him in the living room. They all took seats in the conversation pit, ADMIN-1 and Kathy sitting side-by-side on a sofa.

"Steve and Julie, I hope you won't mind if we take just a few minutes for another celebration?"

They both nodded their heads enthusiastically in agreement.

He stood up and said, "John, come on over here please."

Puzzled, John got up from his seat and joined AD-MIN-1.

"For weeks now, John has been working very hard on our preparations to open the unoccupied level above us for the purpose of bringing in some new recruits of child-bearing age who will join us here to learn what we're doing, and then, along with us, prepare the next generation of scientists and staff so that the work of the Origins Research Team can continue beyond our lifespans. Dick, Steve, and Julie have been working with him very closely on everything from logistics, selection of recruits, to actually getting the physical space ready to house, feed, and care for these new young people who will be joining us.

"When John and I first met to discuss his decision to remain here with us, he expressed his concern that his background as an engineer and training as a military officer may not be useful to the project. However, I think it is now apparent to all of us just how wrong he was about that. His life experience is exactly what we needed to organize this new major addition to our work, and I want to thank you, John, for all of your efforts on our behalf to date." ADMIN-1 applauded and the others joined him as Dillon's face once again turned a light shade of red.

"Please now, I'm just glad that I can contribute."

ADMIN-1 continued before Dillon could say anything more, "But John there is a really serious problem here."

"Uh oh," Dillon replied.

"Yes, and the problem is that for a few weeks now, John has been going about his duties, working with other members of the community, and nobody quite knows how to address him. He's not comfortable with Colonel, and that leaves either his first or last name. But everyone else here has a formal position descriptor.

"So, John," he said as he removed a brand new name badge from his pocket, "it's high time that we correct this problem, isn't it gang?"

His colleagues, now standing too, replied with a chorus of "Yes!" and "Hear hear!"

"Therefore, John, it is my pleasure to welcome you formally as the 416th member of the Origins Research Team. But what about the rest of your position descriptor? Well, I would like to announce this evening that the new recruits who will be joining us, as well as the existing staff members who will be working with them full-time, will carry the highly appropriate position descriptor of LIFE. And finally, John, since I am hereby appointing you as the administrator in charge of the new LIFE level, your badge reads 'LIFE-416,' the first badge to carry this new descriptor."

Everyone applauded heartily and came over to shake Dillon's hand.

"I don't know what to say, except thank you, thank you all again for bringing me into this very special place and making me feel at home, especially considering everything that happened before this. I really don't know what else to say," and his voice cracked with emotion.

"What would your military training have you say, John?" ADMIN-1 asked.

"Yes sir. I'll do my best sir!"

Then, turning to Steve, ADMIN-1 said, "Now as to you, ADMIN-415, since you joined us in ADMIN, you've been working on various projects as assigned and doing a fine job. Your help with the new LIFE level has been particularly appreciated by ADMIN-2 and myself. But now we're going to have to pull you away from fighting fires and get you started on some real work," he said with a smile. Turning back to the whole group again, he continued, "One of the many challenges facing us as we set about to bring in a new group of recruits for the primary purpose of continuing the human species on Earth involves education. Think about it. The new people we bring down here will be in good physical health and will inevitably come to us with many different levels of formal education, as well as many different types of life experience. We also hope that they will be as emotionally healthy as is possible considering that most of the world has been devastated by World War III. Our medical team will, of course, be dealing with the post-traumatic stress aspects.

"But these people will have been removed from their home and work environments, and many of them will want to be productive members of our community beyond just their single most important task of procreation. In many cases, this will require special training to bring them up to speed with whichever part of ORT is best suited for them. Then, of course, we will be having children in the LIFE level. Children who will be needing a full range of educational opportunities. In short, one of our most important tasks in the future will be to provide this education and to do it right. So we need someone like you, Steve, who has a great deal of experience in both the theory and practice of education and educational administration."

Seeing what was coming, Steve said, "I wasn't born in a railroad town, sir, but I can hear the train coming down the tracks."

Everyone chuckled as ADMIN-1 continued, "I'm sure you can, so let me be the first to congratulate you as you assume your new assignment, in effect, as our secretary of education. You won't have too much to do, just design an educational system suited for a small group of both adult and traditional age students that will cover everything from pre-school to post-graduate training in nearly any discipline you can think of. Should be easy for someone with your talents, don't you think?"

"Uh, sure, sir, whatever you say."

"That's the spirit. Look, I know it sounds daunting, if not impossible. But you're going to have a lot of help. Virtually everyone now on staff will be assigned to assist you, and where appropriate, to take on the additional role of teacher or instructor. Think of the pool of talent we've got here in ORT. We have the very best group of physical scientists, social scientists, physicians, nurses, engineers, technologists, and more, than have ever been gathered together in one place. Moreover, we've got the best maintenance staff, talented chefs, electrical experts, plumbers, computer programmers, and...need I say more? Yes, you have a difficult task ahead of you, but you also have an unparalleled opportunity to design a complete educational system from the ground up. And we'll learn as we go. There's no reason to believe that there should be a fixed number of years of elementary school, high school, college, or professional school. We may have fully-qualified doctors and surgeons practicing here in their early twenties. It's your system to design, mold, modify and rework as you see fit. And by the way, you start tomorrow, so you'd better get a good night's sleep!"

But despite ADMIN-1's humorous admonition about getting a good night's sleep, exuberant conversation followed amongst the entire group late into the night, buoyed by Steve and Julie's celebration, the announcement of Dillon's new role in ORT, and now the news of Steve's upcoming responsibilities as "Secretary of Education." Underlying all of their joy, of course, was the feeling that the potential for the project to continue long into the indefinite future was becoming more and more real.

Chapter 48: Null Hypothesis

The next morning, ADMIN-1 pressed the intercom key on his desktop console that connected him directly with Arianna.

"Yes sir?" came her pleasant and always professional voice.

"Please alert all of the team leaders, all ADMIN staff, as well as Facility Services to prepare for an ORT ALL meeting in the presentation auditorium tomorrow at 0900 hours. I want all, repeat all, personnel to attend unless they are dead or dying."

"Uh, yes sir, so that includes MED too?"

"Yes, literally everyone."

"Roger sir. I'll get on it right now."

"Thank you." And the call was ended.

Arianna had been ADMIN-1's administrative assistant since the Epoch, and she had a greater store of institutional memory than perhaps anyone in ORT other than ADMIN-1 and -2, and of course, ADMIN-1's partner, Kathy. There hadn't been an ORT ALL meeting since the initial small group had come together informally after their arrival. With the catastrophic events of the past few weeks on the surface fresh in her mind, she couldn't help but feel uneasy about why this extraordinary meeting was being called. But her boss had offered no explanation, and she knew better than to ask. She began the task of organizing the meeting and requesting everyone's attendance through their respective team leaders. She contacted Facility Services to be sure that the auditorium was spotless, as well as Catering to have them provide coffee, tea, orange juice, and pastries for the huge group that would descend upon the one and only venue in the entire facility and located on the ANALYSIS level that was large enough to host such a gathering.

She also knew that this process would raise the already elevated anxiety level throughout the project, but that could not be helped. She sent emails where possible, requesting confirming replies, and she made voice or video calls where necessary. Within the span of less than two hours, everything was arranged, everyone was notified, and confirmations were received. She also took more than one call from different persons seeking additional information on what was going to happen in the morning. She could only repeat that she honestly had no other information to provide.

———

Interest was so highly peaked throughout ORT that it provided the topic of conversation that evening for many different table conversations. Rumors were rampant. Even the group of highly talented and dedicated people found at all levels of ORT couldn't resist taking part in the speculation as to what could have prompted this upcoming event. Some feared that the meeting would mark the end of the project, and that team members would somehow have to return to a suddenly inhospitable surface, where radiation poisoning was widespread. Others felt certain that the virtual end of the world would be announced.

A few even wondered if arrangements might be announced for their transportation to Lunar One, and those scientists who knew something about space travel were in high demand to describe what the experience would be like. Then again, given the recent nuclear holocaust that had been unleashed on major cities all over the earth, one could easily wonder how there could possibly still be a space program left to transport even one person to the lunar colony, let alone all of the 400-plus current members of ORT.

The social scientists tended to believe that the meeting was simply being called for the purpose of reassuring everyone that life for them would go on despite the devastation above. These things were best done face-to-face, and after all, extraordinary times called for extraordinary measures.

There were a very few people who were absolutely certain of what was to be announced due to their own need-to-know information. And among all of these groups, they would be the most surprised.

People began filing into the auditorium early, some nearly an hour early, wanting to get a choice seat near the front of the hall. Steve and Julie, as part of the ADMIN team, and having had specific tasks to be performed prior to the meeting, were up very early and in the auditorium long before the doors opened. Arianna's thoughtfulness in having Catering provide refreshments was particularly appreciated. The coffee and doughnuts were being depleted as quickly as new supplies could arrive from the main galley. And once the clock reached 0845, no more replenishments would be arriving since the catering and galley staff would also have to leave their posts to take their seats in the auditorium.

Steve saw his former THOT team leader, Vivian, enter the room and they exchanged waves. He wanted to speak with her briefly, but the auditorium was crowded, there were only a few minutes remaining until 0900, and Julie suggested that they find two seats together. They managed to do so, but unfortunately they were near the back of the hall. They were no sooner seated than the overhead lights dimmed, spotlights lit up the podium on the stage, and a chime signaled the top of the hour.

———

ADMIN-2 stepped up on the stage and the audience gave him a round of applause without even thinking about it consciously. Steve had experienced this phenomenon earlier in his life when he had been an undergraduate in college and had been taking a basic earth science course that had been broadcast from the main campus of his university to the smaller regional campus he had been attending for his freshman and sophomore years. All semester long, he and his classmates had watched and listened to their professor via closed-circuit television. Then, on the last day of the course, they had entered the huge classroom only to find that the television monitors were turned off, and when the professor himself walked into the classroom and the students saw him in person for the first time, the same kind of enthusiastic applause was forthcoming for no particular reason other than that they were meeting this "television personality" live for the first time.

ADMIN-2 began to speak and the audience grew silent. "I want to personally thank all of you for being here this morning. I know this is an unusual event, but I am quite sure that you will find our time together interesting, to say the least. Would you now please join me in welcoming to the stage our chief administrator, ADMIN-1."

This time the applause was loud and strong, and the audience as a whole stood up in a gesture of respect. There were many people in the auditorium who had never seen ADMIN-1 other than on video monitors. Their lanky leader approached the podium and microphone, dressed in his signature black turtleneck shirt and blue jeans. He tried thanking the project members in order to quiet them, but instead the applause grew more intense. He waited a moment and then held out his hands in a calming gesture. Slowly the crowd quieted so that he could begin to speak.

He smiled and said, "Well, I guess we need to do this more often!" The audience laughed in response. "Seriously, I want to thank my own staff, and particularly Arianna, for their efforts in getting things organized for our gathering this morning. Please show them the appreciation I know that you feel for them. In fact, I'm going to ask them all to stand and be recognized right now." Steve and Julie stood up along with the rest of the ADMIN team. "Come on, that includes our invaluable support services. Stand up Galley staff, Catering, and Maintenance too." Team members applauded again in earnest for their colleagues who all too often worked long and hard without any overt show of appreciation.

"Now, I suppose you are wondering why it is that we're meeting this morning?" Responses of "yes" and "please" and scattered applause came from the audience. "Of course you are, and we have a full agenda for you. To start things off, I want to call to the podium Robert, TRAN-15, who will provide some background for, and the nature of, one of our important announcements this morning." More applause as Robert came from the audience onto the stage.

"Greetings to you all. My task is to explain to those of us who may not be familiar with statistical hypothesis testing the concept of a null hypothesis." A few groans made their way from different parts of the auditorium to the stage. "What? You're not excited by the always fascinating science of statistics?" he replied jokingly. "I find this to be incredible. Just unbelievable!" The broad smile on his bearded face signified that he was fully capable of humorous self-deprecation. "Well, I promise that this will be at least short if not sweet. Many of you know about our DATA team's effort to find a possible 'maker's mark' for the universe in certain irrational numbers that are defined by constants or ratios that exist within the universe. Certainly the most common example of one of these numbers is Pi, which is the ratio of a circle's circumference to its diameter. For reasons which I had the occasion to discuss with the THOT team many months ago, this is a very difficult search indeed. There are many of these irrational numbers, as well as irrational people to go with them...," the audience chuckled along with him, "and there is an infinite quantity of number systems out there to be examined. It's like looking for a very tiny needle in a very large haystack, and you have no real idea what the needle looks like. So, whenever our colleagues in DATA come across some pattern in an otherwise random-appearing sequence of numbers, we start out by assuming that the pattern is meaningless, and this becomes our null hypothesis. The null hypothesis is treated as valid unless and until significance testing provides enough of a confidence level to reject the null hypothesis and to assume an alternative hypothesis. So, in this situation, the null hypothesis holds that there is no significant difference in a given pattern from its brother and sister numbers on both sides of the pattern, but rather that it's just something that happens occasionally when you examine random numbers in great quantities. However, if significance testing does provide enough evidence for an alternative hypothesis, in this case meaning that there is reason to believe that the pattern found may, in fact, have significant meaning, then we reject the null hypothesis and assert the alternative. Is everyone thoroughly confused by now?"

"Oh yes," "Uh huh," and "Do you think?" could be heard from the audience.

"Okay, well then the most important thing for you to know about our null hypothesis this morning is that, based upon the DATA team's dedicated efforts for years in their search for information relating to our most fundamental mission, that being the nature of the origin of the universe, I can now tell you that a pattern has been found in a somewhat obscure irrational number, and in a number system other than the decimal system which is most familiar to all of us as a result of the fact that we each have ten fingers, which has given us over a ninety-five percent confidence level to reject the null hypothesis and assert that we have, in fact, located something of significance. In other words, we may have discovered a maker's mark in the universe!"

As these last words were uttered, the audience gasped in excitement and then applauded loudly. Robert continued, "Remember, we now have reason to believe that this finding is, in fact, significant, but we have not decoded it nor discerned any kind of a message as yet. That will be the continuing work of DATA and other mathematicians and scientific analysts in the weeks, months, and quite possibly, years to come. But needless to say, we are excited about the possibilities of this find. And so with that piece of news, my friends, I will conclude my remarks this morning and return the floor to ADMIN-1."

Enthusiastic applause followed Robert off the stage. A few members of DATA and MATH exchanged knowing glances at each other, as if to confirm to each other that they had been correct in their assumptions as to the reason for this morning's meeting.

ADMIN-1 resumed speaking. "I know that we all share Robert's excitement in the potential meaning of this discovery, even if we may not fully share his interest in the null hypothesis concept," he joked. "When I was in graduate school, most of my classmates and I regarded the required statistics courses as 'sadistics.' Some of you may have had a similar experience. But thank you, Robert, for bringing us this very exciting news this morning.

"Now, I would like to turn to serious matters which are not quite so optimistically bright with possibilities." The project members became very silent, knowing that there was no shortage of bad news from the world above them. "During the past year, we have watched a totally corrupt and incompetent administration in Washington reject science in favor of a fundamentalist religious belief system which, while it no doubt offered comfort and spirituality to large numbers of people, it never had any business being merged into governmental affairs. Our forefathers who drafted the Constitution and the Bill of Rights of the United States specifically called for a separation of church and state. And, they also warned their contemporaries that a democratic republic would last only so long as its citizens chose to protect it and nurture it.

"When the nation was small, members of Congress were actually accountable to their constituents. But as the size and population of the country grew by leaps and bounds, so did the influence of special interests, which were capable of providing the mother's milk of politics, money. And that became far more important to politicians than individual voters, because without the funding needed to mount a campaign for election or reelection through the expensive mass media, namely radio and television, it became impossible to reach those voters. Time and time again, a few legislators of good intent tried to institute a system of public financing for elections, but the forces of the special interests were firmly arrayed against it.

"Qualities other than those needed to make an effective leader became important in winning elections. Charisma, so-called good looks, a pleasant speaking voice, and a host of other factors, including the ability to raise the enormous amount of money to campaign effectively, became more significant than the ability to chart a course for a nation based on an inspired vision.

"Over time, the electorate became disinterested in and disenchanted by politics in favor of more immediately stimulating fare, whether it be spectator sports, popular culture and entertainment, or, quite frankly, mood enhancers like drugs and alcohol. Politicians themselves were tarred with a broad brush as being corrupt and interested only in their own advancement in the power elite. All too often this impression was accurate. And yet, there were still some leaders with integrity and ability who occasionally made it through the electoral gauntlet. We had an outstanding example of this with the Jeremy King administration, which served the nation brilliantly for eight years, only to be followed by that of the Reverend Brasington, who of course was most directly responsible for bringing along with him his own personal version of the apocalypse, which the world unfortunately came to experience as World War III.

"As a result of our nation's failure to choose good and competent leaders far too many times, it now falls upon those of us here in ORT, as well as the brave colonists at Lunar One, to not only insure the future existence of the human species, but also to chart a course for a more progressive and more rational society which will manifest a strong probability of survival over a long time span.

"With all of this in mind, I now have the distinct honor and the heartfelt pleasure to introduce someone to you who will have a strong hand in helping these things to come to pass. There is no one, and I repeat no one, more qualified in all of the world than the individual who is about to join us here this morning. Ladies and gentlemen, fellow colleagues of the Origins Research Team, please join me now in welcoming the one person who truly deserves the new position descriptor of ADMIN-0!"

The assembled team members were simultaneously filled with intense feelings of awe, wonder, and curiosity. Steve turned to Julie and asked, "Did he say ADMIN-0?"

"Sure sounded like it to me," Julie quietly replied.

The spotlight on the podium dimmed and another one lit up the front entrance door to the auditorium, from which it was just a few steps up to the stage. People craned their necks to see what was happening, and others began to stand. Momentarily, the door opened, and as the individual just introduced as ADMIN-0 slowly walked into the hall and up the steps with the aid of a black aluminum cane, there wasn't one person in the audience whose jaw didn't drop in startled disbelief.

Chapter 49: ADMIN-0

As recognition spread throughout the audience, there were audible gasps and visible signs of bewilderment. Then, slowly at first but spreading to the entire assembly, applause grew louder and louder, and every single person once more stood to honor the most distinguished personage ever to stand before them at the lectern. Finally, ADMIN-1 motioned with his hands for quiet and the audience complied, but no one took their seat.

"To paraphrase Mark Twain, I'm afraid that reports of my death were somewhat premature," began former president of the United States Jeremy Scott King. "Please, take your seats, and thank you for that wonderful welcome.

"Since I know that you're all surprised to see me here in the flesh, let me explain to you some things you may know about and some things you wouldn't know about since the time I left office. When I held my first cabinet meeting as a brand new president, and by the way, your ADMIN-2, Richard Henry, was there that day serving as my chief of staff, I told the cabinet officers that we had a huge undertaking on our hands to try to save the country from the corruption and incompetence of the Tate administration. We were embroiled in a war of our choosing in the Middle East, and the cost was staggering in terms of loss of life, wounded military personnel, as well as the cost to our treasury. The greed merchants of Wall Street and beyond were actually running the country, and special interest groups made sure that politicians fell in line with their wishes. It was literally a dream come true for large multi-national corporations, oil companies, pharmaceutical manufacturers, and most especially the shadowy world of defense contractors. Civil liberties had been eroded as a result of terrorist attacks on our nation, which provided the shock and awe necessary for President Tate to exercise extreme and unwarranted measures while the public and the news media were too frightened to object. The U.S. had secret prisons in a number of foreign countries, we used torture as a matter of executive fiat, we were using warrantless wiretapping and surveillance on our own citizens, even targeting some major news media personalities and the few dissenting politicians in Congress. In short, we were the United States in name only. In a very real sense, we had become the enemy of democracy!

"Because we had to begin taking drastic measures, I advised the cabinet to expect only one term of office. However, the public responded favorably to a move back toward normalcy, the economy rebounded, and a few years of peace for a change had the effect of giving me a second term. We continued our efforts to rebuild the country, and we also undertook two other major initiatives. You fine people here in the Origins Research Team represent one of those initiatives. The other, of course, is our lunar colony made possible by reinvigorating the civilian space program. I can't begin to tell you

how thankful I am that these two projects reached frui-
tion before the catastrophic circumstances now extant
on the surface would have made them literally impossible.

"I had hoped that this kind of progress might have
continued under my vice-president, Celia Wright, who
waged an excellent campaign against the Reverend
Brasington, but as you know, the pendulum was swing-
ing back toward conservatism, and his brand of fundamental Christianity won the day. Even following his
election, I had thought it possible that the realities of
the office might take him far enough away from his pulpit to continue some effort of progress, but as we soon
found out, it was not to be.

"The life of a former president can be quite pleasant, but it is very proscribed by the necessities of Secret
Service protection and the like. The problem was that
there were more things I wanted to do that were perhaps not so appropriate for a former president, who really does owe it to his successor to more or less disappear and let the new administration run the country.
Well, I can tell you that it wasn't easy to get involved
in a carefully staged car accident. Fortunately, there
were a lot of civil service officials in place from my own
administration to assist in making a number of things
possible, including my apparent death and subsequent
disappearance.

"I have to take just a minute to thank Steve Morefield, your ADMIN-1, for assisting me in joining you
here. And by the way, he was totally unaware of my life
after death experience and was every bit as surprised

to see me as you were. I also want to apologize to his security assistant, Julie, as I arrived in her presence heavily disguised. In fact, Steve introduced me to her as his Aunt Marian!" The audience laughed and cheered. Julie looked at her partner and could only shrug her shoulders.

"So now here we are, and we find ourselves in the unpleasant position of carrying the burden of the survival of the human species, along with our friends and colleagues at Lunar One. However, there is some good news to report. There are a few, and I mean a very few, areas of the earth that are so far unaffected by radioactive fallout. Very soon, we will be gathering together some young people of child-bearing age from one of these areas to join us here in an as-yet unoccupied level of this facility. They will of course be able to reproduce, and part of your mission now will be to educate them to take your place over a period of time. They will hopefully do the same with their children, and so on for generations to come." This brought more applause from the ORT members.

"As for me personally, I'll be hanging around here until my time comes to leave this world, and I look forward to engaging all of you in spirited conversation from time to time. And while I thank ADMIN-1 for the position descriptor he has bestowed upon me today, it will be honorary only, and he will continue to run the Origins Research Team. I will be of whatever service I can to you, as well as the colonists at Lunar One, from quite a distance, of course.

"There is just one more thing I want to discuss with you this morning, and that is the necessity for maintaining the absolute secrecy of the location of this facility. But right now, each and every one of you is going to learn that location! Please observe the projected video screen behind me."

With that request, the stage lights went black and a satellite map was revealed on the large screen visible to the entire audience. Slowly but surely, the map zoomed in to a smaller and smaller area, but with more refined detail with each step. A brief pause occurred just a few times for the resolution to shift. Then, with a sudden impact, the exact location within a much larger area was pinpointed by a green bulls-eye circle. A collective gasp rose up from the entire ORT team assembled for this one historic meeting. Slowly, the conversation amongst team members quieted down, and Jeremy King continued.

"So now you all know our greatest and most important secret. And given the very different type of threat which may now face us, you certainly deserve to have this knowledge. It's also a matter of practicality. Some of you will become involved with our new younger recruits, and many of them will likely come from areas close to us on the surface. Total secrecy within the project itself will no longer be practical or necessary. However, I'm sure the events of the past few months, and particularly the assault on Cheyenne Mountain, have made a vivid impression on you regarding the reasons for keeping your location secure. While there is obviously no longer a threat from the former government of the United

States, due to the most tragic events imaginable, there is the possibility of future assaults by survivors of the war, and we have very limited space here for a finite number of additional people.

"In closing, all of this has been to emphasize that one of your most important obligations is to maintain the covert nature of this facility from the outside world as time goes on. In fact, and this will be my only directive to you as ADMIN-0: Never, ever, reveal your location to anyone who is not a member of the project!"

Epilogue

On a clear and beautiful sunny day, a private pilot began his flight from Dunedin, a city located on the east coast of the South Island of New Zealand, to his home in Westport on the opposite coast of the island. He was flying his cherished Cessna 421 Golden Eagle, a twin-engine plane that could seat six and that had cabin pressurization for flying as high as its service ceiling of 27,000 feet. He first circled over Port Chalmers, where many small fishing boats and pleasure craft could be seen in the waters below. Prior to World War III, Port Chalmers had been a frequent stop for cruise ships carrying passengers from all over the world to visit the North and South Islands of New Zealand, as well as New Zealand's huge neighbor to the north, Australia. Thankfully, the small nation had so far been spared from the radioactive fall-out that now blanketed much of the world.

Setting a course for north northwest, he flew over the train tracks leading from the main station in Dunedin, once used extensively for sight-seeing trains carrying tourists from the city into the rugged terrain inland. South Island is the largest land mass of New Zealand, and a range of mountains known as the Southern Alps divides it along its length. The pilot always looked forward to flying over the highest peak of these mountains, known as Mount Cook, which rises to over 12,000 feet above sea level. He routinely used Mount Cook as his waypoint, where he would slightly alter his course to take him home.

While this route was not the most direct one for his trip, he enjoyed flying at about 13,000 feet around Mount Cook so that he could revel in the majestic view of one of the most prominent and rugged features of South Island. Today, as he circled around the peak, and with conditions of near-perfect visibility, he briefly saw the bright sun reflect off of what appeared to be a shiny red sport-utility vehicle parked near the base of the mountain far below him on the ground. For a moment, he wondered who would be so adventurous as to drive the rugged country roads all the way to Mount Cook, but just as quickly, his thoughts turned to home, to his lovely and devoted wife, and to the tasty dinner she always had waiting for him upon his return.

The End

Visit www.the-origin-project.com

Acknowledgments

This novel is dedicated first and foremost to my wife, Mary, whose never-ending encouragement over the years of my work on this project truly made it possible. Secondly, it is dedicated to the memory of my parents, Gerald and Doris, who gave me the ultimate gift of unconditional love and support during every day of our lives together. I miss them terribly.

There are countless others who have served as inspiration and sources of information for me, and I won't attempt to name them all. But special thanks must go to Alice Martin for her invaluable help in too many ways to enumerate here, and to Carol Jones for her editing assistance and suggestions that became important to the final product which you now hold in your hands.

And last, but certainly not least, it is dedicated to you, the reader.

Randy Patton

13644623R00215

Made in the USA
Lexington, KY
11 February 2012